INDIA, DAVID, AND THE DEVIL

MICHELEE MORGAN CABOT

This is a work of fiction. Names, characters, places, and incidents either are the product of the author's imagination or are used fictitiously. Any resemblance to actual persons, living or dead, events, or locales is entirely coincidental.

India, David, and the Devil

Copyright © 2017 Michelee Morgan Cabot. All rights reserved. No part of this book may be reproduced or retransmitted in any form or by any means without the written permission of the publisher.

Published by Wheatmark®
2030 East Speedway Boulevard, Suite 106
Tucson, Arizona 85716 USA
www.wheatmark.com

ISBN: 978-1-62787-424-3 (paperback)
ISBN: 978-1-62787-425-0 (ebook)
LCCN: 2016940658

CONTENTS

Prologue 1
Guardian Angels 3
India 5
The Escape 9
India at Eighteen.. 15
The Die Is Cast... 26
The Job, Gliders Up 28
The Burglary 40
Boxing the Wake 50
Dave and Women.. 55
White Knight 60
Afterward 66
Drug Addict's Needs 71
Sunday Dinner 74
A Clue?.. 79
Mark's Itch 82
A Conundrum 84
Mark: Persona, M.O.. 87
Ginsberg and Taylor 90
Vernon 93
Fire Doors 97
Mama – 0 India – 2 99
If It Walks Like a Duck 103
No Lights at All 106
Mark on the Carpet 110
Av-Speak in Numbers 113

Overbooked?	117
Claudia	120
Vern's Concerns	123
India Plans; Mark Plots	130
Ups and Downs	138
Soaring with the Best	144
Storms Afoot	151
Low-End Ride, Low-End Girls	156
Cheers and Beers	162
Markie's Next Kill	169
Children's Aid Society	176
Mark Versus India	180
Obscene Villainy	188
Sunday Soaring	194
Landing Out	200
Back at the Airstrip	208
The High-End House	211
Retrieval, Celebration	214
House Heist	219
Things Tighten Up	228
Relationships	233
Parents' Field Trip	238
Vern's Girlfriend	241
Mark Schemes	243
India and Dave	248
The Flight Test, the Future	253
A Hidey-Hole	257
The Cookout	262
Closing the Net	265
Lost Child	267
Epilogue	273

PROLOGUE

She had flashed through the woods like a bright butterfly, yellow silk catching lingering shafts of sunlight. Something out there had prickled her scalp, had made her flesh crawl. Holding her breath, she listened for signs of being followed—a crackling twig, an absence of bird calls? No, nothing. She shivered. She laughed softly at herself. Why would she be followed? Wishful thinking?

Good lord, India.

She trembled and gulped, pushing thick, flame-red hair from her damp forehead, tendrils catching in her fingers. It had been a wild, anxious run. Drawing deep breaths to calm herself, she paused beside the brook, listening to it chatter over stones. The new yellow dress, now smudged with dirt, was a splash of gold against the rocks. The water tumbled down into the valley she had left behind her. It had taken some effort to leap over fallen branches in her hidden path, a thin trail vaguely discernible in the tangled mix of forest growth. To lengthen her stride, she had hiked her narrow skirt high up over her bare legs while trying to move noiselessly. As she made her way, her dress snagged on the odd briar. Her fear was intensified by . . . what?

Accustomed to making her way to the top of the crag,

she had disturbed little in her upward trek. It was her favorite outlook, her safe place.

Nearing the crag's jagged top, she planted one hand on a granite shelf and hoisted herself up, the other holding her skirt away from rock scrapes—never mind scuffing her skin. Here was the sunset view over the valley and of her house below. Firmly seated, she relaxed, feet swinging, bare thighs pressing down on rough rock. A shadow flickered in front of her.

She lurched and gasped in shock, in terror. Her hand went limp; the skirt fell out of her fingers. She froze.

He dropped down beside her and reached for her, eyes crinkling with laughter as he took in her panic.

Mmm.

He liked a quivering conquest. He felt strength power up his arms. He was high, he was aroused. Her rosy color from the run was a further turn-on. She was flushed like a luscious peach . . . and he wanted that peach.

GUARDIAN ANGELS

The holy man stirred where he sat, and looked at me. He passed a finger over his lips, then spoke. "You need to meditate upon your guardian angel."

"My guardian angel? I have a guardian angel?"

His eyes twinkled out from under his cowling hood.

"Yes, of course," he said. "Sit quietly, close your eyes, rest, allowing your mind to focus on nothing. Empty your mind of all thought. 'Go in,' as we say here at the monastery. Clear your mind of all things. It may take time to have nothing in your mind. Then allow yourself to pray, pray to meet your guardian angel."

Later, at home alone, I did as he said. A hazy cloud of pure white slowly filled my mind, floating as a veil in front of me. After a few minutes, a shape took form in it and drifted toward me. It was a misshapen thing, angular and lumpy, of no particular color.

"Don't you know me?" came a voice into my mind. "You don't recognize me, do you?" I had to admit I did not know what this thing was, and said so.

"I'm your guardian angel," it said . . . "I look this way because of all the blows I've taken for you."

I felt an enormous flood of love coming from it, and joyfully I reached out to embrace it. But it faded away.

I later recounted my experience to the monk, while he nodded. I asked him if everyone has a guardian angel. He said he hoped so, but thought there were some so opposed to goodness, they weren't allowed in.

"In?" I queried. "Into where?"

"The heart," he said. "The soul." He was silent, then said, "Remember, God is love. Agape. Where there is love, there will not be evil. That will take you far."

I thought for a moment, then said, "All right, now I know there are angels. I always hoped for it—but now to know it? It's an amazing revelation. But what about the devil, what about demons?"

"Well—we do not speak or think of that. It is said that what the devil wishes is to hear his name, to be acknowledged, for us to open the door. So we do not 'give him house.' I believe this is true. I do not think on, nor do I speak on that."

He looked at me with his penetrating gaze. "Best you don't either."

ONE
INDIA

India had been day-dreaming, lying on her bed, listening to distant house sounds, clinking plates and glasses, and murmuring voices.

"India? Here, honey, try this on. I just got it for you," her mother said, peering into India's bedroom. Mrs. Elizabeth Hammond, Dr. Hammond to the public and Mama to India, had an affectionate mother-hen nature for her children, expressed often in directing her daughters' dressing up.

"Come on in, Mom. Let's see," said India, bouncing up from her bed.

She entered, handing her daughter something in lush yellow silk. She had gone shopping earlier; now caterers were setting up downstairs for their cocktail party.

"This evening is important. I'm counting on you to help out. And anyway, it's time you stepped up to being an adult." Her mother twinkled and eyed her conspiratorially. "This will help you look the part."

Her willowy daughter took the dress, looked it over interestedly, whipped off the teen-jeans and tee, and slipped into it. It was a sleek cocktail dress. Her mouth opened, her green eyes widened, and her cheeks flushed pink. Coquettishly looking over her shoulder, she flipped her thick coppery hair into an alluring swirl and swished this way and that in front of the full-length mirror. Turning and thrusting a hip, she looked at herself with approval. She tossed her head and lowered her thick eyelashes, flirting with her reflection.

India fully looked the part of a young adult. At well into her sixteenth year, she was already on the cusp of becoming a grownup. Many cultures celebrated fifteen as a coming of age.

Nature has its mandate—best to welcome it; fighting it didn't work too well. India was there.

Her face lit up. "Oh, I love it, Mama. That yellow is just right!" Her mother critically eyed her daughter. She cocked her head, assessing.

"Okay, the décolletage is not too much. I was worried it might be, with your full bosom, but it's elegant. You'll be on stage this evening. Be sure to circulate and speak with everyone. Now that you're growing up, sometimes we will want you to be with us, joining us in hosting our groups and greeting our colleagues. This is your first run." And off she went to get ready to welcome guests.

"We're very proud of you, India," she said. "Wear your silver sandals," she called out as she disappeared down the hall.

"What? Those have high heels." India frowned. "I hate high heels."

India had been taught the elements of poise—"airs and graces," she called them, giggling. She understood the importance of the social contract, about taking up her side of conversations and speaking with eye contact. She was advanced in intelligence, advanced in maturity, already poised and elegantly composed. She slipped off the dress, vigorously brushed her sun-streaked ginger hair, and applied some makeup, working carefully on her eyes. A stroke of mascara, batting her thick lashes to check the handiwork, and a light brush of shadow to enhance her green eyes. She did not want to overdo and look cheap, like some of her classmates. The party was now getting under way. Back on with the dress . . . Yes, it was amazing. Now down the stairs to join the group.

"Dang those heels. Hand on the railing, India," she cautioned herself, steadying a wobble. It would never do to wobble or teeter. That was kid-like. What had her mother been thinking? But oh, she loved her new look. So did her little brother and sister, wide-eyed and gaping, watching from the large stair landing. Sister looked so *old*.

India's parents had blessed her with her exotic name, feeling it was attractive and had strength. But India herself had struggled with it, sometimes feeling it unfair to be set apart from other girls who had lovely plain names like Anne, Nancy, or Mary. Hers demanded that she be somehow more special. That was their intention, of course. But for a girl becoming a woman, she found it embarrassing.

Sometimes boys taunted her with "Hey, you do Indian stuff, India? Where's your bindi, babe!"

The girls looked on with envy at the leering attention. She was not markedly beautiful. Not yet. But her name was striking and gave her an aura that would always hold well for her. And it was hard to forget.

Quietly, gracefully, she moved to the edge of the group,

stepped in, and introduced herself. They turned to her. She was a glowing young female in full bloom.

Holy cow, they thought. In those heels, she could meet most men's eyes on their level. She smiled serenely.

She was pleased that finally she could nod, smile, and say: "Hello, my name is India. How nice to see you."

The name went so well with the dress.

TWO
THE ESCAPE

They had been introduced. He had snapped to attention, riveting in on her youthful attractiveness, pouring on the charm. At first she had been flattered. She had been poised, she had been conversational. But he'd been leering in his admiration. Menacing? She was too inexperienced, too naive to decide what was just annoying, what was merely friendly interest in her youthful good looks, and what was too much, inappropriate. His bold attention finally made her uncomfortable. Skillfully she worked her way through the gathering to the patio door, and out. Once outside, she kicked off her shoes, picked up her skirt, and leaned forward into a tiptoed run.

Her hill beckoned.

Pennsylvania's ridges, mountains, streams, and wide rivers attracted settlers early in America's history. Their quiet farming villages slowly grew into townships, then eventually brought in city people looking for a more picturesque, rural life. On her father's side, India's family had farmed, but her city-born mother had transitioned to the countryside after educating herself—and meeting and marrying her lawyer husband. She was a Pennsylvania native too, but found her kind of business, psychiatry, to be more at her pace in the suburbs and beyond, and equally needed there as anywhere.

The state was surely William Penn's forest. Trees grew high and thick, covering the carved geology of gorges and plateaus with splendid specimens both deciduous and coniferous, a patchwork of stunning colors in the fall, a waving sea of flowering branches in the springtime. Ravines led brooks and rivers through the state's valleys and highlands; the mountains' orographic lift of passing air masses delivered bountiful moisture to the landscape. Quaker Penn and his deep faith had to have influenced the settlers and probably gave them to believe this abundance of good earth and nourishing rains were God-given on their behalf. The rock-oil discovery and subsequent strip coal mining had come after a time. But not in Penn's time. But they made a living possible for a man, so probably he'd have offered up thanks for that, too.

India grew and flourished against this background.

Now nearly at her hill's apex, looking downwards at the spring as it swelled into a bouncing stream, she turned her widened eyes nervously up to the crag and wondered if she ought to stay put until full dark, or climb to the overview and see what was happening below. Was she being silly? This man who had admired her so just now—maybe she should encourage this attention. He was handsome. And she had been attaching "teen" to her years for a while. She surely was not a child anymore. Yes, it was time to grow up. But it was overwhelming. She just didn't feel ready. And he was way over twenty-one. A man, unlike the boys she was used to.

She took a breath and got up rested, a barrette falling unnoticed from her thick hair onto the path. Carefully, step by step, she snatched her skirt up around her waist to climb up further, braving brambles that scratched her long bare legs and snagged the silk dress, leaving the odd thread behind on thorns.

Finally she dared stop and turn around to check the path behind her. She raised her eyes to scan the darkening dome of blue sky. The hawks were done with their circling, and the sky was beginning to streak with pinks and corals of the waning day. In the distance she saw a plane descend toward an airport to land through a misty haze on the horizon. Tranquil, bucolic.

"Well," she sighed. All seemed serene, nothing at all alarming. But the vague impression of something sinister beside her in the woods persisted. That feeling had pushed her into her desperate race. She shivered with anxiety, and prayed anxiously. As she did, the dark sense of evil slid away, retreated. She laughed nervously. What a silly girl she was.

A shadow flickered. He dropped from above to crouch at her feet. He stood up in front of her, laughing.

"Ah, don't be afraid," he said, offering his hand. She ignored it, staring at him, stunned, speechless. How could he be here?

"You move as fast as an Indian. You about outran me," he said, chuckling with amusement. Tall, long-limbed, and athletic, he had starred in track in high school—it was a solitary sport that suited him.

Her speech returned. "What are you doing here?" she demanded, voice quavering, eyes large and frightened, pulling back from him.

He smiled down at her, rocking slightly from foot to foot. "Oh, come on now, relax—I'm just having fun. Come sit with me and watch the sunset. Isn't it beautiful?" He opened his arms in a sweeping gesture.

India smelled his sweat, acrid through the shirt sticking to his chest. She imagined she felt warmth coming from his body. "You, you—scared me witless. You're having fun? No!" She shook her head, getting control of herself, eyes glaring angrily.

Now she heard crashing footsteps coming up the hill, searchers confirming their chase route by the occasional yellow thread of silk. They were loudly hurling "India, India" at the hillsides, echoing. Hearing their calls, she grew confident. She slipped off her shelf, ducked around him, and spun around to bolt toward the voices. She glanced behind her, just once. His intense eyes had bored into her and had crinkled too warmly.

But . . . where was he? He was gone, vanished like smoke. Had the voices scared him off?

What was going on? Had he actually been there? She did sometimes fantasize romances, silly day dreams with the unattainable movie hero. All her girlfriends had their favorite stars. Now she was off-kilter. She slowed her downhill run, realizing that, after all, she had not felt any actual touch of that reaching hand.

He fingered the silver barrette he'd scooped up off the path and thrust it into his shirt pocket. Maybe someday he would return it. He felt a pleasurable heat strain at his loins.

Oh boy. He threw his head back, shoulders shaking with silent laughter. Good God, those amazing sexy bare legs.

Once again at home, explaining her disappearance to her parents had been tricky. She was puzzled and embarrassed about the man, and didn't want to talk about it. But they had observed her furtive exit.

"Well, I was bored with the party," she explained. "I had talked with everyone, done what you asked—why not?"

However, her mother had watched some interchanges with the young man that had distressed her. Quietly aside, she had asked workers to go and look for her. Now her parents took in the scratched legs, dirt-smudged dress with tiny pulls in the silk, the bare feet—and felt a worry creep in. But all in all, their daughter seemed all right.

"India, where on earth are your sandals?" asked her mother.

"Sandals? I like to go barefoot, Mom. The high heels hurt. I kicked them off on the patio."

Like Shakespeare's Juliet, India was on the cusp of that dangerous age. Later in bed, burrowing down between the soft sheets, she brooded. Wonderingly, the stalker's face in her mind, her hands traveled down her body, seeking pleasure. She sighed, closing her eyes, finding that familiar comfort. Busy little exploring fingers had discovered that bliss years ago, during naptimes, long before she ever knew about babies. Anxiety brushed away by pleasure, she snuggled down to sleep—to dream of her pursuer? She knew where children came from, in full detail. Her doctor mother had made sure of that, as she moved into adolescence. She wasn't even close to all that.

But *sleep*? Her mind wouldn't stop. She threw off the covers and sat up. India in her sixteenth year was in a full tailspin. What was going to happen to her, in growing up? Juliet had been barely fourteen, much younger.

Nature had an insistent, unrelenting imperative.

What had that man said, Dr. Freud, the one who antagonized her mother?

"A forerunner of modern psychiatry," jeered her infuriated mother. "A scholastic of his time with no knowledge of women at all!" She had often lashed out at Freud, berating the air around her. Freud had said about women, "Anatomy is destiny."

"No!" Adolescent India was defiant. "Not *me*!" she announced to her mother. "I will not be driven, I will not be victimized by love, by urges. I will *not*. I will be very, very careful."

"Hang on to that thought, dear," advised her mother.

Deep in the ethers of the cosmos, Eros dimpled in mirth.

THREE
INDIA AT EIGHTEEN

*H*er cheekbones now sculpted fetching shadows on her face and India had beauty to go with her ripe body, enhancing the intrigue of her name. Pheromones having their dictates, boys orbited her like tail-wagging dogs. But she plainly, disconcertingly, was not interested. She had her secret fantasies; those were plenty for her. Reality could wait. She had things to learn, places to go. What occupied India's mind was the draw of what she might find around the next bend in the road. She was smitten by the allure of uncertainty, the mystery of what might come next.

Her intelligence and integrity served her well. Most importantly, her strong core of self-preservation—the kind that kept her skirts clean. One could say a "Goodie Two-Shoes," but that wouldn't be right. No one would call her that because she was sweetly compassionate and unjudging. Some muttered "Saint India," but those were a snarky handful of miscreants nobody liked. She was a happy person that people liked to be around. She enjoyed learning and applied herself conscientiously without being smug about it. She usually made the honor society, and as a social service option, regularly reported for duty as a Big Sister at the Children's Aid Society, the high school's adopted charity. Being an actual big sister herself, she felt an affinity for younger ones. Her sister Claudia had entered her life when India was three, becoming her own live baby doll to love. As a teen, she had seen that casual, irresponsible sex often brought unwanted children to Children's Aid, wonderful little children that brought sadness and misery both to mothers and offspring. The adolescent fathers? Most disappeared into a hidden world of irresponsibility.

Her parents were rightfully pleased with her, cooing to friends about what a good daughter she was, never giving them any worries.

They didn't know of her dreams, her secret agenda to one day spring loose, to savor the world away from Valley, their not-so-imaginatively named township, and to probe ancient, earthly secrets. Always the face of her erstwhile pursuer hovered on the edge of her imagination, but his features had become hazy.

India's rich inner life led to daydreaming in classes, sometimes infuriating her teachers. Chemistry was her favorite. She didn't daydream in there.

"India, would you please pay attention. Look at me when I'm teaching the class; you are a part of it you know," teachers would fire at her. That endeared her to her classmates.

They reveled in Saint India's embarrassed blushes, eyes lowered and mouth turned down, on the receiving end of impatience. Trouble was, she learned quickly, then her mind simply left the room. She had a robust curiosity about things far beyond her small town world. She grew into an adventurer—at least in her own mind—devouring books of faraway places, getting dreamy over songs of wandering, and setting great explorers as her models. Charles Lindbergh and Amelia Earhart topped the list. She regularly settled into a carrel at the library, first attending to her homework, then digging into books pulled from stacks by the friendly librarian.

And so she had read up on, and hidden, her interests from the world. Saint-Exupéry, the French aviation pioneer, was her favorite author—but not his *The Little Prince*. What she dreamed over were his *Flight to Arras* and *Wind, Sand and Stars*. There had been a seniors' Job Day recruiter trying to draw volunteers into the air force, and she pictured that route to flying. But to be a United States Air Force pilot you needed a college degree, and she couldn't possibly wait that long. Anyway, she wasn't at all sure she wanted to be what the guys called a jet jockey.

She had set herself a goal. She would graduate at seventeen, but her eighteenth birthday would come right after that. Somehow, she would learn to fly without the Air Force. She would, no matter what. Her mind was set. Her parents had no idea, and she wasn't going to tell them.

A few days after graduation, her family threw a surprise eighteenth birthday party for her. The whole class was invited, the boys exuberantly exercising the right to the birthday spanking. That provoked a hilarity that had the crowd racing around the patio, grabbing an exhilarated India for the soft-bottom spank.

That party, with celebratory champagne glasses filled with sparkling cider for its guests, set her off and running. Then and there, bubbles tickling her nose, she decided.

INDIA, DAVID, AND THE DEVIL

———◆———

It was a sparkling post-rain Saturday morning in June when she bicycled out to job hunt. That was expected of her. Her parents were disciplined, self-made successes, Dad a lawyer and Mom a psychiatrist, both of whose genes she was built on. But en route to scour for opportunities, she strayed off course. Oh, yes . . . she strayed. "I'm free!" she sang into her slipstream, bicycling joyfully forward into her future.

"I'm free!" she shouted, kicking her legs out to the side, and rolled along unpowered for a block or so. *Hey*, no one would know. A dog, sniffing at parked car tires, turned to look and considered a chase—but feet back on the pedals, like that she was gone. The dog returned to the tires. What a heady feeling, to be completely away and out of touch.

But not exactly guilt free. All her life she had steered the course, no attention-getting deviations. (No credit for goodness; it was her nature.) Her parents had always been reasonable, monitoring their daughter. But now India felt, well, noncompliant. Defiant? She was eighteen, why should she account for every action? In a rebellious, rules-defying move she whipped off her helmet, tossed her head and let the wind blow her thick hair. But only for a moment. Whacking her brains out in a bike spill was not on her list.

She was exhilarated by her freedom from school, and wound up by thoughts of the future.

Perverting her day's plan, the glider port outside of town whispered *Come on over, come over here.*

Her mind said, "See? It isn't far—just right over there, at the base of that ridge." For years she had wistfully watched gliders circle and swoop like hawks, and wished she could do that.

"Frivolous," sniffed her mother to her tomboy daughter. "And dangerous. Get any idea of doing that right out of your head."

Oh, yeah? Pedaling rapidly, passing by fewer and fewer stores and houses, she came to terra incognita at the edge of town. The road curved; she came to a split. A dirt road took off westerly to the right. She slowed, gripping the handlebars. A small airplane sign with an arrow pointed the way. This was the moment. She smiled and leaned into the turn, pedaling resolutely, stirring up a dust trail behind her, wheeling down the dirt road.

Puffy clouds were arranging themselves overhead in a line, known to pilots as a street. She hardly noticed as she was rolling along, eyes on the roadway. Each white growing wisp capped a rising column of air, up to where the water vapor cooled enough to condense into clouds. These upward currents, called thermals, were caused by the sun heating the land—a parking lot or a farmer's field could jump-start an upward rise of air, like heated air from a stovetop burner. Just like wiggly air rising from the stovetop, the heated air shimmered over a freshly plowed field as it warmed and rose. A pilot would maneuver the aircraft up an updraft to its top, and then he'd zip away from it, grab onto the next updraft, and in that manner steer the flight along a de facto aerial path, or street, leading away from home base. There were competitions to see who could range the farthest and climb the highest, and there were medals to win.

She followed the gravel drive to a wide sweep of grassy runway, the gliders' home base, bicycle tires crunching and throwing up a stone or two. There were some cars parked at a weathered clapboard building. A sign said VALLEY SOARING CLUB.

The door was open. Nobody was there. There was a counter, a desk, and clipboards hanging on the wall behind the counter. She glanced around. The place was dilapidated. Ratty old sofa, cushions concave from years of backsides. The path-worn carpet's color was anyone's guess. Ugh. *Discouraging*, thought well-kempt, fairly pampered, India. Well, here she was, no giving up yet. She stood still, feeling the silence. Hesitating, feeling foolish, she called out "Hello? Anybody home?" filling the emptiness.

"Well hi there!" greeted a tall, sandy-haired young man, popping out of a back room, startling her. He wore khaki pants, light blue shirt (broad shoulders pulling the top buttons open, showing a glimpse of tanned chest) and sneakers. The shirt pocket had a glider emblem on it. "Sorry I wasn't out here at the desk—most everyone is up already," he said. He took in this gorgeous young female, standing in front of him. "You're looking for an introductory flight, right?"

She stared at him, and nodded with questioning eyes. "An introductory flight?"

"Sure—a trial flight." She seemed dazed. "O-KAY! I'm available. Only twenty-five dollars." He pointed at the list of glider club prices on the board behind him. "And if you find you like it, we can log it as your first lesson," he said, giving her the usual sales patter. "The money basically goes for fuel and airplane maintenance. We don't pay ourselves."

She looked vaguely at the cost list of club membership, tow charges, and plane rentals. Her mind was stuck back on "introductory flight."

This flight could be a lesson? An actual lesson? Her head wobbled in agreement, as she grasped onto that thought. He slid open the display case and got out a small blue booklet, a swooping glider imprinted on the front and the words "pilot log."

India went very still, pushing her hands into her jeans pockets. He peered down at a large lined scheduling pad spread open on the counter, his eyes moving over the page.

"I see there's a glider available. You're lucky. It's a fantastic day for soaring. The lift is tremendous—and everyone who can is out taking advantage of it."

A lesson? "Lift?" Holy cow. This was happening too fast. Whoo-ee, was he ever cute.

Her mind whirling with the thrill of this spontaneous leap into the unknown, she struggled with it. Well, it was just a demo ride. Nothing more, really. She wasn't committing to anything. Just a demo flight.

Ah, but there it was, that trail winding out in front of her, rising into the skies. This is what she had always dreamed of, right?

He grabbed a clipboard; they strode to the tie-downs and the one leftover glider. Glancing down at her, he liked the way she matched his strides. He hollered to a guy sitting in the shade of the towplane. They made their arrangements, and hooked the two planes together with a long rope from tow-plane tail back to the sailplane's nose. He showed her the weak link that would break if the pull got to be too much. He did a walk-around, checking wing bolts. The men motioned for her to take the glider's front seat, and she climbed in with a bit of a hoist, plopped down, and sat.

ABsent She took a silent moment to question herself. *Heavens, what on earth am I doing?*

Her breath made a sudden intake, as the instructor leaned over her, said "Excuse me," and stretched down between her legs, pulling up webbed straps from under the seat, a harness contraption with a seatbelt that went right between her thighs to attach to others coming over her shoulders.

What? She had not expected that kind of move.

Coolly detached and deadpan, he explained, "You must wear this type of seatbelt when in flight. It keeps your body in place, keeps you from rising out of the seat, under certain circumstances."

"Oh, I see."

"I'll show you what I mean, when we're up," he promised.

Her heart pumped faster.

"Wait. You don't get motion sickness, do you?" he queried.

She thought for a moment, shaking her head. "Never. At least never carsick, never seasick."

He looked at her and nodded. "One of our club members used to be called 'Mr. Green.' He always barfed from motion sickness whenever he went up. But he was determined to learn. He just kept at it until he beat the nausea."

She giggled and said she didn't think she'd be a "Miss Green." Her thigh tingled where his hand had brushed it. His fingers deftly adjusted the straps and buckles over her chest, careful not to get too personal.

A man ran out from the shed to help, and grabbed a glider wingtip, lifting it so the wings paralleled the ground.

The towplane fired up and roared forward into position, carefully pulling the rope taut.

India gave herself over to the plane, the flight. She leaned back against the thin seat padding and thought about the seatbelt. It felt tight across her hips and breasts, tight against her shoulders, like a trap, full of hard buckles and D rings embedded in nylon canvas straps. She wriggled her bottom to shift position.

Mistake. He watched her. Wriggling didn't help. She flushed and squirmed at his closeness, looking down on her. His gaze made her aware of her breasts, modestly concealed under a collared shirt. She knew she was being assessed. She was glad she was not wearing a snug tee, her usual teenage uniform.

Were eyes really ever that pale a gray? His were, shaded by thick blond eyebrows and lashes, and his gaze smoked.

"Uh-oh, too tight?" He scowled and moved a hand toward the chest buckles. "I can loosen it."

Oh no. This was no high school boy. This was a man, a full-grown attractive one. "I'll manage." she licked her lips and swallowed. "Um, what's your name?"

"Dave," he said, "David Ridgeway," and leapt easily into the seat behind her, strapping himself in with a V-shaped contraption of his own. "Yours?" he asked, as he gave the tail-waggle signal to begin the takeoff.

"India Hammond," she called out, over the blast of the towplane's prop wash.

India had continued to mature into a luscious young woman, the kind that might have been fashion model material had she been skinnier. Her beauty and warm personality were legendary in her high school. She was the green-eyed Queen of May and Homecoming. And, she smirked to herself, she didn't have to put out to be popular. That made for prurient rumors. Was she a lesbian? The gays at school said not. When the few lesbians trolled, she ignored the hints. The girls snickered, watched her, and thought maybe she might be anyway. They themselves really liked the sweaty writhing and deep kisses they got into on their dates. But not India, reported the few boys she'd been out with. Sexual activity was a subject of intense interest at Valley High.

Now it appeared she too was finally entering the danger zone.

After the flight, she had trouble steadying herself. They had climbed and swooped, circled and descended, and she loved it all. But her equilibrium got whacked, sensing unaccustomed variations of gravity. After landing, she nearly flopped out of the plane. Walking seemed to be a slight problem, and she leaned lightly on his arm. She had wheeled and soared, feeling the lift and pull of G-forces against her seatbelt, seeing the horizon tilt and spin, knowing for the first time what it was like to absolutely not be in control, except for the time in the roller coaster. Knowing her life was in the hands of the man behind her, she liked it. What power. She thought she might like to have that kind of power for herself, that kind of control. Life or death control was what it was.

And him? She shouldn't think about that.

"You enjoyed your flight?" he asked, smiling down at her as they walked back to the building. "Do you think you'd want to learn to fly, to soar?"

She looked sideways at him, grinning. "You bet. I loved it. Imagine being able to lock eyes with a hawk at his level!"

His pulse raced, feeling her on his arm, thinking about having her as a student.

Whoa there, boy! She's hardly more than a kid, he thought. *You're twenty-five, middle-aged compared to her.* He had to rein in his reactions. She might be a tidbit he was not entitled even to try for. Probing for her age, he said, "Well . . . to get your license you must be sixteen."

India looked up at him in surprise, and said, "Oh, I'm old enough. I just had my eighteenth birthday. I'm considering colleges now, and I'm sure that having a glider license would look good on my applications."

He placed his hand on her back (delighted that she had reached the legal age of consent) and guided her up the steps into the office.

"Well let's check the scheduling then; you have all summer to accomplish this."

She wondered at herself, and how much she liked his touch. She was tall, but he outreached her upwards by at least eight inches. Nice, she thought. A tall, rangy guy. And a cleft chin? Mmm. And those eyes.

FOUR
THE DIE IS CAST

They arranged lessons for Saturdays and Sundays for the next two months. He explained that the club operated mostly on weekends, since flight instructors were volunteers who held weekday jobs. He himself was a computer software programmer.

"My kind of work often lets me make my own schedule. I actually prefer off-hours, at home or in an empty office, free of coworker interruptions, to concentrate on programming and systems analyses." He suggested he could probably teach her occasionally on a weekday when he could round up a tow pilot—they too had day jobs.

"Weekdays?" she said. "Probably not weekdays." She was looking for work, but now her pay was going to have to support what she could see might be costly, although not as expensive as getting a power-plane license. After her birthday she had quietly phoned about lessons at the next township's airport. Now she was surprised and happy to find out glider instruction would cost by far the lesser of the two. Glider, powered plane—all the same to her, the uninitiated. It was all flying, and cheaper was better.

Unlike power-plane lessons, although towplane costs had to be paid for, the volunteer instructor's time was gratis with glider club membership. The club was not a money-making venture.

She said she would have to let him know about that later. She planned to keep her new interest hidden from her parents. She had no illusions of their being happy with it. Too bad, she shrugged.

She paid her twenty-five dollars, said good-bye until her lesson the next day, and left, wondering how ever was she going to find an excuse to get out of the house.

Maybe I could let some girlfriends in on this—they could cover for me. Pondering this new unsavory idea of deception, she spent the afternoon checking into restaurants, gift shops, and clothing stores, looking for work. Not a position in sight.

Disconsolate, she went to a drug store, the old-fashioned kind with a lunch counter and grill, a few booths, and sat down for a Coke. Looking up, she spotted a yellow highlighted notice taped up on the big wall mirror above the soda fountain, nearly swamped by signs touting bacon burgers and fancy sundaes.

WANTED, DAYTIME HELP IN PHARMACY, it said.

"Yeah, they need another set of hands, big time," said the soda jerk. "Ask in the back if you're interested. The Phelpses are the pharmacists." He swept appraising eyes over her, as he wiped down the counter. Wow.

Her depression floated off like morning fog. She would have that job.

FIVE

THE JOB, GLIDERS UP

*A*t the back of the store, she stood at the prescriptions pick-up window and rang the bell for the pharmacist. There was movement among the shelves.

Again she was glad she hadn't worn the tight tee. Her mother had made her read an old book, *Dress for Success*, when she was opting for teen gear, saying "That garb is fine for now, India. But you are growing up and need to know some business facts." And so she had prepared herself a little, when rummaging around in her closet for job-search attire. Best to look collared up and disciplined.

"Are you Mr. Phelps, the pharmacist?" she asked an older man, working among the tall shelves of boxed and bottled medicines. He heard the bell and turned to peer at her over his glasses.

"Yes, I'm the pharmacist, Roland Phelps," he said. "My partner is in the back. Can I help you with something?" He took in this good-looking girl with a glance, cynically figuring her for a consult on birth control pills.

"I'd like to apply for the position you need filled; there was a sign at the lunch counter."

He straightened up and looked her in the eyes. *You can always tell by the eyes.* She appeared intelligent and calm.

"I need work for the summer. I probably would not be available after September. I've just graduated with high honors from Valley High. I did well in chemistry, if that's important, and I could bring you my grades. I've been active in the school's childhood charities. I really would like to work here. I'm smart and learn fast."

He was taken aback. She was assertive, calm and confident, but not pushy. Maybe this could work. The sallow-faced kid from last month turned out to be lazy and unreliable, and seemed to have fingers that trailed over workstation surfaces for drugs to pinch. Couldn't have another one of those. Well, she didn't look the type. But would Maudie be willing to have such a beauty here? He doubted it. He sighed.

"Just a minute," he said. "I'll get the other pharmacist, my partner. My wife."

He disappeared behind the tall stands of shelves and returned in a few moments with a stern-faced woman. "This is Mrs. Phelps, my assistant pharmacist."

In the meantime, India had quickly pulled back her drifting, lush, sun-streaked hair into a modest tidy knot. She now looked the part of a serious worker. Surprising what a hairstyle could do. The two women eyed each other.

"Your name, dear?" asked Mrs. Phelps.

"I'm India Hammond, Mrs. Phelps. It's nice to meet you." India weighed her approach, and decided on direct. "I'd like to work here over the summer. I have good organizational skills"—a useful buzz-phrase she had picked up—"and feel I could do well for you." India pointedly let her eyes pass over the piles of unsorted inventory languishing on countertops.

Mrs. Phelps looked at India, and thought for a moment. "Aren't you Dr. Elizabeth Hammond's daughter, Elizabeth Hammond, the psychiatrist?"

Surprised, India replied that she was.

To herself, Maude Phelps mused, *Dr. Hammond is a good woman. Perhaps her daughter is as good a person.* And she smiled and quietly recalled that unlike many of her profession, India's mother rarely relied on drugs to solve problems; as a pharmacist, she was privy to her prescriptions.

"Well then, if my husband feels you would work well with us, you're hired." She too had been exasperated by the last failure to pass through. She sensed better luck with this one. They were overstressed by just managing supplies, never mind all the paperwork put aside while filling customers' needs.

India viewed the clutter with interested eyes. Nothing she liked better than putting things in order. She had her father's methodical mind. And she had her mother's compassion, a condition that sometimes caused sadness when working with neglected children.

"Oh, my word, that's terrific!" exclaimed India. "When do you need me to report for work?" The two pharmacists had followed her eyes, as she took in the disorder.

Mr. Phelps looked at her. "Well, can you start right now? If you are free, we can show you how to arrange the products. We can spend an hour doing that now, and get a head start on things. Then come to work Monday morning at eight-thirty. As you can see, we are pretty backlogged."

India paused and thought about this, then said, "Gosh, as much as I'd like to, I do need to know how much the job pays. I'm thinking about college, or perhaps taking off a year to work and travel." And held her breath.

They quoted a number that India rapidly worked out as being doable, and they agreed on it. She thrust her arms into the clean white cotton jacket they handed her, shrugged it on, folded up the cuffs, and stood waiting for instructions.

"May I first call home and tell them my news? I know they'll be pleased. I think they were worried I might get a job at Hooters!" she laughed. The town, though rural and out of the heavy mainstream, was as American as any other, replete with the strip mall chains of restaurants and watering holes found across the country. "By the way. I would not dream of working at Hooters."

They quickly became a team, separating, alphabetizing, categorizing, and filling shelves with packages awaiting attention. Rollie, as she came to know him, stayed mostly at the prescriptions window taking and filling orders, while India and Maude Phelps ("please call me Maudie, dear, everyone does,") began to make reason out of the chaos. Rollie moved carefully between them when necessary to get items, trying not to break their stride.

"Nice job, India," praised Maudie. "It's hard to work and think when the desks are a mess."

India nodded. "I feel the same way. I can't concentrate until the surface is totally clear in front of my computer screen!"

They looked at each other and cocked their heads in complicity. This was going to work out. Maybe. The pay would cover her flight lessons, but not put anything into the bank. How would she explain that to her overseeing parents?

She would simply have to be open about it. Just as well. She had always been open and trustworthy. Never mind. She could manage this. She could argue as skillfully as her father in the courtroom. She would justify the importance of a pilot's license, accenting its weight on college applications. They'd go for that. Logic would win them over; for someone reviewing applications, it would be an affirmation of independent thinking, of self-initiating—those senior year buzz-phrases she had ringing in her ears. The kid with ten gold stars on her forehead. Yes, they'd go for it. Anyway, it looked like the only way out.

Bicycling home at the end of the day, sunset not far ahead of her, she reviewed what the day had brought. A good job, and glider lessons. And an amazing guy to teach her to fly. Astonishing.

Besides the exhilaration of a new discipline, she would be near Dave. She figured she would not mention him.

And so it was that she presented her plan, and won.

After the kudos from her parents and getting them to knuckle under to glider lessons, her father even offered her the first year's club membership as a graduation present. She thanked her dad over and over with hugs and adoring smiles. Then she said good night and disappeared up to her room.

Happy India. Having dreaded a possibly stressful confrontation, she smugly applauded herself for her successful interchange with her parents. She meant to review a flight manual Dave had given her. *The Principles of Flight*, it said.

But she soon drifted off to sleep with the words "lift and drag" and "stall speed" blurring in front of her eyes,

Dave's face a warming backdrop. Her lesson was at eleven in the morning.

"Good timing for thermal buildups," he'd said. "We'll catch one and circle up to the top, watching out for hawks. I'll begin going over with you how to control the aircraft." That was her last thought until the alarm went off.

There had been a parting word from her parents. They needed to be reassured that Sunday church and the Sunday dinner would not be blown off.

India wasn't particularly religious, but she and her family had always gone to the early church service on Sundays, and she would not skip that. The nine o'clock service would enable her to be at her lesson by eleven. She liked the peacefulness of the church, the friendliness of its community, and the occasional bits of wisdom she gleaned from the pulpit. And in her mind, as she knelt for prayers and the benediction, she sensed a warm love surround her. Nice. Odd.

It was a particularly radiant India who shared the sign of peace that morning, glowing with happy excitement.

"Good morning, India!" Dave called out from the doorway. She was walking around from where she had propped her bike against the side of the building. She was fairly jiggy with excitement, and nearly greeted Dave with an enthusiastic hug. Oops—no no no. Whew! He was just as yummy as he'd been yesterday.

India had read about thermaling, but she had no idea how confusing and tiresome that could be at first, getting accustomed to going around, and around, and around . . . circling endlessly in the thermal's invisible updraft rising to cloud base, a column shaped liked an inverted cone, widest at the top . . . until finally one day what she was seeing would suddenly click into just one scene, a panorama—not waypoints endlessly flashing past. Her brain would do that for her. Then would come the full joy of soaring.

They did the walk-around preflight check, attached the rope, went over the maneuvers to be done, and strapped in. The lesson passed quickly, the landing coming sooner than she wished, and her new logbook was filled in with her first lesson entry. She examined it carefully, dazed by what she had started.

The flying part was intriguing: handling the ailerons and rudder to make turns, extending spoilers to slow down for landing. All of it. But the best part was when Dave settled his eyes on her and said, "You know, at the end of the soaring day, around five, we all usually meet at Checkpoints Bar and Grill for a beer and burger. An early supper, for some. We talk flying. There's a lot of hand-flying gestures, and I believe you could pick up some points just by listening. What do you think?"

She was flattered that she was being included in this older group. It was true. She wasn't a kid anymore. She had a good job, and she was learning to fly. Might as well move up.

She took in a breath and smiled. "Thanks for wanting to include me," she responded. "But there's a problem."

He had been holding his own breath. Good God, she was beautiful. And apparently untouched. That was significant.

"Dave, I'm not of drinking age. I'd love to go and be

with the group, have a soda or something, but I'd have to be accompanied by someone at least twenty-five. It's the law."

"No problem," grinned Dave. "So happens I'm twenty-five."

But it didn't matter, not yet, not today. Snapping herself back to her life, she realized she could not join them this time. Or maybe not any Sunday.

"Dave, I'm sorry, but my Sunday afternoons are taken," she explained. "My family is waiting now for me to come to Sunday dinner." She did not add that she didn't want to stir a pot that needed to stay tepid, not boiling; that her parents were not ecstatic over the glider lessons. This was Sunday, a family day, with an unbroken tradition of Sunday dinner.

He nodded and hid his disappointment, coming up with a smile. India noted again how good-looking he was.

Sunday dinners. It was a Pennsylvania country custom, left over from farming days. They would sit down together in the afternoon to feast, laugh, and talk around an antique trestle table, a massive, handsome table, one with history, passed down from her great-grandparents. It had been built by them and used in their kitchen. When her father was a child, he had sat at that very table. He told them how he had judged his growing up by how far his chin was, first below and then above, the table top.

"You didn't sit on cushions, Dad?" queried India.

"Sure, at first. That's how they figured how many cushions," he laughed.

Weekdays, meals had been prepared on it: sour dough breads kneaded, vegetables chopped, cream whipped by hand. Hard-laboring farm workers, first ducking their heads and hands into the cool stream of the farmyard water pump to clean up, came in at midday to sit down with the family and refuel, scarfing down piles of good cooking served from large platters.

Nowadays, the Sunday dinner ritual just involved immediate family and a few neighbors and friends. The old family farm over the ridge to the east, its wide cornfield rows tall and lush with tassels in late summer, had finally gone for a high price to a developer. The family hadn't wished to be farmers anymore. The buyer put in a monotonous checkerboard of real estate. Monotonous, but the houses had great views of the valley and ridges. Today at the table, India's sister and brother would want to know all about her new life. Big changes for their big sister. They had already been awed by her new job, her responsibilities at the pharmacy.

She had worked late the day before clearing the computer and how it was set up for inventory, matching items as they put them away, checking them off against the list in the computer.

Something was off.

She hadn't said anything at the time, because she couldn't be sure of what she had seen. Not being able to locate some items in the computer inventory, she had been puzzled. It looked like some packages on the countertops were simply not registered. Had somebody been mucking with the supplies? She would discuss it in the morning, Monday, with Rollie and Maude.

She would have to be careful how she brought it up.

It would be her first real workday. She was keyed up thinking about it. But she threw herself into the meal's conviviality, eagerly diving into the conversation. As well she should have. She was the center of attention, with her head-whirling news of flying lessons and a new job. The outlook was so rosy. And that made her a little uneasy, like it might be too good to be true, to last? But with her eyes shining happily, she told of the thrill of handling the glider, of circling with hawks, and seeing their town from above.

She did not mention her attractive instructor.

It would be a whole week—no, make that just five days—before she would see him again. She would be lost in a many-days-long sorting of little boxes in her new workplace, tapping data into the computer. And she would study the flying book.

She wanted to impress him.

The next-door neighbors had been fondly watching India for years, wondering how she would turn out. She was lovely, perfect. They wanted her for their son, now away at a summer program. But this adventurous spirit, risking life to fly with birds? No, horrors no. They smiled thinly at this disappointment.

India launched out of bed early the next morning with a new intensity. A job! She had a real job, one where people were going to depend on her. She would be an important part of a team. And she would get paid. It was a rush of happiness she held onto as she threw on clothes and took the steps two at a time down the stairs to get breakfast.

Her parents were already at the table, ready to send her onto her path into the adult world of commerce. Their baby, off into the workforce.

For her parents, it was a melancholy moment. A new stage of life. Her mother, being a mother, scrutinized India's clothes. Sigh. There was nothing to critique. India had already donned her long white work jacket, covering her clothing, unbuttoned at the neck to show a blue oxford cloth collar. Her thick hair was pulled back into a coiled braid, framing her high smooth forehead and half-covering her small ears that sported pearl earrings. Shoes? Her mother peered down. They were sensible cushion-soled sneakers, showing below trim, utilitarian khaki pants. Sneakers were allowed. They were good on concrete store floors, even if these were an unbusinesslike jaunty pink. Her mother sighed again. Her daughter was ready, and there was nothing for Mama to do but say "Good luck darling, I love you, have a good day—and please tell the Phelpses hello for me."

The time to travel to the pharmacy on her bicycle would be twenty minutes, with cross-town traffic. Her father frowned, unhappy about her maneuvering in the rush hour, and insisted on taking her.

"I'd love to give my daughter a ride to her first job," he said, dropping the frown and smiling at her.

"Well, Daddy, that would be great. I think probably my ducking and shortcutting the backstreet way I know would probably get me there sooner, but I'd love for you to take me," she tossed back, returning his smile.

He thought to himself, *Thank heavens I haven't lost her yet. She still likes to be with her old Dad.*

She arrived at eight thirty, just as the store was opening; the cashier was just swinging wide the front door as she got to it, the store keys dangling from her hand. India turned and blew a kiss to her father, and disappeared inside.

Ashamed, he blinked back tears. His little girl was clearly on her own way into her own life. He choked up. "Never mind. I have cases to see to," and continued to his office. She would call when she needed a ride back home.

SIX
THE BURGLARY

The Phelpses were already there when she got to the back of the store, but they were in a state of hand-wringing despair. The organizing they had done on Saturday was now a total shambles. They turned frightened, hollow eyes to her.

"We were broken into and burglarized!" Maudie exclaimed, sagging helplessly against the counter. "Look at that! The back door is jimmied open. And no alarm went off!"

No alarm? India surveyed the damaged door and took in the fact that no alarm sounded. They were pale with shock. "Good lord," she exclaimed, looking at the mess. "Have you called the police?"

"Not yet," replied Rollie. "We only just came in ourselves—through the back. We got here just before you!"

India reached for the phone and dialed 911. The pharmacists were paralyzed, stunned into inaction. India quietly took over.

"Please come immediately to the Phelps downtown pharmacy. There's been a break-in and burglary." The dispatcher took the data and radioed for someone to investigate.

India turned to her bosses and said "I was going to mention this on Saturday. I noticed irregularities, discrepancies, with your inventory on the computer. Items didn't match up. What's that about?" They looked at her numbly, uncomprehending.

"We don't do our own computer work, we just make entries. The rest? That's all hired out." India looked at them, wanting to say something about the older generation, but wisely kept that to herself.

"I know it would have been a lot more to do, but if you could have been more hands-on," she said, "you'd have noticed, as I did, that there were more items on these counters than you had originally ordered. Maybe they were entered to be paid on another file, another category. Let's see." She booted up the computer and quickly browsed the files, looking for suspects.

Sure enough, there it was, hiding under cosmetics. Items ordered and already paid for—a nice little list of controlled substances. But who had access besides them, and who would do that? The hired accountant?

She turned and looked questioningly at the owners.

"If you don't mind my asking, who is your accountant, and how often does he work on this computer? It might be important."

They mentioned the company they said many used in the town, one that came highly regarded and recommended. She decided not to tell them what she had found. She wouldn't bring it up until her father arrived and she could tell them all together. She also noticed there was a camera function on the monitor. Why would they need that? Probably just came as part of the equipment, like her laptop.

Hm. Unlikely that the accounting company would be the criminal. Had they been hacked? That was beyond her expertise. But something tickled her brain. Dave had said he was a computer programmer. Could he help?

Next, she quickly called her father's cell phone. He answered as he was parking in the office building's garage.

"Daddy, the Phelpses have a big problem here," said India in a low voice.

At that very moment, the police arrived at the pharmacy, started cordoning it off, and immediately began their investigation.

"Dad, you need to come back, come back here *right now*. There's been a burglary and we need your help." She hung up, turning her attention to the mess behind her.

"I'm Sergeant Moore," said the policeman in charge, turning to the pharmacists. His experienced face reflected his concern. "I need you to answer some questions." He looked at them intently. "Are you all right? Can you do that?" he asked the pale, shaken owners.

"Oh, of course," Rollie responded, subdued. "What do you need to know?"

The sergeant began taking statements from the pharmacists, his men yellow-taping off the products part of the pharmacy, which was pretty much the whole of it. The owners were aghast, watching their livelihood being barricaded off from them. Their hands covered their mouths in consternation, wondering how they could do business. This was not going to work.

Clients were already starting to line up for prescriptions, and the pharmacists looked confused, unsure of what to do.

THE BURGLARY

In his company's parking garage, India's father stared at his cell phone. He had heard the background commotion, wondering what on earth was going on and noting how quickly India had hung up. She had said something about a burglary? He quickly put his car in reverse and pulled out of his slot, proceeding as fast as he could to the exit and back down the street.

In the front of the store, police were questioning the store's buxom cashier.

"Maisie, when you unlocked this morning, did you notice anything strange, different?" the sergeant asked, trying not to ogle her plunging neckline.

"No, Sarge," she slowly shook her head, wide-eyed. "I always come in the front door. Nothing out of order up this way," she responded, hoisting her décolletage just a bit for a better viewing.

She was put on call to be available for questions. But curious, she quietly moved toward the pharmacy, following the sergeant. Nobody was checking out now, anyway. There was a sense of waiting, hanging over the store.

India and her employers sat down on stools at the soda fountain counter and stared at each other. Customers drifted around, stealing looks at them, some offering condolences. Condolences? Well, it was like a death, or an assault on your person. An invasion of your home, your business, makes you feel violated. Your faith in your fellow man gets shaken. It was worse, perhaps, than losing the goods.

"Don't worry Mr. Phelps, the police will get the bastards," a worried client offered, and commiserated. The pharmacists smiled dolefully.

"Oh, we know they will. We have a great police department. Sergeant Moore is the best. We'll be up and online for you soon."

But Rollie's eyes said he didn't believe it. The drug problem had come to the valley; he had heard that the hospital was already troubled by thefts, and not all done by the staff.

India was impatient to put forth her idea of a hacker, but she had been around the law long enough to know to keep her mouth shut about anything and everything until her father got there, and until they could talk about the possibility together with her employers. She hoped they would want her father's counsel—pro bono, naturally. She would unobtrusively suggest that to him. He arrived even faster than she expected, and she murmured the pro bono idea in his ear as she hugged him.

"Of course, honey," he said, and turned to speak with the police and the Phelpses.

"Good morning, counselor," said the officer in charge. "I didn't expect to see you outside the courtroom today."

"Right! Good morning, Sergeant Moore. What's the story? What happened? I'm here answering an urgent SOS call from my daughter," he said waving his hand in her direction. "A burglary? What a way to start her first day on the job. Doc Phelps, do you want me getting into this? Things look to be gridlocked."

"Mr. Hammond, we have been burglarized. What a mess," sighed Rollie. "We can't even move around, much less attend to our customers. Whatever you can do would be appreciated."

"I'll do what I can, gratis of course, and help you get back into action," he said. "Sound okay to you, Sergeant? Not that there's much I can do here. This part is police business." He turned back to the Phelpses. "We have to get out of the way and let them do their jobs. Do you need me to stay? I could wait out there," he said, gesturing into the store's shopping aisles. "If you need me in the future, that's when I actually would be more useful."

The sergeant said, "No need. We can quickly dust for prints, take crime scene pictures. You haven't touched things since you came in?" he asked, getting an emphatic *No!*—"I need an accounting from you of what's missing. Then I believe we can leave you alone." He nodded his thanks to India's father, then indicated to the forensics team just coming onto the scene what they should do, and they went at it.

The process took longer than they'd hoped. There was back door damage to investigate, also the area outside in the back alley, tire tracks to examine—all the things even crime show viewers knew about, only this was happening right under their own eyes. A reality show that they did not need. The Phelpses listed what they could see was missing from a quick look around, and promised they'd come up with a complete list later.

"Whoever did this was familiar with the layout. The partially hidden surveillance camera is broken, and the alarm system is dismantled. I hate to tell you, but it looks like an inside job." Sergeant Moore turned his piercing eyes meaningfully toward India, forgetting that her father was standing right there.

"Sergeant?" barked Hammond. "My daughter?"

The Phelpses recoiled in astonishment.

Mrs. Phelps patted India's arm reassuringly. "No. She couldn't have done it. She's a fine person. Anyway, her first time in the back here was on Saturday for a couple of hours only, and she was working hard with me. She certainly didn't have a moment to learn anything about the place."

India became more certain than ever that the break-in had been done for drugs, undoubtedly by the one who had hacked the computer system. The police also felt it was probably the work of an addict, seeing the short list of missing drugs, but not knowing about the hidden computer file. Yet.

The police finished up their on-site investigation, removed the yellow tape, and allowed the store and its pharmacy to get on with business.

"Okay, Maisie, you're back in action," advised Sergeant Moore, seeing she had followed him. She slowly swung around and swished her hips, sauntering back to her cash register.

Rolling his eyes, Moore turned to the pharmacists and announced, "If you can manage it, please do not discuss this with anyone. We need to make as low-key a search for the perpetrator as possible; we do not want to send out any warnings."

Right, thought India. As if the store's gawking customers weren't going to spread the word as fast as they could. Small hope for keeping it quiet. The four of them, the Phelpses, India, and her father huddled in the back to discuss strategy. India revealed to them what she had found on the computer before the police had arrived. Her father was pleased India had the wit to keep her own counsel on that until she could tell the Phelpses. They were flabbergasted.

India observed that more products had just been delivered, and wondered if those would be the target of another burglary. "Rollie, Maudie—what do you think of this? It scares me, I'll tell you." The couple agreed.

Since she had been sworn to secrecy about the thefts, she could not discuss it with Dave. Anyway, she had days to go before her next glider lesson; she needed to concentrate on learning to fly. She hadn't been able to separate herself very well from her job concerns and her studies of the flight manual, but she hoped it wouldn't show. She was going to learn to handle that plane.

The day unfolded in disarray, even with India's organizational help. The thief had torn the place apart; Mr. and Mrs. Phelps were completely rattled. But there was already another mess, one of skewed recordkeeping. India was stumped. Maybe they needed to start at the ground floor, from the beginning. What a thought. Regrettably, the pharmacy records had been shabbily kept; the owners were chemists, not bookkeepers.

At some point, modern technology had left the pharmacists behind and woefully out of touch with recordkeeping. They were functionally stuck back in the age of written slips and ledgers, but since they switched to computers those had gone untended, the new system being managed by an outside accounting firm with online access to the pharmacy's financial records. They had been relieved not to have to learn a lot about computers—their forte, expertise, lay in a different arena. They were advanced chemists, trained to mix and compound complicated formulas. They certainly didn't want to take time to learn a new discipline, one they knew came easily to youngsters. When introduced to computers in school, they never took to them.

Maudie spoke. "You know, India, we tried to learn the technology, but it just wouldn't take. We tried it, didn't like it one bit." The pair looked at each other hopelessly. "It was tiresome and frustrating, wearing ourselves out with frozen screens and hung up cursors. They called those screens the Blue Screen of Death. So when the option came up of an electronic link to an outside accounting firm that could handle all that, we grabbed at it."

But in doing so they lost control; they no longer had personal hands-on tracking of their inventory. They could do data entry of their orders, but that was it. The accounting firm gave them updated reports; all orders were tracked by the firm. Reports they didn't bother to read. The Phelpses became too relaxed, too confident, too complacent, too trusting. They felt they had no reason not to be.

India peered at the tiny camera eye on the monitor and wondered if access to the computer's camera function was possible from the accounting firm. If so, that would explain outside knowledge of the pharmacy layout as well as information about the pharmacy's security camera.

India looked around, thought for a moment. Where to start?

"Why don't we begin with the mess that's visible, and put that in order?" she proposed. "The intricacies of the business can be addressed later, with your accountant."

Maybe they needed a different accountant? Her full lips pressed together, forming a thin line; a frown mark appeared on her brow, altering her look of lighthearted maidenhood. Suddenly one could see a hint of the older woman to be.

Maude was watching India's face. *Well, well... Except for the red hair and youth, India looks just like her mother, minus a few years.* She quickly put a hand to her mouth and sighed. *No matter... a handsome woman, Elizabeth Hammond.*

India was quite impressed with herself, seeing how her college prep courses—in particular advanced placement in marketing—had prepared her for this. She had figured she was simply getting ready for college, notching her belt with interesting courses. Her opinion was that nothing she learned in school could actually prepare her for real life. How was she going to apply algebra, please? Philosophy? (Well, languages, sure.) But here she was, applying spreadsheet know-how to the real world. "I'll be danged," she marveled.

The week passed quickly, and soon it was Saturday. She had spoken with her father about the computer expertise of her glider instructor; by now she was referring to him as "Dave." He took that in.

"India, you don't know this fellow. He may be okay, but you do not really know him," he asserted, hoping she would not get to know him at all, Phelpses' problem notwithstanding.

"Stick to flying, India" became his father-mantra in his head. He looked at her and saw a new expression, one he didn't like. One that meant bye-bye Daddy.

SEVEN
BOXING THE WAKE

Saturday arrived with little fanfare from her household. Her father watched her getting ready to depart with uneasiness. Her mother was already off for appointments at her clinic.

She had reviewed the first part of the manual before she scampered down the stairs for a quick breakfast of bagel, jam, and butter, and a sip or two of cocoa.

"Hey! You need protein to stick to your ribs," chided her father.

"Okay. I'll have a hard-boiled egg on the way," she said, peeling it quickly and slipping it into her pocket. Throwing a kiss behind her, she leapt onto her bike and whizzed off. The path to the airport whispered *at last* as she pedaled hard to meet her handsome instructor.

After a few blocks, out came the bare egg, now linty, from her pocket. Oh, well, she thought, glancing at the bits of lint. She chomped it down in two bites, lint and all. Cripes, now she would have to get the caked yellow yolk out of her teeth before she could smile a hello at Dave. How dim was that?

Pedaling on, she futilely worked and worried her tongue around her teeth. Dodging past Dave at the doorway, waving a perfunctory hello, she barreled into the bathroom. Swoosh, swish, swish . . . she checked her smile in the mirror, and was good to go.

"Sorry Dave, had to do what I had to do!" she giggled as she emerged to greet him.

He beamed at her, thinking how maybe he had actually forgotten how captivating she was. She turned her green eyes up at him and dimpled sweetly.

The lessons proceeded according to the syllabus. This day they would practice boxing the wake. A plane leaves a wake, a path, behind it as does a boat—except you can't see the airplane's wake, because it's invisible air. But the same sort of churning disturbance, turbulence, exists as a choppy path of air behind the moving towplane, as there is a choppy path of water behind a moving boat. One must learn where it is by flying a square, like a picture frame, around the envisioned path behind the plane. And get the feel of the wake. Not amusing, to be trapped in it. One flies the towing process above the churning wake.

Again she thrilled as he leaned over her to make her snug in the seat harness, but this time she helped him with the buckles, allowing their fingers to brush. He smelled good.

And as he leaned over to help India into her seat harness, his brain buzzed. *How can I concentrate—boy, she smells good.*

She was a quick study, a good student. This day she learned how to keep the wings level, balance them equally as they took off and climbed out, and how, in turning, to aim the nose at the towplane's higher wingtip, keeping the rope tight. She learned how to do a peeling turn up to the right as she pulled the towrope release, in the opposite direction from the left-diving turn the towplane made, to keep from running into it.

In the next day's lesson, a day forecasted to be clear and sunny, she would learn how to look for gray flattish bottoms of piles of small white clouds, opting for the most concave, a clue to the strength, the velocity, of the rising air. A cloud bottom like an upside-down saucer meant nice lift. Down below that cloud would be the best place to start a round-and-round upward spiraling in the thermal column, up to cloud base, a method hawks use to rise while scanning for prey. If it was to be clear and sunny, maybe there would be no gray-bottomed clouds after all. It didn't matter. She had plenty else to learn. Anyway, like today, maybe the summer sun would again bake moisture out of the ground, invisible water vapor to be lifted and cooled to condense into those puffy clouds.

Her lesson over, her logbook was duly filled out by Dave with notations made by India, too.

"It's your logbook India—you have to keep track of your flights," he had said. "Write what you like. What kind of weather, what you learned, what you saw. Whatever. The log is a little diary. How long the flight lasted in hours and tenths. An hour is one, a half hour is point five. Things like that." He explained his role: "I am required only to write what I taught you and my instructor time."

That done, she moved to go.

Dave looked down at her. It was hard to let her leave. He shoved his hands into his pockets and cleared his throat. Then he offhandedly suggested she could hang out at the airport to help crew the gliders as they took off, and then again later when they returned. Glider clubs were very sociable; everyone pitched in to help everyone else.

India looked up at him. He sounded casual, but she felt more. *He wants me to stay.* She felt her stomach flutter.

He laughed a little, his gray eyes serious under his thick sandy eyebrows. She made his blood rush. "We might even have to go help someone trailer in a glider from an emergency landing out if a pilot runs out of lift and can't make it back past a farmer's field. Lots of hands needed then. We take the glider apart, put the pieces into its trailer, and haul it back here. Wing bolts come out, wings come off, fuselage and wings are slipped into its long skinny trailer, side by side. Like those trailers over there. Then we tow it back by car. Most of us have a trailer hitch." He gestured to a lineup behind the tie-downs, and waited for her response. He chuckled. "Soaring can be a full-day activity, if you can arrange it."

Oh, the temptation. She struggled hard. Her palms were sweaty. But India had told the Phelpses that she would work this Saturday afternoon, and she had to stick to her promise. However, when she had committed herself to work, she promised them only a few hours, claiming a previous early engagement. She had wanted to join the glider gang for their postflying fun; she wanted to make sure it would be possible. She figured she could get away by five to join the group at Checkpoints.

"Dave, I can't stay now. I have to go to work at the pharmacy. But I could join you later, if last weekend's invitation still stands? I could easily bicycle over."

Like how wouldn't it? Dave thought. Who could turn her away? Happily they said "See you later," and she pedaled off to downtown, carefully weaving her way through traffic, and on to the pharmacy.

Maybe, he reflected, *if the soaring ends early enough, I'll go look her up at the pharmacy.* Then he thought better of that. She might not appreciate it. "Aw hell," he muttered. "I need some shaving stuff; might as well go get it there as any other place."

EIGHT
DAVE AND WOMEN

Dave had taken up soaring as a teen and had gotten his license at sixteen. Sailplanes were so beautiful, but it wasn't a sport that often attracted girls. He didn't care. He loved soaring, being alone, feeling at one with the glider and the sky.

Next came computer programming, also a solitary activity. So the quiet computer guy had a quiet personal life to match, but not by choice. It was a side effect of his chosen field.

When in college, he'd been a target for coeds, being good-looking and smart—and maybe very well off? His family was not showy-wealthy, but successful enough with their Pennsylvania-wide auto parts business to buy Dave a top-notch education.

In earlier days, his techie fraternity had held those popular drunken foreplay toga parties, a passé ritual forgotten by the time he joined. But the fraternity's jolly open-door hospitality lingered on, and there were always girls floating around, checking him and others out—archetypal husband hunters, there to gain the MRS degree. They knew where their preferred economic future lay, and figured Dave to be good material. But he hadn't hooked up with anyone permanently. They seemed to be, well, acquisitive, predatory. He extracted more from his education than most, and got job offers from the best. But now that he was placed securely in the mainstream market, there were few opportunities to find dates. Hard to find a mating pool where he could satisfyingly rubber-hip a prospect elbow-to-elbow at a bar, the way he had done at college. Somewhere to gaze into pretty eyes and flirt. Bars here seemed to be discouraging whore haunts, and the water fountain at work didn't draw any women. Needing quiet to concentrate on programming, he usually ended up closeted away in solitude to do his work, sometimes in off-hours at the company, or at home. And there were no interesting women at his gym. They were the earnest, muscle-building, hairy armpits sort. The glider club was his only social outlet. But for a handful of female pilots who were wives of the men, no women there either. So now he found he was a little lonesome.

India got to her workplace after a brisk twenty-minute ride. She had sighted a few of her old classmates as she rolled along, and hailed them cheerily. She was flushed from exercise and looked amazing. News of her flying lessons had flowed out like a flood, saturating their youthful community with awe.

"Aha," they said to themselves. "It looks like she's coming from the airport. Maybe she was in one of those gliders we saw swooping earlier. Is Saint India cutting loose, finally?"

They talked about it for a while. "Well, she was always thinking about adventures, you know, always reading about them. And remember the Ouija board?"

Against her best intentions, she had joined them when they had all played the Ouija board. It was a big fad. India suspected it was not a good thing. Besides that bothersome nudge in her head, her pastor had declaimed vehemently against it, saying evil forces managed it. But that, thought India, had to be pure nonsense. How could black forces rule the Ouija? "Come on," she sniffed.

Then one day one of her girlfriends asked the board, "Who is God?"

The Ouija board froze up. It was silent for them, ever after. They were stumped, creeped out, and a little frightened.

But in the meantime, she liked how it had always pointed her toward a future of roaming and rambling. The needle would slowly spell out faraway places and exotic enterprises, from alpine ballooning to Thai acupuncture. That one made her roll her eyes.

Rollie and Maude were still at loose ends from their break-in; their demeanor showed how demoralized they were. It was hard to accept. At least some order had been restored and the business was functioning smoothly—or so it appeared to customers. India shook her hair and pulled it back into a tidy bun, pulled on her white jacket, and stepped up to help out.

They worked for four hours straight, breaking only for a moment or two to sit and ponder who could have done it.

The Phelpses had thought it might have been the kid who had worked there before India, and had expounded on their suspicions with the police. Immediately, the authorities had hauled him in from his gas station job for questioning.

"Huh? Whattaya talkin' about . . . I was on duty until midnight that night!" he sulked, worrying a chin pimple. "Then I went right home and my folks can swear to it! They're always up watching *The Late Show* when I get in."

His alibi proved out. Also, the pharmacists said that realistically, he hadn't seemed clever enough to pull off something like that. The kid was a bumbler who could hardly make his way around the stacks. He was not up to the work, and they'd had to politely let him go. Oh, he'd indeed had opportunities to place orders and mess with the computer, but he wasn't smart enough or sly enough. They were out of ideas. India still felt it looked like an inside job. The database could have been accessed from the accounting place. After all, the store's computer was linked to the firm for data processing. Technology was convenient, but it could have downsides.

They worked for a while more. India furtively watched the clock, seeing five o'clock approach. But while they had categorized and shelved products, they had observed with distress that there were more controlled substances in the pile, way more than anything they had ever needed or ordered. Maudie had unboxed the last delivery only that morning, when FedEx left it off, stacking it on the counter. Now, studying the items, they became quite unnerved, considering what might happen next. Somebody clearly wanted this stuff, and soon. Another burglary was up, that was clear.

What should they do? They dithered over that. The security camera had been repaired and repositioned, and a night watchman was going to sign on at eight o'clock. They really didn't want to stay that late—they were tired and worried about putting themselves in the middle of something bad. Better to go home. India agreed. She gathered up her backpack, said a troubled good-bye, and went to leave out the back.

By now it was five thirty. She was in an eager hurry, not paying attention to things around her. The alleyway was cast over by long, deep, late-day shadows.

Out of a dark corner a figure lunged at her. Terrified, she opened her mouth to scream, but a hand clamped down on it, and a fierce blow landed on her head, stunning her. She began to sag. She looked up as she went down, and to her shock, glimpsed a face distorted with lust. Maybe the one of years before? The man from the long-ago party, the man on the crag who had tracked her. Then all went black.

The man snarled and hissed, coiled over like an evil snake, bending over her, one hand gripping her by the hair and the other yanking down her jeans, fingers clawing at her panties, probing.

A powerful blow sent him sprawling.

NINE
WHITE KNIGHT

Dave had told the guys he was going to run an errand and would see them at Checkpoints in a while.

"Don't forget your beer hat, buddy," one hollered jovially after him. "And that gorgeous girl!"

When he arrived at the store, he decided to pump up the surprise and park around back at the pharmacy, just before she was to leave. He could knock on the door. The rest was more fantasy. He would play it out.

He was just driving down the alley when a shadowy action grabbed his attention. A gun butt was flashing down to meet India's skull. He jammed on the brakes, and like a rocket, ejected from the car and leapt onto her attacker. He wrenched the man's head back and, seeing crazed eyes, rabbit-punched him in the neck. But he wrenched out of Dave's arm-hold and staggered away running, leaving a collapsed India and a frantic Dave holding her up off the ground, limp in his arms.

"Help! For God's sake, help!" Dave roared, bellowing toward the door. Then he got up from where he was crouched, putting her down carefully so as not to harm her further, and began banging on the door, disrupting the Phelpses' systematic closing up process.

"Help!" he shouted. "Please help! We need help out here! India has been attacked! Call the police!"

Frightened, the two carefully cracked open the door. Panicked at seeing the stranger, they tried to slam it shut.

"No, no!" He yelled and stopped them. "I'm her flight instructor, here to take her out! Some guy grabbed her. He was hitting her when I came around the corner. I slammed him and he ran off."

Rollie and Maudie, aghast, retreated further inside to call police.

Dave gathered India back into his arms.

She was starting to come to. She focused on the face above hers.

"Dave? What are you doing here?" she asked. "Where is that guy who attacked me? Ohhh, ow . . . ." She groaned. "I think I've seen him before."

"Oh, dear God India," he said, alarmed, scrutinizing her. "We made a date for Checkpoints, remember? I thought I'd come pick you up and drive you over, stashing your bicycle in the back of my car. Thank God I did. What a beast that was. Crazy, *crazy.*"

"I don't know him," said India, eyes half-closed, her hand on her forehead, "but his face was familiar."

"The paramedics are coming. Your boss called for help. Someone will check you out. How do you feel?"

"My head is throbbing," she whimpered.

"Look at me," said Dave. "Let me see your pupils." His face bent close to hers, holding his breath as he held her lightly in his arms, both of them sitting on the ground. He carefully eased up her partially lowered jeans. No sense in making this worse. The graveled blacktop was uncomfortably hard and rough. Leaning back, supporting himself on one arm, his hand ground into sharp loose pebbles.

"Maybe you ought to be flat, with your head in a Thomas collar," he said, more to himself than to India. "At least the bend of my elbow is holding your head and keeping it immobilized."

Dave was thankful for his emergency medical training, something he had accomplished while at the university. Needing quick first responders in such a large complex, the university had offered an EMT course for full credit.

He now considered her injury, muttering "Should your head be down? Are you in shock? No, not down, that would make the bleeding worse." He would not lay her out again on that harsh surface; best keep her whole body elevated on his lap, even if the weight of them both on his sitz-bone was pretty painful.

"Oh, my head really hurts," whispered India, raising her hand to touch her forehead.

"Well, your eyes, the pupils, look okay as far as I can tell. Probably it isn't serious," he comforted her gently. "But we'll know soon."

The back of her head was slick with blood; whatever the guy had struck her with had cut her scalp. Head wounds bled dramatically. Blood was splattered onto her white jacket and oozed onto his sleeve. Not a particularly religious guy, he now prayed silently that there was no hematoma, a dangerous cerebral bruise, to clot up on her brain. With that, a certain peace came to him. He held her closer. Distant sirens grew louder, howling up the street, bringing their flashing reds and blues into the alley, rolling to a stop in front of Dave and India.

After paramedics examined her eyes with a light and found no bleeding behind them, India was treated briefly on-site for a laceration to the back of her head, then loaded into the ambulance to be taken to the ER.

Her parents, called by Maudie, had arrived soon after the police and EMTs. They and the Phelpses followed the ambulance.

Dave fumbled through pockets for his keys, striding to his car to follow as well.

What was *this*? The car door was hanging open, the engine was running, idling. The keys were still in the ignition. In his urgency to stop the attack, he had jumped from the car without turning it off. At least he'd thrown it into park. Now he released the brakes, put it in gear, and drove down the dark alley around the building and out into the evening's brightly lit busy main street to follow along after the ambulance.

At the ER, the doctor quickly ran a scan to check for foreign materials, and found none. It was a small two-inch gash. Appreciating her thick, lovely hair, he did a minimal trim at the wound site, drawing the edges together with a few quick stitches. Being rusty red, the blood hid itself well, but was already drying in brownish clumps, gluing strands together. Someone would need to wash it cautiously.

She was good to go.

Dr. Hammond was a physician herself, so India was released into her care to go home, after the ER nurse explained how it was necessary to check India's pupils regularly during the night, and not to let her sleep too soundly, to wake her up periodically. Her doctor mother kept silent, impressed by the competence and compassion of both the responders and the hospital team.

Dave and the Phelpses stood waiting anxiously in the lobby.

As India left the ER with her parents, she saw her instructor and smiled weakly.

"Dave, thank you. I guess we'll have to do Checkpoints together another time. I hope I'm feeling like having a lesson tomorrow; I'd hate to get too far behind."

Her father scowled. "Who is this?" He queried coolly. Arriving when he did, he had not seen India cradled on Dave's lap, or he would have been doubly uneasy.

"Oh, Daddy, this is Dave Ridgeway. You know, my glider instructor. Dave, these are my parents." She was tired and sagging from the painkiller she'd been given. "Mom, this is Dave. You've heard me speak of him." She was beginning to feel dull and sleepy.

Her mother gazed at Dave and could see possibilities. Dave appeared intelligent, a fine-looking grown man. She smiled gently and said, "I understand from Mrs. Phelps here that it was you who rescued India from this assault and beat off the attacker. God bless you for your bravery. Who knows what he might have done?"

"Glad I was there," he murmured, extra glad he'd had the wit to tug up those jeans. He continued, "I was just lucky to get there when I did. Who would think anyone would do something like this, daylight and all. His eyes looked like a lunatic's. To me, he seemed high and drugged out."

The police had taken statements and fingerprints. The attacker had staggered against the wall after Dave struck him and left a full bloody handprint. He'd grabbed her bloodied hair to accomplish his viciousness. Now maybe they had something to go on—both for today and perhaps for the incident the weekend before.

TEN
AFTERWARD

Dave awkwardly said his good-byes and, not knowing what else to do with himself, headed off to meet his friends at Checkpoints. It was hardly a jolly Dave who joined them.

The pilots were waiting, wondering why he was so late. Where was India? Did he ever have a story to tell. But besides the attack, he would say nothing about the protective tenderness he had felt for the wounded India. His backside hurt from the parking lot; the warmth of her body was a memory on his skin. He couldn't speak of that either.

Would she be all right? Morning wasn't soon enough to find out. He cut short his part in the club's whoop-'em-up and looked up the Hammonds' number. Dare he call? Yes. It had to be okay, normal, to see about her, to do that. And so he did, around eight in the evening. Time enough to let things settle down at her house.

Her little brother, gangly twelve-year-old Eli, already almost six feet tall, answered the phone. When Dave announced himself, he got all cranked up. With his eager adolescent voice breaking, he demanded to hear how Dave

AFTERWARD

had hit the guy, the whole story. India had come around enough to weave the tale for her family, once she was resting at home. They were shaken, shocked, and worried. And impressed by Dave, the hero. And hugely grateful.

"How is she?" asked Dave.

"Ah, she's good. You want to talk to her?" asked Eli.

"Sure, if she wants to," he replied.

"I'll ask," said her brother, and called out, "Hey sis, you want to talk to Dave?" A telltale flush spread up from her neck across her face, as she came across the room to the phone.

"Ok, I'll take it," she told her brother.

Eli noticed the blush.

She took Sunday off from church and flying lessons, still plagued by a slight headache and general scalp soreness. The nurse said she needed to keep the area clean until it healed over. She gently pulled the bandages from her head and held a mirror up to survey the damage. Hm. Not too bad. A cut, stitched up, about two inches long, disagreeably laid bare by the shearing done by the EMT. She mostly hurt from the bone bruising blow. Oh, well. She'd be able to pull her hair across it. Maybe Claudia would help her.

"Claudie?" she called out. "I need you."

Her kid sister, fourteen-year-old Claudia, was almost paralyzed with worry. She wanted to say how sad she was, hug her sister and tell her how frightened she was that this had happened. But she hadn't known how to hold her with her head all bound up. She idolized her. She came running.

Now with India's head exposed, it was even harder. She held her arms out to her tentatively, tears in her eyes.

"It's okay, Claude. Heads bleed like crazy. I'm all right now, but my hair's a mess. Help me with it? We'll soak it out first; let's be careful to not wet the stitches."

Claudia gently washed her hair at the kitchen sink, using the spray attachment to swish out the dried blood. The water ran reddish brown, making her shudder, but she was pleased to be called on. And besides, she wanted to know if India could identify her attacker.

India figured her sister had questions and began speaking before she could start in on her. She wanted her to know something in particular and would tell her story in her own way.

"Claude, remember the party three years ago when I slipped away and people came to find me? You must have been twelve."

Claudia nodded and said "Yes, you were still fifteen, same age I am. Almost. Only you were more grown up, somehow," she sighed wistfully.

India looked at her severely. "Ha! Maybe I seemed it. But I wasn't, believe me." Her sister was listening. India paused, then said, "The reason I ran off, Claude, is because a man at the party was bothering me and I wanted to get away from him. And you know what? He followed me. *Followed* me! He actually came after me up our little mountain, and, shocker, surprised me at the top. He scared me to death. Then he just *vanished* . . . like a ghost, Claude! It was spooky. I think maybe the people who were looking for me scared him off. And you know what else? I think the face I saw last night in the alley, the guy who attacked me, was his face. I've been thinking about it all night. I'm scared, Claude."

AFTERWARD

Her sister wrapped a towel around India's wet head, leaving the bandaged stitches open to the air. They looked at each other.

"You have to tell Daddy and Mama. Right *now*," said Claudia, vehemently. She wasn't such a kid after all, thought India.

Forensics at the Valley Police Department had come up empty in identifying the handprint from the assault scene behind Phelps Pharmacy. Too blurry and streaked. Undaunted, the chief of police had sent the print to Pennsylvania State Forensics and was awaiting results. It would take some days, he knew, being as it was not a priority with the state. That is to say, no one had died. But Sergeant Moore had a sixth sense about these things, and had a notion something interesting would be forthcoming.

Sure enough; mid-week a report arrived. A vague smudged partial print emerged. Not much from the smeared blood, but perhaps enough to be useful, if put to trial. The print could belong to someone involved in drug use.

They found a conviction from two years before, a sentence reduced to community service, a sleight of hand of the attorney. Where did he work? At Ginsberg and Taylor, Accountants. Employed as a minor accountant and tech operative. Before that he'd been in sales at a pharmaceutical supply company. He'd been with Ginsberg and Taylor for five years. What a nice coincidence, thought Moore, who did not believe in coincidences.

Was it his print? Maybe. But there certainly wasn't

enough to make an arrest. Absolutely not enough there for a real ID. Merely circumstantial, any lawyer would argue.

The man was twenty-eight, unmarried. He had had some connection to the psychiatric clinic of Valley Hospital, through sales of pharmaceuticals. He had since gone to work for Ginsberg and Taylor Accountants. Dr. Phelps had met him briefly, thought him presentable and nice, and had included him in the group from Ginsberg and Taylor at their party some three years ago.

The Hammond home was a showcase. It had a view of the mountain ridge to the west, part of the vista from the elegantly arranged, sprawling patio, one made for parties. The perpetrator had sped back unseen that night of India's little sortie.

Well, not unseen.

The caterer had seen him darting into the shadows, and wondered about that. The caterer was the one who had pointed the way for the searchers.

ELEVEN
DRUG ADDICT'S NEEDS

Reeling from Dave's blow to his neck, the whacked-out druggie staggered out of the alley and walked around the corner, shoving a pistol into his jacket pocket as he went. His distraught appearance drew glances from a few pedestrians. Good-looking chap, but "off." The intense way he looked put off any offers to help. "He's drunk, honey," said one fellow to his date. "Let's stay well away from him."

Regaining his equilibrium, he straightened up and strolled carefully into the deepening night, making his way slowly back to his neighborhood, many blocks away.

"Shit," he muttered. He was jittery from the onset of withdrawal. Where was he going to find a fix? He had stupidly run out of his supply. He only kept a small stash for himself, after doling out the odd pill to his low-end friends. A few he had met at that soup kitchen when he did his community service.

Sharing his stash was a pleasant routine he had developed through the years, one that elevated his status in the eyes of those in his circle. Made them more amenable to favors he'd occasionally need. A ride here, an introduction there. Things like that. He liked being The Man. Status was important to him.

He'd been counting on easing into the pharmacy's back door via his usual M.O., his treasured master key. But he'd lost it. *Lost it!* He agonized over his carelessness, his stupidity, having to crudely crow-bar himself in. New supplies would be heaped tantalizingly, haphazardly on the pill-counter. They always were. He almost salivated, picturing them. Those pathetic Phelpses, both lazy and stupid, he sneered. The tidy counter had surprised him.

The addict wasn't unintelligent and had always understood the adage "no civilization, no success, without organization," a tenet of good business. The Phelpses were sloppy. No matter. Typical of addicts and sociopaths, he just wanted to reap the results of others' efforts.

And that girl. Right out the door and smack into my arms. She felt so good. I never wanted to do someone so much and so fast, in all my life! He shook his head at his urgency.

Arriving at his building, he leaned against the door frame to steady himself. Yeah, she was something else. Looked like the one he hadn't humped on that hill. Those eyes. Yeah, had to be. He shook his head at his thoughts. *You're losing it, buddy.* He had to be more careful. He had almost ripped her pants off, her knocked out and all.

In the darkness, he felt for his fly to be sure it was closed, passing his hand interestedly over his bulge. Although coming down from his last dose, and definitely needing another, he was still engorged by amphetamine-enhanced heat and desire. He decided it was time for its release. Oh, that would feel good. He could pump himself, but more interesting to find a chick who'd be out hunting.

DRUG ADDICT'S NEEDS

After washing up, he went down the block to a bar. He'd heard you could buy a quick fix from Sam the bartender, so he would do that then corral something for sex.

"Hey honey," he said, boldly staring at a snockered blonde, his eyes aggressively roving over her body. She raised her drink and smiled, lolling her head coyly, arching her back, thrusting her breasts toward him. He smiled and indicated a "wait for me," and caught the bartender's eye. He jerked his head toward the men's room.

Sam knew immediately this was a customer for a fix; he had that tightly wired look. He and the bartender went in together.

The addict pulled out some cash, rolling a bill into a straw. The supplier laid a line on the sink edge, which he snorted up, deeply and gratefully. He waited a moment for the euphoria to hit. Oh, yeah. "Thanks, man. Good stuff." Should have been mellowing, but not exactly. Cocaine, it turned out, could have different effects after long use. That, combined with the residual amphetamine, was an interesting combo.

The bartender shoved the cash into his pocket and returned to his post.

The blonde sat beside him and stroked his thigh, looking down and giggling pleasurably at his straining pants. Her legs were spraddled open on her barstool, skirt raised invitingly above her knees. She brushed a breast against his arm, and eyed him questioningly. He smiled and nodded, putting his arm around her. They left.

TWELVE
SUNDAY DINNER

"Mom, Dad, I have something I need to tell you," said India, her sister at her side, holding her hand.

What was this? Her parents took in the sisters' strength-in-numbers approach, looking at them with curiosity. What was happening here?

"Mama, Daddy," said Claudia, "India believes she might know something about her attacker, and she's frightened."

India held her sister's hand tightly. She looked at her parents and took a steadying breath to speak.

"Well, I'm not sure that I *know*, but the face I got a glimpse of looked like the man at your party, Mama, the one where I escaped up the hill. "I never said anything at the time, but a guest of yours followed me up there, scaring me with his weird attention. The thing is, I never said anything to you because when I turned to look behind me at him, he wasn't there. *Not there!* I thought maybe I had imagined him, fantasized him, I was such a dreamy kid. I thought maybe I was crazy." She began to cry softly, again wondering if she was maybe a little nutty. Her mother, the psychiatrist, might think so. She didn't want to even go there.

SUNDAY DINNER

Her mother took her in her arms. "Oh, how I wish you had said something at the time, India. That young man was seen by the workers leaving the party when you did; he went racing out through the tree shadows. That's how they knew where to go hunting for you. And later on they saw him getting into someone's car. I had questions about his behavior myself, India. You poor lamb. All this time . . . "

India sobbed and shuddered her relief, hugging her parents.

"What do I do now?" she asked. "I don't know who he is."

"I'll check my party guest list. I never throw those out. We'll figure it out. He has to be taken in for questioning about the assault on you, if nothing else." Her mother looked at India intently. "But I'll bet there will be plenty else."

———◆———

Dave called about noon, asking about India, not knowing if it was too forward of him to call again so soon.

Forward? He was the hero who had kept her from suffering God knows what. No worries there. He asked if India would like a visitor, and her mother suggested he join them for Sunday dinner. He quickly checked the skies and his schedule. The skies were overdeveloping, meaning too many clouds were crowding together for any good lift, and his schedule was clear. He had planned on working on some programming at home if he wasn't going to be soaring. But Sunday dinner with the Hammonds? Work could wait.

"Thank you, Dr. Hammond. That would be really nice." He grinned.

Ah, hooray! The day was not a loss, thought India. Her

headache was minimal, her hair was clean, her scary memories had been put right, taking an old weight off her chest, and she was going to see Dave. Yes, her scalp was sore. But she'd have danced around the room if she hadn't wanted to hide how happy she was to be seeing him.

Today the neighbors were all bringing extra covered dishes out of consideration for overstressed Elizabeth Hammond. They all knew how frantic she had to have been over India's attack, and wanted to help her with the Sunday feast. That is, if Liz would even be having company, what with India's condition. But yes, the feast was on. You need your friends in times of stress. Here they'd all fretted about India's exposing herself to danger while flying—and good grief, instead she had tripped into it through earnest work. They tsk-tsked, shaking their heads, muttering that there was no justice.

Guests came at the appointed hour, curious to see the victim and to hear from her own lips just how it had happened. They had watched her grow up and shared her parents' relief at her escaping a major catastrophe.

The table was laden with Elizabeth Hammond's roast beef, Claudia's dumplings, Edie from next door's scalloped potatoes, Edie's sister Susie's two apple pies with crisp, thin, sugary crusts, Paul Hammond's steamed broccoli with oregano-lemon garlic butter, and neighbor Elliot's own garden greens tossed into a bright salad with avocado vinaigrette dressing. Dave arrived a few moments before the rest to greet and look over India on his own. Then he took his place at the table.

India motioned for him to sit beside her.

The neighbors' noses fairly twitched with curiosity,

eyes shining with interest, turning toward him. Elizabeth Hammond introduced him around the table, briefly explaining his role in the affair, and about his being a flight instructor.

India joined in. "Dave actually is a computer software engineer, a programmer, working for—who did you say your company is, Dave?"

He glanced sideways at her. *Sweet. She's trying to present me as a stable, grown-up wage earner to these serious folks, more than just a risk-taking wild sports guy.* He responded aloud, "I work for Edwards and Burnham, Systems Managers."

Nods of approval passed around the table.

Paul, India's father, took that in. So this young man was not just a brave jock, rescuer of his beautiful daughter—he was a responsible adult. This took him aback. He could object to and run off horny boys, but this man? He struggled with his water, recovered, and announced that he would now say the blessings. Heads bowed.

After the last pie crumb had been whisked off the table and the dishwasher was whirring in the kitchen, guests gone with their emptied platters—the family settled in for some sincere questioning. Dave was ready. He knew he would eventually be spotlighted by the lawyer's steady gaze, and would have some pithy questions to answer.

"So . . . you from around here, Dave?" asked Paul Hammond, casually.

"No, sir," he responded. "I'm not from Valley. I grew up in Pittsburgh. After I graduated from Carnegie Mellon, I got a job here. Nice town."

Ooh, that was heavy. Here his daughter hadn't even thought of where to apply to colleges, and her boyfriend—was he her boyfriend?—was already done and finished with all that, and from a top-of-the-line university. Elizabeth saw the problem, too. The Hammonds were not stupid.

Dave was wary. He was not about to cave to suggestions of a liaison between him and India. They had only just met, and he figured she was too young for a permanent relationship. He recognized this, despite his enormous attraction to her. What he wanted to do, besides keep her company for a bit, was to make her into the pilot she wanted to be. How could he make them see that? A conundrum. And how to handle India, now under his spell as the white knight.

Scary thing was, he liked being her white knight. Even as he sat there with them, his mind whirring with arguments against their matchup, he was sinking. He was smitten. But he had to be the responsible one, didn't he? His feelings were too new, but he was sure this was not going to be the scarfing up of a tidbit that he had at first fancied. Oh no.

THIRTEEN
A CLUE?

Monday morning, headache mostly gone, India felt well enough to go to work. But the first part of the day involved a visit to Sergeant Moore at the police station, accompanied by her dad, to tell what she felt she knew, or suspected, of her assailant.

"Good morning, Sergeant," said India, joining her father in his salutations.

"Sergeant," said her father, "we may have something for you."

Her mother had trotted out her old party list and figured out the man's name was Mark Brissante, employee of the accounting firm of Ginsberg and Taylor. Maybe he still worked there. They conveyed this information to the officer, who was plainly glad to get it.

"I'll start digging for information on this chap right away," said Sergeant Moore. "Thank you counselor, thank you India. I'll let you know what I find out."

"Brissante . . . Brissante . . . " murmured Moore to himself, as India and her father left his office. There was an arrest a while back, and maybe a petition to commute the sentence? He couldn't remember. French kind of name, setting it apart. Names around here were usually more Welsh or Germanic. But he did recall a tidy fact. The accounting firm where Brissante worked had direct access to the Phelps Pharmacy computer—this he had learned in his initial questions after the burglary.

"Lydia!" He called in his secretary. "Please, look up records on a Mark Brissante."

"Funny how small the world can be," he said to no one in particular, smirking into his coffee cup.

The Phelpses were relieved to see that India really was all right, and that her beautiful hair was none the worse for the EMT's handling of it. Today it was in a loose braid, not back in its bun, crisscrossed over the wound, more relaxed so as not to pull at the stitches or the strip-bandage covering them. Maudie watched Rollie duck his head in awkwardness in his shy appreciation of her beauty.

She smiled to herself, and patted his arm. "She is a looker, Rollie, isn't she? I think so too. And a fine human, a good worker. We thank God for sparing her worse violence."

She took India's hand. "How's the head, India? Did they have to take off much hair? How do you feel?"

"Oh, Maudie, the EMT was very gentle, really," explained India. "My scalp, my head, is only a bit sore back there. I think I got whacked with a gun butt. I'm very, *very* lucky, really—we all are—that by pure chance my instructor happened around that corner when he did. Well . . . maybe not by chance.

Oh, Maudie, doesn't that make you wonder about fate, or guardian angels?"

They both stared at her, nodding vaguely at this revelation of India's character.

"Now we just have to start listing the inventory again. Checking to see what you ordered, and what someone else might have ordered. It will take some in-depth inspection."

India was now certain that Brissante, or someone in that company, had insinuated extra orders via the accounting firm and gotten whatever he wished, any items he wished, at his leisure. There was a regularity and a sameness to it. What else could it be? They of course were unaware that the thief had accessed his pile of goodies through entry with a master key. Things were always such a mess, they hadn't noticed the growing and diminishing pile.

The drug store was this druggie's candy tree, and that had to stop. But how? They needed a computer-savvy tech. Again she thought of Dave, and as she made stacks and inventoried, she wondered how she could bring him into this.

FOURTEEN
MARK'S ITCH

*B*rissante tossed a few bills at the bimbo after some vigorous, grunting satisfaction, and then firmly handed her out of his apartment door. "Any time you want to, honey," she said. I'm always there at Sammy's if you get lonesome." She didn't fool herself that she could make something more of this. She'd been around too long and had too many years tucked away on her face and body.

"Okay, babe—thanks for today," he grinned, and patted her bottom farewell. "Careful on the stairs," he said. "No fancy elevators here." He grimaced sourly.

Now to come to grips with those drugs waiting at the store. Sheesh that had gone badly. He would just have to do a midnight patrol tonight or tomorrow night. Or maybe he would leave the Phelpses alone for a while. He had another couple of accounts he figured he could tap satisfactorily, with a little work. He could have possibly become a dealer with his access to drugs, but it would have been a full-time endeavor, and dealer was not how he saw himself. But he would need another fix soon. He thought maybe he could ease some Sudafed from a display at a different pharmacy, and work up some meth in his kitchen, but the process was dangerous and smelly, and he had nothing on hand at the moment.

As he brushed his teeth and swished himself through the shower, he continued cursing himself for his knee-jerk attack on the girl—but particularly for losing his hard-gotten master key. Breaking and entering wasn't really his style. Very low. He thought of himself as much slicker and cleverer than that.

"How dumb was that, nitwit?" He reproached himself, looking in the mirror. "She saw you, I know she did," he muttered. "Jeez, you coulda killed her with that whack to the head. That's all you need to answer to now, a murder charge. Mark, you have got to get yourself together." He acknowledged to himself that drugs made him wild.

Alas, he relished that wild feeling.

He walked dripping, naked, to his dresser and pulled open the top drawer. He found it under his socks. "There you are, you little silver doodad," he said to the barrette. "Hers, I think. No?" The air was cool on his wet skin. He liked that. It was an improvement over the perfumed sweat of the barfly. He rocked back on his heels, spreading his legs apart so he would air-dry. And fondled the barrette.

FIFTEEN
A CONUNDRUM

*E*lizabeth Hammond pondered her daughter's situation. She agreed it would be an interesting plus for India to have a pilot's license on her college applications, but involvement with her instructor? Not. As a devoted mother, she became agitated, committed to safeguarding her baby. But good heavens, her "baby" was already eighteen, a legal adult. She prayed she had done her parenting well. But how much common sense did India have, how much good judgement, wisdom? So far she had shown maturity beyond her years. But her mother didn't think she could count on that, now that it seemed love was stirring in her heart. And loins? Never before this. For whatever reason, India had always stayed aloof from romance. There had been no young crushes.

Dr. Hammond looked over her office appointment calendar. It was clear for the next few hours. So she had time to put her attention to something else. She had another reason to worry about India. The workplace that had seemed so safe, so secure, the job that they were so delighted about, was just another hot spot of danger. Should she encourage her daughter to leave it?

A CONUNDRUM

India and her bosses took a brief break from the tedious inventory, and sat together at a booth for coffees. It was still early.

India spoke. "It might seem obvious, but how about barring the back door and only use the front? It is a solution. That would steer burglary attempts away from the alley around to where it's open to public view, where there's lots of foot traffic. That would make it harder for anything sneaky to take place."

"Well—there are fire laws decreeing a fire exit. How do we get around that?" queried Rollie. "We have to have a door back there."

Maudie spoke up. "Let's call the fire department in on this. They may have a one-way exit door solution for us," she said and pushed herself up to go to the phone, not wanting to delay action.

The fire department, being the fire department, came with sirens howling on the chief's car, pulling up and sliding into a space it could barrel out of quickly. The chief rocked himself out of his seat, big belly almost exiting the door first, cradled by his thighs. His uniform was being tested at the seams. Chief Baxter liked his vittles.

"Good grief, Ed, it's just a consulting visit, not an emergency," growled Rollie. Everyone at the strip mall had gathered outside, necks craning, to see what was going on. The chief waved them off, with a shake of his head.

"Oh, heck, you know I forget to turn that thing off. I

hardly hear it. It usually *is* an emergency when I go out, so it's set to blow. Sorry about that."

"Well, come on back to the pharmacy, and I'll show you the problem." Rollie took his arm and began leading a procession of fire chief and assistant, then Maudie, India, a couple of sales clerks. Maisie, too, fell in line, naturally curious. That would not do.

Rollie turned and said "Maisie, you are needed in front at the cash register—and take these clerks with you. They need to be on the job. The chief is only here to consult about the back door."

"Okay, boss," said Maisie, disappointedly snapping her gum and gathering the clerks, sashaying away, one on each arm till she propelled them into the aisles, back to work.

Customers were looking on inquisitively, but returned to their errands when the action cleared.

Mark, lurking there to see if he had any chance of recovering his loot, was one of those slouching about, hidden inconspicuously behind the others. He caught the words "back fire door." India, who was in the pharmacy, never knew he was there.

SIXTEEN
MARK: PERSONA, M.O.

*H*earing the conversation about a fire door, Mark saw his source dry up. He knew he wasn't going to be able to get supplies there, not any more. Not with one of those one-way fire doors. Nothing less than a bulldozer could get through one of those. And he hadn't slipped to the hooded thief stage yet as far as a front door approach was concerned. Bad news. He would be seen easily at night, in the illuminated, patrolled parking lot.

He strolled out casually, turning his face away from Maisie's inquisitive, birdlike gaze. It would take days before the door was installed; maybe he could grab up his booty before that happened. But how? No . . . he would have to write off this supply. Time to move into another avenue.

Of course he could try to dry out, go cold turkey. That would eliminate all of his problems. But having done that once already, he knew it was a hell he wasn't eager to go through again. And the lure of drugs was too powerful. He hadn't lasted. He'd had a drug rehab counselor a couple of years ago when he'd hit bottom. Maybe he would look him up.

In the meantime, he needed to get something to calm his

nerves. He went to Sammy's for another quick fix. Sammy opened up by nine for alcoholics and hair-of-the-dog folks. The broad wasn't there—too early. He was glad. Nerves settled, a high established, he reported in to the accounting firm to see if they had work for him to do that day.

Mark was basically a jobber, one who worked when needed. When calmed by drugs, he was charming, nice looking and intelligent, and he presented himself well. He had a good track record in their sales department, corralling new accounts, and they knew he could handle their clients' accounting records well.

He had access to an amazing amount of information. He scrupulously kept the clients' spreadsheets up to date. He was not college educated, but night courses in accounting and IT training served him well. He had been their highest-ranked student the two years he was there. He was born intelligent and strong, the son of grassroots Americans.

Underneath, though, he didn't fit the all-American profile—honor, faith, loyalty—all that Boy Scout stuff. Being a thief or manipulating people did not bother him. He felt he deserved the good things in life. He'd been into party drugs since he was twelve, snitching from his damaged Gulf War veteran dad's supply of pain killers, getting high with his no-'count friends. He was not ashamed of robbing his pain-racked hero father of relief. He wasn't a hero to Mark. His father was just a handy path to his kicks. He was not crazy about his dad. His father had not been around much, always off somewhere in therapy treatments or sleeping off a pain med, and when he was up and about, he wasn't much company. The invalid took up most of his mother's attention.

Mark, charming on the outside, was a bitter kid on the inside. He was glad to find companionship outside of his home, a gang who liked him. Anyway, once he started on drugs, he didn't wish to quit, or couldn't quit. His Dad had become so addled he didn't notice missing pills. His mother had seen changes in her son, but she didn't understand what was going on.

"Are you okay, Markie? You seem strange."

"I'm fine, mom—don't worry," he would snap impatiently.

Besides intelligence, Markie had peasant cunning, a sly cleverness better than street smarts. He made sure his grades didn't reflect his slide into the dark side. Public schools were too easy for him to let that happen, especially to a high-IQ kid like Mark. When once he did poorly on a trigonometry quiz, his teacher took him aside for a talking to. But Markie was a warm-eyed, charming faker and fraud. And he was clear headed at the time. He successfully, craftily, reassured the math teacher. The event was a heads-up for him. No more hints to adults suggesting he might be a lazy badass kid, one looking for a free pass. Especially since he was and felt he deserved it.

SEVENTEEN
GINSBERG AND TAYLOR

"Morning, Mark. You up for some sales calls?" asked his boss, as Mark sauntered into the offices of Ginsberg and Taylor. "There are a couple of new prospects we'd like to add to our client list."

"Sure," said Mark, grinning. "I'm in the mood to conquer worlds. Lemme at them."

Mr. Ginsberg tore off slips of paper with the information on them, and waved him on his way.

"Boy, Mark is certainly a positive, upbeat winner of a guy," he said to himself. "Nice that he found us. He's been good for business."

Off went Mark, noting that these hoped-to-be clients for the accounting firm were new hospital supply companies, with branches in other towns. Oh, that was good. He requisitioned a company car for the sales calls, and headed on his way.

The phone rang on Ginsberg's desk and was answered in the anteroom by his secretary. In a moment her head appeared around the door. "Mr. Ginsberg, I have a Dr. Hammond on the line for you." He indicated he would take the call, and picked up his phone.

"Hello Elizabeth," he smiled into the receiver and looked out at the sunny day. "How are you this bright morning, and what can I do for you?"

"Well, Ephron, this is a little touchy I'm afraid. Do you recall the young man you brought to our party a few years ago?" she asked hesitantly. "Can you tell me something about him?"

"Sure I do," he answered. "Great party, Elizabeth. I think I told you that at the time, and how much our team appreciated being included. Lovely situation you have there, your views and all. Well—the fellow we brought, Mark Brissante, with whom I believe you already were slightly acquainted, is our best salesman and accounting tech." He paused, wondering what was up. "I think you had previously met him as a sales rep. Is there something I can help you with?"

"This is most awkward, Ephron. Our daughter India was assaulted by an apparent drug addict the other evening, and is plagued by the notion that she recognized his face. She thinks it was the young man from that party we had. So. What is your take on your employee, this Mark? Any possibility at all that it could have been him?"

"Good heavens, Elizabeth—not Mark! He's eminently trustworthy. You do know his dad is an honored veteran? The poor guy got shot up in the Gulf War fiasco. Good people. I would never imagine a boy of his to be capable of physical violence toward a woman. She has to be confused." He stopped for a moment, and thought. "You say she was assaulted? What happened?"

Elizabeth explained that India had been knocked out by a blow from her assailant, and glimpsed his face briefly as she crumpled. She did not go into the robbery aspects of the scenario.

"That's it, then. She no doubt had her senses addled and didn't see right. It just could not have been Mark."

"Very well," said Elizabeth, wondering about the clarity of India's observations. "We'll leave it at that." And they rang off.

Sitting back at her desk, Elizabeth picked up a pen and began doodling hearts, what she always did when thinking of her children. She reflected on her interchange with the accounting firm, and decided Ephron must be right. She would speak with India.

About that, and the wisdom of keeping the pharmacy job.

EIGHTEEN
VERNON

Seeing how his supply line had collapsed, Mark wisely decided to try a different route to replenish his cache. He had friends in neighboring towns: a few other addicts, some who owed him. He decided to call in a favor. One man in particular had talents and skills that could be useful, one to whom he had passed along little friendly freebies in his role of good buddy. Mark didn't dare go the computer hacking route again, at least not for a while—and this guy was a skilled burglar. His best characteristic? He had an everyman's face. He looked, well, in all ways plain vanilla medium. Medium height, medium coloring, bland features. He could be a maintenance worker, a doctor, a bank teller. No one would ever remember him, he was so indistinguishable. Nope, no one would remember him, even if they saw him clearly. After they had executed their plan, even if seen, witnesses would not be able to pull up his face. Markie stood out more. He would have to be the guy in the shadows.

But what were they going to steal? Silly question. Drugs, of course. Vernon sometimes also clipped the odd piece of jewelry—not enough to be immediately noticed and reported as theft. He targeted anything small and not tacked down, anything he could get rid of, fence, quickly.

The plan? Markie figured they could reap the fruits of hospital supply cabinets, particularly in the next town's General Hospital. Those so-called secure cabinets that nurses carelessly left unlocked until the ends of their shifts would be Vern's targets. Mark knew that particular hospital well enough. That was where he had been taken when he overdosed a couple of years ago. That episode was something he'd carefully hidden from the sunlit world outside his dark one of addiction, especially from Ginsberg and Taylor.

It was an old-fashioned hospital, a rabbit warren of corridors and special care sections. When his friend Vernon had come to see about him, his friend had outfitted himself in green cotton hospital scrubs that he lifted from a rack in a back corridor. So costumed, he had surreptitiously perused the hallways' work stations, coming across as merely one of the constantly changing teams of orderlies. He added the handy garb to his closet of getups.

They knew they shouldn't be seen together, Mark and Vernon. So they arranged a meeting in an iffy part of town where their first target would be. Mark pasted on a mustache and wore glasses. Corny, he thought, but it did change his looks. He tugged tousled hair down to his eyebrows so that he looked dorky and bookish.

Vernon, having such an insignificant profile, didn't wear anything unusual. He merely pulled on unaccustomed sweat pants, sneakers, and a hoodie. Good camouflage for him. Usually he presented himself as a dapper dude—polished tasseled loafers, neckties, and buttoned-down shirts. He liked to cultivate the style of a successful broker type. If asked, he would claim some large workplace that handled mortgage bundling. Fact was, he lived nicely and entirely off proceeds of small jewelry thefts and drug trafficking. But no fancy car or dangling gold chains for him—such a cliché, waving the "Here I am" flag to investigators.

Instead, he did his light-fingered work in the bathrooms of hotels and homes where he could discreetly slither in. It was easy, and he liked the elation of working on the edge. In the hotels, there was always a distractible maid—"Sweetheart, room 223 is looking for fresh towels"—or sheets, if he needed more time.

Then there was always a garage entry into high-priced residences. He had a remote control with enough codes to open Fort Knox, rigged up by a geeky pal of his oldest boy living in New York with his mother. There were nearly always goodies to pocket once he got in—tubes of heroin, baggies of marijuana, and even the odd plastic bag of crystal meth. He was sometimes troubled about how addicted the nation had become, then shrugged it off. Their loss, his gain. A hotel room theft of drugs would never be reported, nor would a home theft. These he would fence on the street via certain shadowy contacts he had cultivated over the last decade or so. He had never been caught. His contacts had also remained unpinched.

Vernon considered himself lucky, but he knew luck wasn't enough. He also knew he was, and had to be, very damned clever. And he had recognized a similar gleam of intelligence in Mark Brissante. He and Mark made a good team. Markie had a problem with drugs, and Vernon knew it. Vern liked him anyway, even though Vern himself had never ventured farther than grass in his search for head trips. So he put up with Mark's peccadillo.

And also, Markie could find him some bedtime action when he needed it. Mark had the sexy looks and ways to round up sweet stuff. He had done so and shared generously. Yes, he owed Mark.

NINETEEN
FIRE DOORS

The next morning, Tuesday, the fire chief came by with a catalog of doors. They had but to choose one, and he would get it for them at discount. They called in Charlie, the grizzled, bearded maintenance man, to bring him up to date and ask for an installer reference.

"I can do it myself, don't you worry about that," said Charlie. "I worked in construction before I got too arthritic. But I can easily do this, especially with the help of my other guy. It's a requirement of the frame being well-anchored to the outside wall. See this frame here?" He thumped a stubby finger on a catalog picture. "This door comes with its own secure frame. You'd need a tank to get in, after we mount this thing. See the push bar? It's the only one on the door, see? Only way to open it. And it's on the inside, see? Only way that door can open is to push out." He hitched up his pants. "It's the law, you see."

He rambled on. "Yup. Ever since Boston's Cocoanut Grove nightclub fire way back in 1942 when most doors generally opened in—didja know that? No laws on that, back then—and a god-awful disaster happened. A fire started in that nightclub's basement bistro. Flames leapt from burning decorations, flames and smoke filled the place, people panicked, they piled up like rats on top of each other trying to get out, *and burned up.* The pushing, panicking crowds trampled each other trying to push down the door. The only doors, a revolving one and a regular one beside it—except for one down in the basement kitchen, where a few slipped through—only opened *inward.* They could not get out. Trapped. It was grisly. Hundreds died horribly. Since then, all doors in the US of A open *outward.*"

Charlie stepped back to see their reaction, fingering his beard. They nodded in unison. They knew all about this urban tale of horror, but would not spoil his moment.

"So this here only opens out. Actually, all of 'em in this here catalog open out. Like I said, it's the law. This is what you gotta have, and I can see it's put in right. I have experience with this sort of thing," he said, flexing a bit of authority.

The owners made their choice, and the chief made a note to order it. Charlie said he'd be watching for the delivery; he would line up his construction guy to help install it.

Then the fire chief made his way out the front, hoisted his stomach into the front seat, and left, again forgetting to turn off the siren.

TWENTY
MAMA—0
INDIA—2

India went to work, this time to conquer the paper filing, getting orders put away properly. Things were settling down and her headache was gone. The Phelpses seemed calmer now that a solution was in the works to safeguard their business.

Maudie pulled India aside. "India, let's see if we can separate out the things I know we never ordered. I'm pretty sure I can quickly peg the strangers. Almost anything starting with 'oxy' for starters. I want to contact the drug companies and see about returns. Drugs for pain are hatefully expensive, our hacker's apparent head-numbing drugs of choice—and I'd like to minimize our losses. It will take some work; a lot of these items we hardly see, weird names made up mostly from the chemical derivatives."

This was work that appealed to India—a reason for stacking and sorting, more than just alphabetizing things on shelves. Checking chemical compounds would be a pleasure. She threw herself into it with enthusiasm. But soon, digging deep into archived data on the computer, she saw befuddling concoctions that went way beyond her meager knowledge of chemistry. Her eyes itched with fatigue. Pharmaceuticals were so complex. They rose into the stratosphere of chemical equations, equations that would add, divide, and multiply their components all the way around a room of blackboards, top to bottom. Well, she thought, touching her stitches. This won't do.

"Maudie . . . do we need to check, confirm, actual compounds' formulas? I doubt the formulas would be challenged. Geez, public high school chemistry hardly got us past NaCl—table salt, you know. These look like hypotheticals behind the Big Bang."

"No, of course we don't need to do that. Just look up the names of pain drugs. There should be an online category for those. Check and see what we have on the counter here from that list. Our thief wouldn't be pilfering in any complicated way." Maudie viewed with amusement the relief on India's face. "That's a lot easier way to find our troubles. If you want, focus on drugs whose names start with 'amphet,' 'oxy,' or 'hydro.' That should do it."

India put in a hard day's work, picking and checking, as well as doing the usual stacking and alphabetizing. Keeping track of inventory was ongoing and interminable. She was glad to leave at five, and would be glad to get home.

She called her father for a lift home. She did not trust that her attacker was through with her. When she finished up in the pharmacy, she departed through the front door, keeping herself alert as she walked into the parking area to meet her father.

"How was work today, honey?" her dad asked.

"Fine Daddy . . . mostly just a lot of sorting and filing," replied India. "I'll tell you everything when we're all together at dinner. Easier that way."

Her father nodded agreeably. His curiosity could wait.

And tell she finally did, all about how she was checking off items against an online drug list. And about the fire chief and the new back door, with maintenance man Charlie front and center. Including the Cocoanut Grove history. They listened without interruption.

But a set-to was brewing.

Her mother was obviously agitated about something. At India's insistence, she finally broke her silence.

"Well. All right then—my turn." She straightened up in her chair, and looked seriously at her daughter.

"I called Mr. Ginsberg today, and asked him about the employee he brought to our party three years ago. It was awkward, of course. I told him that you had been assaulted, and that you felt you recognized your attacker. I gave him the name from my guest list. He was shocked, acknowledging his employee and swearing to his good reputation. He insisted this man would absolutely never hurt a woman. He was appalled at the idea, India." Her mother peered at her closely. "So, my love, are you quite sure it was him? Mr.

Ginsberg believes you must have been fuzzy from the blow to your head."

India looked at her mother with astonishment. "You called about this man?" she asked.

"Yes, I did," said her mother. "And another thing. I do not think it wise for you to continue working at the pharmacy. There is obviously danger there."

"Oh, Mama. You can't *mean* that," wailed India. "My job at the pharmacy means everything to me. I'm sure it's not dangerous. I mean maybe it's dangerous in that they sell drugs, but every place has its dangers. Good heavens—a liquor store could be dangerous. Well . . . I'm not going to work at a liquor store, so scratch that. But any place with a cash register is potentially dangerous. What do you want me to do? Give up the place where I'm using the marketing skills I learned in my honors course? Give up a job at a place where I'm respected and appreciated? All because some meth-head tried to rob it? Please. Don't do this to me. You know I respect your opinion and love you, but this is something I found for myself and I am truly needed by these people. Actually *needed*. You have no idea how far behind the times they are in tending to their business affairs. I am their answer."

India rallied all her skills, ones genetically handed to her from her father, to argue her case with her mother. And her mother backed off, at least for the moment.

"Oh, India—I worry so about you."

"Well don't worry Mama. I will be fine. The Phelpses will be fine. All will be well. I'm sure of it."

Her inner voice was suggesting otherwise, and she chose to ignore it. People do that, when it's bothersome to heed it.

TWENTY-ONE
IF IT WALKS LIKE A DUCK

*B*ent over beers in a dimly lit bar, a smoke-filled one on the sorry side of a neighboring town, locus of Mark's next target, the two men, Vern and Markie, began formulating their plan—one they would initiate the next day. Their drugs were running out. Markie could get a hit or two more from bartender Sam, but Sam himself was looking for a fresh supply. The sort the bartender provided was not so easy for Markie or Vern to find.

Sam was bulbous-nosed, cheeks mapped with spidery red veins, the bushy eyebrow type—a sociable sort with a big smile for everyone. And a good listener. He knew who needed what, and he was always available to place and fill orders. Sam understood misery.

But his kind of merchandise was controlled by the local larger underworld and had to come from the Network. "Network" was the euphemism for a dangerous worldwide drug-merchandising organization, anchored in and powered by Eastern Europe. Vern and Mark operated on their own, intentionally small-time, not a part of the bigger supply scene. But they said they'd keep an eye out for some stuff for him. Sam sensed they had plans, but not how or where. Nor did he want to know.

Vern already had his idea of how and where; the only thing was to line up Markie with the getaway vehicle. Since Mark was not privy to company car use after hours, the deed had to be done during normal nine-to-five working hours. That suited both of them. At the moment he had no other vehicle sources, and the hospital drug cabinets would be locked up by the end of the workday. The hospital pharmacy was never a source for Vern. Way too secure. So Vern was good with all this.

Ever attentive to details, Vernon had cunningly taken a cell-phone photo of a hospital orderly wearing a hangtag id. With that photo, he had gotten something made up for himself. Not his own name, of course. He donned those snitched orderly's scrubs and went in by the back way. There he was checked by a guard who glanced perfunctorily at his hangtag, waving him by unchallenged.

Equipped with cleaning gear, he took an elevator up to the hospital's interesting parts. Head down, moving a mop, he shuffled down a corridor, watching for a vacant nurse's station. Bingo. With eyes as if they were in the back of his head, he pilfered the cabinet, leaving a few things behind to divert nurses from the fact that supplies were missing. He sneaked the items into a waist pack, then strolled with his mop to another floor, and accomplished his business again. And so it went off perfectly, unnoticed by hospital staff.

His stomach pooching out quite a bit more upon exiting than when he went in, Vernon strolled nonchalantly past parked ambulances and hospital workers, cigarette smokers having their own kind of fixes. Sticking his feet out ducklike as part of his disguise, he ambled down the block to Markie's awaiting, idling car. Not unusual at hospitals. He was glad the car bore only a discreet logo, not large letters trumpeting the accounting company's name. He opened the door, slid in, and worked at removing the pack filled with his haul. He arched and writhed until he got it off, all while Mark was driving down back streets, cautiously avoiding pedestrians. Soon they were speeding down the highway toward Valley, smug with their spoils. Still, Mark watched carefully for any signs of police attention. A little paranoia was good.

Markie himself had had his own successes earlier that day. Before he and Vern had gone out on their sortie, he had called on the prospects assigned by his boss. The people found Mark to be pleasantly professional, calm, knowledgeable, and very reasonable. He had been quickly passed along to higher-ups to make his presentation to those with more authority.

The two companies had been attracted to the concept of external accounting, especially someone local with a reliable reputation like Ginsberg and Taylor. They liked the idea of nearby control of their affairs. They signed up.

Mark, later on, would bring up how a direct connection to the firm could be worked out easily, and would be in everyone's best interest. He would wait until enough inconvenient internal blunders surfaced, causing delays and snarls in the company's invoice system. That would happen. It always did. And Ginsberg and Taylor would be there, solicitous, ready with the solution.

TWENTY-TWO
NO LIGHTS AT ALL

The day had been successful. He had left Vern off near his apartment and returned the company car before five in the afternoon. Good timing, good harvest.

In the darkness of his room, a glass of Scotch in his hand, Markie popped a pill, the stronger dose of amphetamine that Vern had plucked from the hospital. He settled into his easy chair to wait for it to take effect, looking out the window onto city lights. His next thought was to see about harnessing himself some action. He felt it building. He was getting high, feeling that power and itch of wildness wanting an outlet. He thought about the easy slut at the bar. He thought about young tender green-eyes. Ah, red-headed green eyes. Yes. He would follow her and see about her. Not right away. But he would find her, and he would have her. In the meantime, he would look for easy blondie. He didn't need a challenge today.

The fire had kindled in his groin, and he had to get it taken care of. At least once tonight, maybe more. He bet the bimbo could do whatever he wanted. And down he clambered, jacket over his shoulders, out the door. Sam's bar was just down the block and around the corner. He looked in—it seemed nearly empty. He went in.

Spotting his prey, he grinned engagingly and descended on her. The bartender was away from the bar. He should buy her a drink first, those were the rules. Also, he must pretend he thought she was a special tidbit, one he'd been looking for ever since the last time. She said she didn't need the drink. She opened her lips and opened her legs, there on the barstool, as she had the first time. Now she also reached up beneath her skirt, caressing her inner thigh, and indicated he should too. He shook his head "Not here—let's go have some private fun. I'm a private kinda guy."

"Well there's nobody here to see nothin', but ok," she sniffed, smoothing down her skirt. She retrieved her purse from where it hung under the bar, and they went out.

"You wanna come to my place?" she asked. "It's a little bit comfier than yours. And I have a mirror where we can even watch what we're doing," she giggled. "It's not far—just a coupla blocks."

"Okay babe, let's go watch ourselves," he laughed. The drugs were acting a little funny, he thought. He felt a meanness start to course up into his brain, along with the urgent drive to get into her. Oh well—that would probably wear off.

They started walking the two blocks in inky darkness; the street lamps were burned out. "They're supposed to fix those," she said.

He said he had cat eyes and could see in the dark.

There wasn't even a pair of passing headlights. She laughed, and put her hand into his pocket, feeling for his hardness. He opened his pants, fired further by her touch. He yanked her around and rubbed against her, pulling up her skirt, forcing her legs apart and driving himself into her, slamming her up against the wall below the defunct street light.

"Oh, yeah, yeah," he growled.

With each thrust, each movement, the raging wildness intensified, and he began to strike her, cutting her lips. She moaned with desire. She didn't cry out. She liked to be hurt. Her mouth opened, her throat hissing in pleasure. So he hurt her some more, tearing at her blouse and biting at her breasts. His fist went for her open mouth, cutting his knuckles on her teeth. She shuddered and sagged against him, legs splayed against the wall, jerking and climaxing in a strange bliss. He pumped her hard and came with violence. Rage completely overtook him, and he began grunting hoarsely and beating her senseless, until she no longer breathed. She fell lifeless, and he let her lie there, no longer bleeding.

Looking around, he saw no one. No one had seen what he had done. It was a place with all the light drained out. The light of her soul, certainly. And his? Markie didn't believe in souls. He sucked on his knuckles in the dark, breathing hard. The blackness of the street seemed blacker, shimmering with glee.

Fortunately for Markie, Sam had not seen them together. He had been in the supply room when Mark came into the lounge. When Sam came back and saw the woman, a neighborhood regular, was gone, he shrugged. "Ah, crap, now I got no customers at all."

Sam liked to talk to the working girl. She was company on a slow night. The place was now completely devoid of business. He idly polished a glass, first breathing a mist on it.

"Oh, man," Mark muttered to no one. "What now?" The intensity of the craziness was waning, leaving him shaking. He went to his apartment and cleaned up. He sat still in his chair, thinking about the night. After a few hours he heard sirens coming down the street, past his building, past the bar, to the place where he had left her body.

"Jeez, I didn't even know her name."

But he was not sorry. Oh, not at all. On the contrary—he was pleased. He was wallowing in the enjoyment of the way he had felt as he killed her. How could he describe that feeling of overwhelming power? Ecstasy? He flexed his sore fingers.

"I want to do it again," he announced to his room, smiling.

He sat there through the night, slumped, nerves jumping, random thoughts passing though his brain with no apparent connection, one to the other.

A childhood melody plucked momentarily at the edges of his mind, gliding in through a terrible blackness. His mother had held him and gently crooned, "Jesus loves me, this I know." The darkness expanded, blocking and stifling the memory, and the faint melody flickered away. He desperately clawed at it, trying to bring it back.

"Christ, what was that about," he growled. He was perturbed at the intrusion.

Was Markie irredeemable from his descent into wanton evil? Was it the place of no return? All he could think of was the ecstasy he had felt, and now needed more of, from taking another's life.

TWENTY-THREE

MARK ON THE CARPET

At the pharmacy, things were looking up. The week was filled with the hoped-for pharmaceutical refunds, or at least promises. Companies had been contacted, and they would honor product returns with repayments.

Refunds came in sooner than they expected, after shipping out the drugs, a FedEx process. The inventory tracking was proceeding well, but there were barriers they came up against, computer-wise. They called the police in.

"Mr. and Mrs. Phelps, next we will have to contact your accounting firm," Sergeant Moore announced. "That's Ginsberg and Taylor? We'll be going there next. It might be a good idea if you advised them we're on our way."

The firm was shaken. At the office, Mark reviewed their records together with the help of a couple of other employees, but they came up empty. The devious thief had carefully hidden his tracks—through multiple international routings? They could find nothing.

The Phelpses decided to write off their losses and start anew. This time, with a different accounting firm.

Ginsberg and Taylor were askance at losing this good

customer and thought they'd have to put Mark on notice. He dissembled and put on the best innocent act of his life.

"Mr. Ginsberg, I am truly sorry," lied an apparently chastened Mark, brows furrowed with anxiety. He clenched his hands in an affectation of worry. "I am astounded that such a theft happened on my beat. I'm good at my job. I'm careful and intent on making these accounts as safe as Fort Knox. But we know that the Russians, and the Chinese particularly, are like damned electronic ferrets. They are not hindered by distance and have their scanning eyes and searching fingers poking deeply even into our US government's most protected programs.

"I have combed our databases, and have found nothing indicative of errors on our part. I wish I could have tracked the thieving hackers. They had to have found a chink in the security armor, the firewall."

The account had been deactivated, so there wasn't much more he could do to find it. He no longer had access, he explained.

He went on to expound on the modus operandi of the drug cartel. No doubt cartels had gotten into it. There was something simply called the Network, a drug peddling organization, one that electronically bored, or linked, into private computer systems all over the world, through gaps or flaws in firewalls—all for the purpose of making robotic use of them, vastly expanding the main computer system's storage and capabilities, all the while using each newly grabbed computer as a treasure chest of things to steal. Yes, that had to be the answer. He would immediately reconstruct new shields, unbreachable firewalls, on all their clients' accounts.

He did not say he would have clandestine backdoors for

his own use. Anyway, maybe he wouldn't go the hacking route again. It was getting too risky. And he liked the drugs they were scooping from the hospitals. Man, that combo with the Scotch was over the top. His nerves had finally settled, but he still was feeling good, a whole twelve hours later.

Mark was very believable, and they wanted to believe him. He was well-spoken, fluent—even glib—at technobabble. He glazed their eyes with excess information.

That aside, Ephron Ginsberg wondered how Mark had scuffed up his knuckles. Those knuckles would not have anything to do with his job description. Perhaps this was another facet of Mark, an unpleasant one he hadn't thought of. What did they really know about him? They had done a due diligence on him when they hired him, finding all the data available about his scholastics (top grades) and criminal records (there were none). But about his life now? No information available. Thinking back on Elizabeth's call—could he have attachked India? Mr. Ginsberg's gut told him he should send his private investigator out again, to check.

Oh hell, leave well enough alone, Ephron, he advised himself. *Mark is a good employee.*

A mistake.

TWENTY-FOUR

AV-SPEAK IN NUMBERS

*I*ndia was studying her flight manual with deep interest. At the moment, she was flummoxed. She had a major difficulty understanding something called the Coriolis effect, a phenomenon of the earth's rotation affecting the directional flow of air. She just couldn't get it. She was smart, but she couldn't understand the principle at all. Dave might explain it, come Saturday.

These days she found herself injecting phrases into her conversation used around the airport. Compass references filtered in first. "You need to do a one-eighty here, Dad—you didn't turn off when you were supposed to." That was for turning around to go back in the opposite direction.

Then came "ceilings" stated in thousands plus hundreds of feet, the above-ground elevations of clouds. "Looks like the ceiling today is around four thousand feet." Like that.

Wind direction?

The tow pilot would say, "Surface winds today from two-forty (degrees) at five (nautical miles per hour)." Then he'd tell them, "Winds at three (thousand feet) from two-seventy (degrees) at fifteen (knots)."

She knew from her studies that MSL was short for Mean Sea Level—an arbitrary altimeter setting that all agreed would be sea level all over the world, above or below the water level, no matter. Water levels rose and fell all over the world with tides; the MSL had to stay put. Standard pressure was 29.92 inches of mercury at fifty-nine degrees Fahrenheit. All over the world, the atmospheric pressure would push the mercury in a tube up to 29.92 inches at sea level, all other things being the same.

Dave commented, "It is a little complicated, but isn't it fascinating? See that gadget there on the panel for the pilot to set, showing altitude? That's the altimeter. That's the Kollsman window on the altimeter."

In 1939, German-born engineer Paul Kollsman had invented the sensitive altimeter for airplanes, and made millions on it.

Dave continued. "With that knob, you turn the small dial seen inside that window. Watch the numbers change in there till you have the setting which you got earlier by phone from Flight Service. That will now show your altitude above sea level, where you and your glider currently sit.

"You know," continued Dave, "failing a connection with Flight Service, just dial in the elevation of the airport before you take off. It's on the aeronautical chart at your airport symbol. Here, it's even on the sign over the door." He tipped his head toward the building.

"See there? One thousand two hundred twenty feet, the field elevation." Sure enough—there were the numbers. She hadn't thought much about them, but had wondered what they meant.

"That will do it too. Dial the field elevation into the

altimeter, and the numbers in the little Kollsman window will give you the barometric setting." All pilots were required to set area altimeters correctly so all aircraft would be flying at the same indicated altitudes. India liked that. In flight, air traffic control would also give the local area altimeter setting.

When Dave said, "Turn to a heading of one hundred degrees"—or any other heading, for that matter—she became confused, until he pointed out how to look at the compass and turn the plane until it made the compass needle point at the desired number—then straighten it out. "Yeah, exactly like that." He praised her when she did it right.

A month had gone by. She had avidly studied and passed written tests on weather, aerodynamics, federal aviation regulations. She was happy in her new sport. As much as she loved Dave's presence, she was looking forward to someday flying alone.

She was having an outstanding time, all the while wishing she could fly during the week as well as weekends. She just couldn't get enough of it. Maybe the Phelpses would be okay with her occasionally taking off a weekday afternoon or morning.

She would approach the pharmacists with her plan.

"Maudie, I think we have finally gotten everything straightened out," exclaimed India, scrutinizing the counters and tidy shelves. "It surely looks like the records are in order. I have to say I am astonished. Don't tell me Dudley did all this?"

Dudley. For extra help, the Phelps had contacted the local college placement dean, who found a perfect fit for them. A top honors young man who loved nothing more than tracking and filing numbers needed a job. They hired him to work on site, in the pharmacy, not connected to any outside internet. No more easy outside path to their supplies.

"We have had the greatest good luck, India. Dudley stuck with the mess—even working late—to get us organized."

India had pitched in to rearrange the banks of tall shelves to form a private alcove, a workstation, for him. Dudley was an introverted, numbers-focused geek who seemed to communicate best with spreadsheets. They had thought they couldn't afford him, but with the savings from no more thefts, they saw a significant rise in the angular black line of the earnings graph.

No crook had been caught—it appeared none would be—and India was miles away from her license.

She had to convince Maudie and Rollie to help her out. Now that Dudley had done so well for them, it looked like she had a clear shot at winning them over. Twenty hours of dual instruction were required for solo, but she only had eight logged hours of dual in the month since she had begun. She *had* to speak with her bosses. She had been coming in on Saturday afternoons to work, and now wished she could take a second lesson on Saturday, instead. Or on a weekday, if Dave could work it out.

TWENTY-FIVE

OVERBOOKED?

*H*er life was getting overcrowded. She thought when graduation freed her from confining classes she would have plenty of wiggle room to pursue a fun new life, but she was seeing that life beyond school was even more demanding. And just yesterday, out of the blue, she had gotten a call from the Children's Aid Society asking if she could give them some time.

Those children had been so close to her heart. Once, from the pulpit, she had heard—when her mind wasn't wandering from a stifling sermon—"Suffer the little children to come unto me." What did that mean? "Suffer" might mean, "allow," she figured. Well, all right for Jesus. The disciples back then in the Bible story were shooing clamoring kids away from him. They were taking up his attention and time, and the disciples didn't like it. And Jesus didn't care for their being shooed away. But what about me, India? Was that a message for her, for the congregation? India was not at all pious, but sometimes she picked up some, what she called "important life tips." Usually the minister taught from the Bible.

One of the lay ministers referred to the Bible as a book

of love letters from God—life guidance, on any subject. And it was a history book. India was a little bored by all the "begats" and said so.

The teacher had smiled and said, "Look at it this way. Those old boys were proud of their lineage, and didn't want anyone to forget about it."

India was a bit of a history buff, and that gave her new ideas, views, of the tribes of old and of her own. Begats? There was plenty of begetting now, in her own time.

So when, after that Sunday, she next went to Children's Aid, she knew what she could do. Hold the children on her lap, the little suffering, poorly loved creatures. She could show them God's love, a love she felt could come through her to them. It wasn't all that easy; a few were so little they leaked and reeked. So. That would be her gift. She would take it upon herself to housebreak them. That would be useful. India was practical.

She once overheard a conversation about angels. Someone had said "Oh, there are angels, all right—and sometimes we ourselves are nudged to be angels to each other."

What could she do? The call had come in at home; her sister had taken the message. She must return the call.

"What did they say, Claudie, the Aid people, when they called?" India had asked. "Can you tell me anything more?"

"No, sis. They asked me to ask you if you could spare some time for them. They didn't say when, or anything."

Claudia looked at her, wondering where this was going. Would India want her to help out? She would like to go with her and help at Children's Aid. It was going to be an option for her at school in the fall—maybe she could start early and learn the ropes. And anyway, she loved being a sidekick to India.

"The trouble is, Claude, I don't have an extra minute any more. I do love those little ones—I should find time for them. But to make time, I would have to give up flying lessons. I don't want to do that. I just don't think I'm self-sacrificing enough." She bit her lip as she thought about it. "Maybe I can cut back here and there on my work schedule. I need the money, but I could make adjustments."

She picked up the receiver, dialed the number Claudia had written down, waited for someone to answer, twirling a lock of hair on her index finger. She brooded. Finally a recorded voice came on.

"You have reached the Children's Aid Society. If you are receiving this message, it is after hours. Please call back between 9:00 and 5:00."

Well, noted India, it was five fifteen. Reprieve. She thought she would like to talk it over at the dinner table. Maybe her parents would have some insights. But she didn't talk to them then. She put it off. Maybe today? She would not call to speak with the organization until she had discussed it with her parents.

TWENTY-SIX
CLAUDIA

"You know, I could work with you, India," Claudia had said, looking eagerly at her sister. "Really I could. I've always enjoyed babysitting—I'm good with kids. I plan on majoring in child development when I go to college. You know what? I'm not a child anymore. Maybe they'd even like to have someone my age at the Children's Aid Society, working with them."

India smiled at Claude, thinking what a great girl she was. Who knows? Maybe. And, reflecting on it, she remembered she had been her age when she first started.

And listen to that—Claudia, my little sister, already has a life plan. That brought her up short. *Whatever am I going to do with my life?* she asked herself, moodily.

She looked at her again, assessing. "Come stand here by me, Claude." Claudia came over, stood in front of her. Their wide green eyes met on the same level, their hair was alike, thick and auburn red. "Oh, look at that, Claudia—we're the same height!" India looked more closely . . . no, they couldn't be twins, but, lordie, they were surely cast in the same mold. She hugged her sister and giggled. "How could I have been so caught up in my own doings that I missed how much you've grown up?"

Claudia laughed happily. "And how alike we are!"

And Eli? Her russet-haired brother already towered over them both, and he was just barely thirteen. Their mother was not tall—but their father had basketball player dimensions, his high school sport. Her mother always muttered she had a phalanx of giants to get around, just to put together breakfast. It was true.

The next day came and she slid through it. Dinner time. India spoke as they ate. "Okay, my clever family, what's my solution here? How am I going to help at Children's Aid? Any ideas? I feel I should put some in time," she said. "I probably could cut back on my work hours. I know the Phelpses are pretty organized now, and have their accounting under control. What do you think?"

India waited for them to chew over her quandary and to respond.

She went on, "Daddy, Mama—I really don't want to stop my flying lessons. That would be my other option, if you can call it that. Besides loving the challenge of learning this new discipline, there's pure joy in it. And honestly, I still feel it's a plus on college apps. Which reminds me. I've got to start getting those out. I'm already too late for fall admissions, but I'd be good for the post-Christmas semester. Of course, I still might take off next year . . ."

They continued staring at her, wondering what she wanted to hear, how they should respond.

Finally her dad said, "Sounds to me like you need to call Children's Aid, find out what they want, discuss it with them, then talk to your bosses. If their business is as straightened out as you say, it might be that the new accounting guy has usurped your place. Maybe that would be a shame—but your mother and I wouldn't mind at all if you didn't work there anymore." His hands had clenched into fists as they rested on the table. "That crisis we had with your attacker was quite enough, India." He relaxed a little, but spoke sternly.

"If you do continue—well, you had spoken of trying to work in another flying lesson each week. As it is now, I can't see how that could happen. Your days are scheduled fully—no gaps."

India looked at her father. She sat stiffly watching his face, immobilized in consternation. This is not what she was looking for. She wiped her mouth and set her napkin down.

"I'll talk with Dave. Maybe I could start each lesson earlier, adding a bit of time to each hour. He says it's not wise to push the learning curve, but maybe it could work. I'll ask."

Her father nodded. Her mother could see she was not about to leave either the pharmacy or the flying. Well, she would have to work it out herself, and she told her daughter so, patting her arm reassuringly.

India was horrified at the thought of leaving her job. The new accountant they'd hired did indeed keep the records straight and the inventory tracked, but he was not the hands-on worker that she was. They needed *her*.

Surely they must?

TWENTY-SEVEN
VERN'S CONCERNS

Mark was getting twitchy again, and Vern didn't like it. Markie had subtly changed since he'd gone onto what they dryly called the hospitals' high-potency "perfect panaceas," and Vern found it worrisome. It was nothing he could put his finger on. Just sometimes there was a queer light in his eyes that hadn't been there before. An occasional fleeting odd expression. For the next couple of weeks they continued to pull off a few successful hospital heists, although Vern felt they were running out of handy locations and would have to search further afield.

"I think I should work the hotels for a while, Markie," he said over their coffee meeting one morning. "There's often a nice little something in the medicine cabinets, hoarded by the weekenders. I do enjoy dipping into those bathrooms. Always a thrill." He mused . . . "You know, I haven't been into a house in a long time. I've got this handy garage opener for those jobs. Only thing is, I usually pull those off at night." He chewed his toast and studied Mark for a reaction.

"Well that sure won't work with a company car," Mark stated firmly, twiddling his fork. "I can only have access to a car in the daytime, and then not that often. You know Vern, I have to be cagey. I get one only when they figure I'm going on sales calls. Those can't be done at night."

"Oh, right," sighed Vern. "Maybe I can get some wheels. I'll check around. We could always swipe one for a job—possibly from one of those off-street commuter parking lots—then slip it back in when we're done. That could work."

Mark frowned, thinking. "Aw, hell, that's way too risky. Those lots always have vicious watch dogs. Hey, haven't you seen those fangs, those dogs snarling and leaping against those chain link fences? And what if you don't get the job done quickly? What if someone crashes into the car? What if the guy comes to get his car early and puts out a 'stolen vehicle' on it? Way too many 'what ifs.'"

He thought quietly for a moment. "A borrowed car might be doable, though. Depends on who it's borrowed from. Now, take my parents' car. There's an idea. My mother doesn't often drive at night. My Dad doesn't drive at all anymore, he's so incapacitated. Maybe they'd let me borrow it. I'd have to think up something really good, because she knows I always have a company car to use. But since it's not available at night . . . I could say I have a date to go to a concert somewhere."

They went quiet, thinking.

Vernon certainly didn't want to stop his pilfering; he was building up a nice stash of money. His clientele, a small but needy group, counted on him. And it was a pastime that was not only lucrative, it was fun. Such fun that it sometimes made him quietly chuckle with pleasure. Escaping detection was a thrill, and the closer he came to getting caught the more fun it was. He always enjoyed the jobs. His future? He didn't plan far ahead. Not beyond a dynamite Caribbean

VERN'S CONCERNS

vacation sometime, taking a willing chickie with him. He was counting on Mark to help in that direction.

Meanwhile, Markie was entering a dark period. He was brooding, fantasizing, aching for another domination conquest, another kill. It was now always in his thoughts. Even at work, pouring over electronic spreadsheets, he had that sick desire teasing the corners of his mind. He had been looking for opportunities whenever he and Vern went barhopping. As a precaution, they rarely went to the same place twice or stayed long enough to make an impression—or attract attention. Vern in his hoodie or knitted cap, some drab color, and Mark with his horn-rims and shaggy hair, a disguise he changed around with different glasses frames and varying hair styles. Interesting how many sleazy bars there were in the world. But Mark never saw worn-out broads any more, none worth picking up. Where were they all hiding? Maybe they'd tarted up and gone uptown.

Maybe it was time to look for the redhead. He knew exactly where she lived. He remembered from the night of that party. But no, not yet. He wasn't sure he wanted to off that one, anyway. It would be a waste. But she'd be good for a whacking-great robust rape. He dreamed to watch her suffer, barely enduring pain. His loins heated up, thinking about it, and he shifted in his seat, pulling on his beer. The kill, the murder? He'd prowl for another eager, disposable slut.

That other one? No one knew who she was. No identity at all, nothing on record. No driver's license, no fingerprints, no files. Her teeth apparently had never been touched—no dental history. So strange . . . as if she had never existed. He doubted he'd keep that lucky streak.

Vern looked at him, noting his black expression. "You

okay, Markie?" Vern asked nervously. Mark was beginning to concern him. Not good. He needed a dependable partner.

"Sure, Vern. I just need a little action, that's all. And one of those pills you picked out of the last cabinet. You got any on you?"

"Yeah," said Vern, jiggling his knee with annoyance. "But Mark, you realize that dips deep into my gross." He puffed his lips out. "I mean, you're not buying. To the high-end buyer, those can be worth a hundred bucks per." Ah, never mind. They hadn't cost him anything. Better to give Mark his fix than have something ugly happen. "Okay. How many do you need?"

"Just a couple. The effect lasts a long time. Good pills. Thanks," said Mark, palming the pills, slipping one into his mouth and putting the other into his pocket. He would save that one for a special occasion, and have it with a glass of Scotch. When he had a victim targeted. He hoped it would be as amazing as the first time when it was so crazy wild, in the pitch dark in the street. De facto public, yet not.

In a few minutes the pill kicked in, his mood noticeably improved, and he grinned at Vern. "Hey Vern, let's figure out our next gig. Maybe we could find a motel with a couple of dumb maids to do, and get some kicks. How about one of those on the outskirts. The Brand X no-tell motels. Those places are good for drugs, don't you think? And certainly a couple of easy lays."

"Now you're talkin'. Sounds good to me." They called for the check. Vern liked it when Markie was in an up girl-getting mood. That meant buddy Vern was going to get laid. Markie, rakish and sexy, would find one who would settle for him.

Maybe not as fine and hot a wench as Mark's, but a good one. The pretty ones generally traveled with a plain, needy sidekick. He was fine with that.

But Vern didn't think chances were at all good for finding stashes at those motels. Those were where sales were made, not where people vacationed and hid their goodies between hits. A downtown high-rise Hyatt type was best for that. But he too was antsy for some poon—and so he went along with Mark. Sex first, drugs later? He figured it would work out.

"Markie, why do people go for drugs in the first place?" queried Vern, looking at the tabletop. Mark stared at him, glassy eyed. What was this about? thought Mark. Jeez, I don't need to go there.

But Vern was not stopping. He raised his head and looked at him. "Mark, I know I enjoy the head-high from cannabis . . . but the heavier stuff? What's that about, the getting doped out and unconscious? Yeah, opium dens have been refuges since the Chinese hit on that piece of heaven, and I've read that even elephants and birds poke about for fermented fruits to get drunk on."

"Did I ever tell you about the pie-eyed birds staggering around on the lawn of my mother's garden?" He snorted. "The redbirds, cardinals I think they were, got drunk from gobbling rotten, fermented pyracantha berries!"

"What is it then, a genetic right or predisposition?" posed Vern. Mark looked over at the people sitting at the bar, and said nothing.

Vern chewed on a pretzel, sipped the last of his beer, put down the glass, and spoke again. "Pushers lure children into a hooked life of addiction to ensure a tidy income—clueless kids that don't have a chance to realize they have an option. I've never thought that was anything less than purely hateful. Not a path for me to follow, for my income."

Mark froze. He did not like it when Vern got philosophical, conversational, about things associated with his ills. But Vern was not aware of how Mark had become addicted, how he had dipped into his Daddy's oxycodone, peer-pressured by bigger kids, ones he hung around with. They were older, snorting powders, patronizing and sneering at the young admiring hangers-on. He remembered how he had needed to impress them, and so he swiped "keep out of reach of children" stuff from his parents' bathroom for them to try.

They liked it. Oh, indeed they liked it. He was in.

He watched them pop the pills, get silly and dreamy—and decided to try that for himself.

That fork in the road. His young manhood to be was about to be trashed. His parents had murmured warning things about drug addicts, and he had seen "Just Say NO" commercials on TV. But sadly, the big kids' sneers were more effective. But it's always like that, isn't it? Except for the rare human who is born knowing, with that strong core of self-preservation. Vernon had it. Markie didn't.

Why drugs? Entertainment, certainly. But Vern had noticed more and more that drugs were a numbing escape. An escape from a boring life, an escape from painful memories. Escape from pressure to succeed, even to find a job. Why did so many successful entertainers end up as stiffs from drugs? Escape from a lifestyle they opted for and then couldn't handle? By then, the drug had its hook into the nervous system. They were lost to it, no escape from its grip. But finally an escape from the skewed life, the ultimate escape, with the overdose.

Vern had heard there were more deaths from overdosing than from automobile accidents. He hoped the trend wouldn't affect his plans anytime soon. He doubted it. But Markie better be careful. Had he the brains left to care? Vern had noticed a subtle shift in Mark's manner, his outlook. Less "up and easy," a little more intense and edgy. Moodier?

The waiter brought their change, and they left.

TWENTY-EIGHT
INDIA PLANS; MARK PLOTS

She made her call to Children's Aid.
"India, oh, how good to hear your voice, India . . . How are you, dear?" Platitudes traded, they got to the meat of it.

"We all miss you. You are such a ray of sunshine and, yes, competence! Any chance you could come back and give us a few hours each week? The children miss you. Now that it's summer, they're here more hours, and those you knew wonder where you are."

Even though she hadn't been a daily volunteer, India had been a reliable and stable point in their lives as they were cared for by the Society. For three years she had come to report for two-hour stints, often three times a week. What could she do? What in her life was going to have to give, now that she was so involved in both soaring and the pharmacy? She felt the children were a clear priority; she knew she could have a positive influence on them. She just had to figure out how. Maybe she had to integrate her life, make all the factors fit together.

"Dave—I have a problem." They were having a post-flight lunch at a local café, just before her Saturday afternoon stint with the Phelpses. India held her head slightly lowered, her demeanor serious. "You know I'm dedicated to getting my glider license, but now I'm getting myself into some other commitment issues."

Commitment issues. That was a buzz phrase she liked, words that spun out importantly, giving weight and a hint of mystery to whatever the person was involved in, worthy or not.

"The high school's optional social work program, one affiliated with the Children's Aid Society, was something I participated in for three years, starting when I was fifteen. It's a fine program, a kind of Head Start on a much smaller scale, one that helps less-well-off children of Valley laborers get good care during the hours their parents need to be at work. Well—they miss me. They actually need me. They're asking me to devote some time to them again." She sighed, obviously stumped. "That's going to be quite a trick, what with my work schedule and all."

He studied her face, searching for a hint as to how he should respond.

"So I had an idea. For one thing, since I really feel I may be on the backside of the learning curve. To catch up, could I start my lessons a little early and wind them up a bit later, adding about a half-hour to each lesson? I'd of course pay for extra tows."

"Yes," he said. "That would be workable. You actually could use more time in the air, practicing coordination; Dutch rolls and so forth. You know—the maneuver where you pick a point on the horizon, put the nose on it, and roll the wings from one side to the other in a half circle around it, never losing the point. That's one thing you need to master. And since you wouldn't mind paying for extra tows, it would be good to get more landings in. You do land pretty well already, but one always needs to practice. You need to get ready for your flight test at the end of the summer."

"Okay! That's the plan, then," replied India. "Next thing. Dave, how would it be if I could arrange transport and permission to give kids tours of the airport and gliders? They could take turns sitting in one. I could give them some rudimentary explanations of flight."

"Ah, nuts," replied Dave. "Think for a moment, India. What kind of liability are we talking here?"

She tilted her head and peered up at him. "No liability, Dave. No actual flights. And their parents would have to sign permission slips. They will, I'm pretty sure. First off, it would be for the older ones only, of course. No toddlers. But even the older ones are pretty young—five to six years. They're inquisitive and absorb information like sponges. They're thirsty for it. I don't think there's a slow one in the bunch." She looked at him, eyes big and hopeful. "What do you think? Maybe I'd be seeding crops for some-day pilots. Not a bad thing, right?"

He looked away, scanned the sky, and thought about it. He had to look away . . . her eyes melted his resistance.

"It would only be at most once every couple of weeks, on a weekday afternoon," she said. "Late in the fall I would like to bring a familiarization of soaring to all Valley school children, not just the Children's Aid. I'd have to sell it to the teachers, of course. I would want you to be a part of it if you can, but if not I could come here on my own. If we arranged one trip a week, each time I could cover some different aspect. I could explain the forces of flight: i.e. drag, how the air pulls at the skin of the plane, and about the wing spoilers for slowing down. Every kid knows about how the wind pushes his hand when he sticks it out the car window; I can start with that."

He saw her differently, now. No longer just a beautiful young woman with charm and intelligence who wanted to fly. She was a part of the bigger picture of the humans in the Valley community. Hm. This would take some figuring, how to help her with this project. "Well, if we're going to do this, don't you think we should get the towplane in on it? But India, please—the club would never condone your being here by yourself. Especially not with this outside group. We need to consider aircraft security, property security. Little house apes wanting to climb all over everything, and all that. We'd need to round up some chaperones." He saw her expression at house apes.

"Oops. Sorry—that just popped out. At home we always called preschoolers that."

She laughed and clapped. "That's funny! They do usually scramble like monkeys." India beamed and did a little sitz-jig in their booth. He was going for it; she had him.

She would consult the aid people; she could talk them into it. They would find chaperones to thwart the little climbers. A field trip. They would not be able to resist her compelling point of view. And they could use their van for transport. Then one day if she did get permission from Valley's grammar schools, school buses could be assigned for field trips. The season was pretty short; it shouldn't be a problem. What would the parents think? Parents like field trips.

Ok, she said to herself, I've got those things cornered. At least a start on it. The school system she would attack later.

"This all sounds pretty positive," he said, smiling down at her flushed face. "Seems like you've got it figured out; you just need to organize it."

Her complexion took on a glow when she was happy. He saw that often, as she turned to speak to him in the cockpit. How could he deny her anything? Anyway, it was a fine idea. One used by Young Eagles volunteers giving rides with power planes, and at FAA Ace camps. This was just starting younger. He was sure he could arrange time with his office.

And who knew? Maybe somebody would come with him, to see what gliders were all about.

"Okay then," she quietly deliberated to herself. "Next, I need to go and speak with my bosses. I hate to lose income, but we all need to know where we stand. I hope it won't be worse than I think."

The Phelpses. It was now Saturday afternoon, and she was heading to the store to put in some time.

Things were back to near-normal there. The door company had said the model they wanted would be ready for shipment in two weeks . . . too long for the Phelpses, but they had to live with it. The delivery date was coming close.

She found Maudie and Rollie in the back where they were happily chatting with Dudley.

Oh no. What was he doing there? Her heart sank, imagining her job going poof. He wasn't supposed to be there on Saturday afternoons.

"Hello everyone." She tentatively smiled a greeting at them. "Hi Dudley. I didn't expect to see you here. Are you working today?"

"Oh, hi India. No. I just came by to tell the Phelpses that I have a full-time job now, but their affairs are in order and can be seen to by someone with ordinary secretarial training. It's just simple data entry work. I've installed a program for tracking the entries, costs, and payments. Easy stuff. I wouldn't have abandoned them if the job hadn't been finished up. You know, this was a wonderful way to step into the world of commerce. I have really liked undoing the Phelpses' Gordian knot, as I liked to call it. It was a puzzling pile of data, but it's all sorted out now. Too bad the thievery could not be traced. The orders came from beyond the firewalls from who knows where. I could not track those, and I heard the police couldn't either. Anyway, if you don't have anyone else in mind, I know of someone trustworthy who can do the work you need. A college friend of my sister is looking for part-time work."

The Phelps turned hopefully to India, wondering if she could fill that role, but didn't say anything. They sensed some discomfort.

She was again at odds with herself, teetering between relief to still be needed and a need to pry loose a little. She was hoping to cut back on her hours to help at the charity, and here they were asking for more time from her to spend in the pharmacy. She wasn't going to go into her problems with Dudley listening in. She was awfully glad to know her job was safe—but her problems were none of his business.

They wished Dudley well in his new position, thanked him profusely for the good job done, and sent him on his way with congratulations. Then India turned to the Phelpses with her conundrum. She would ease into it.

"Do you know of a social services organization here in town, the Children's Aid Society?" asked India.

"Well of course we know of it. We donate to that charity, don't we Rollie? We believe in helping the children of our community in whatever way we can. We also donate prescriptions to doctors for indigent people. Why do you ask?"

"Oh, good. Well, for the past three years I've devoted time weekly to them, helping with the kids; it was an activity I really liked. When I graduated from high school I left the program. It was a social service option for sophomores and upperclassmen." She stopped and watched their faces. "The director has contacted me to ask if I could come back. Apparently the children miss me, and the organization needs me. I'm sort of behind the eight ball on this. Children are a priority in this world. But my time is pretty filled here. The only thing I could do, if you were agreeable to it, would be to give them a couple of hours twice a week, but that would be cutting back on my work hours. It would of course mean a cut in pay. Do you think we could work that out? Do you think there's enough slack in your schedule now that the accounting is organized and the inventory is under more control?"

"Oh, dear," sighed Maudie. "I would say yes immediately, but we don't actually have the office help in place, now that Dudley has left us. I was thinking you could do that job. But maybe it's too much? Don't you know how to do bookkeeping?"

She was afraid of this.

"Only on a very basic level, Maudie. I took a course in school, but never had to put it into practice. I could give it a try if Dudley would agree to show me how the program works that he installed. But remember, at some time I will be going to college. Probably Dudley's friend would be a better choice for extra help."

They talked some more, India filed and shelved, and then she was off to Checkpoints, being picked up after work by Dave. The Phelpses would get Dudley to come familiarize her with the program on Monday.

Suddenly, India remembered how willing Claude was to work with the children at Children's Aid. She would take her to meet the director, and they would talk it over. Brilliant. Problem solved.

Outside in front, hidden eyes watched as India got into Dave's car. He was keeping tabs.

Mark was obsessing. She was constantly in his thoughts; he daydreamed of cruel possibilities. She was becoming the stuff of conflicting dreams. He had no good model to predicate his ideals on, woman-wise, no concept of man-woman relationships. Only his long-suffering, patient mother, anchored to her husband's wheelchair, a man he didn't like who had taken all her attention away from him. A terrible shame, but there it was.

How can we understand the forming of a madman, the shaping of a killer? A killer who, although he idealizes, romanticizes his victim, would not hesitate to embrace the sick, erotic delight of watching the last breath escape her lips, and note the pupils expanding to extinguish sight in death.

TWENTY-NINE
UPS AND DOWNS

"You'd better start thinking of flying all by yourself, India. You're going to have to do it pretty soon," Dave threatened, eyes crinkling warmly, calling over to her from the back seat up at eight thousand feet. The day was perfect. They were skipping along the street of lift, watching the Pennsylvania landscape slowly pass by under them. Long ridges looked like so many ripples and waves of an ocean, frozen in place. That must have been from when the earth was heaving and molten, she'd once thought, and it cooled like that. But not so. She had read that those wavy ridges came from the shifting and pushing of underlying tectonic plates. What a visual to go with the flying lessons.

"Of course I want to pilot the glider by myself," she responded, "but I've gotten so used to your being with me, I wonder if I can."

"Hey," he scoffed. "I won't let you go until I know you're ready. Your life is in my record book. I've put forty licensed glider pilots into cockpits since I started teaching. I haven't lost a student yet. I'm not going to start now."

"Ok. I trust you." She couldn't look at him; he was behind

her. But she envisioned his face, and hoped she was right. No little inner voice said "Don't," so she relaxed and gave herself over to the constant circling and Dutch rolls, and poking around for the next thermal. She got good at finding and riding them.

"Feel it?" he would say, when a wing was nudged upward. "Now turn into it—that's your thermal! Now start circling to catch that rising current!"

That was last weekend.

Now it was Saturday again. Would today be the day? India brushed her hair nervously before pulling it back in a ponytail. The sunrise was behind her. She had gotten up early to review the last lesson before she went downstairs for breakfast. She had worked in a two-hour lesson each time she went, so that was two hours more per weekend, and a month had gone by. She was working on her required twentieth hour of instruction now, and she knew it could happen. Soon, she might be left to fly by herself, soaring high and wide over the hills. She was eager, excited—and terrified.

Pah. She knew she could do it.

But what if . . . What if the tow rope broke on takeoff, would she remember the emergency procedure? Land straight ahead immediately, that was the drill. Fortunately there were plenty of fields beyond the takeoff end of the runway for just such a crisis. If the rope broke higher up? Look for lift, and try to circle aloft in it? No. She had to get back into the traffic pattern and land. Those were the rules. Fine. She knew she could do that. They had certainly practiced it enough.

Weeks had passed. Summer was drawing to an end. Goldenrod brightly brushed now fallow fields, distant mountains looked a deeper purple, and occasionally the air got chilly early in the afternoon. Dudley had familiarized her with the data entry program for the pharmacy spreadsheets, something she could handle most of, but Rollie had also hired a part-time worker, the one Dudley had recommended.

Her sister had met with and won the affection of the Children's Aid director. She had started logging happy times at the charity, making notes at night from her memories of the day, notes about child development to go with a textbook she had found. Claudia had her eye on her future.

India had arranged field trips yet to happen. Volunteer chaperones were not easy to find, but she had drawn up a few little lessons, and she knew it was going to work out.

And now, here she was, back at her favorite place.

She parked her bicycle against the building as usual and came around the corner looking for Dave's cheery "Mornin', Sunshine!" He was there, but he was clearly preoccupied. His tanned face was serious, sun-bleached eyebrows pulled together in a scowl, pale gray eyes narrowed as he looked down at her. His attraction to her showed; he ducked his head and thought of what he could say to make things right.

"Something going on today, Dave?" asked India, searching her memory for a tip-off, looking around at cars and trailers lined up alongside the airstrip.

Oh, right. That regional glider meet was today. Well, they were sure at it early. Her eyes came to just below his shirt collar; her eyes fixed on that vee of his tanned chest. Suddenly she wanted to touch his skin. He noticed her gaze and blushed from the neck up. They looked into each other's eyes, and froze.

It was indeed early. The sun's brilliance still shone low above the horizon, tall neighboring pines cast long shadows across the grass runway. Tiny spider webs still glistened with dew, like wee tablecloths for bug victims. It had been a cloudless night.

Already gliders were lining up for turns with the towplane, their pilots restlessly standing, waiting, beside their aircraft. The towplane itself was even now roaring off down the runway for the sniffer flight, the one to check for thermals, hopeful to find at least little bumps of their beginnings.

Once thermals started building, the gliders would get active. They would be off and rolling, one every seven or eight minutes, the time it took to haul one up to the release altitude and for the towplane to spiral back down to land, dropping the tow rope just before touchdown. Someone would run out, snatch it up, and rush back to hook it up to the next glider in line. The towplane would make a rapid turnaround, taxi back, and get attached to the other end of the rope, roll forward, and pull it taut. After the "I'm ready" tail waggles, the planes would be rolling again.

The meet. A competition. Many more gliders were there than usual, and lots of unfamiliar faces. These cued-up early birds would be ready for the wingman's circling arm-wave start sign. Besides a point-to-point race triangle, some were going to try for endurance and altitude medals, medals they would pin to their caps. Volunteers were in place, checking for approved flight recorders and cameras. Pilots had to prove they had flown over the checkpoints. Some had mounted cameras in their planes to photograph those landmarks, as well as secured timers to log the flights. Not that anyone would cheat.

Dave sighed with frustration. "Well, as you can see, it's pretty busy around here this morning. It turns out I'm going to have to be the one to check out the participants in this competition. The guy who was supposed to be in charge got sick and couldn't make it, and I'm the only approved Soaring Society of America authority on site today. I'm so sorry, India. I knew this event was coming up. Remember? I mentioned it last week. Now my time is locked up. You and I will be late getting off, if at all."

Her face fell; she looked like the bottom had dropped out of her day.

"Hey—I didn't know until I got here that I was going to be hog-tied like this," he said, wondering how he could fix things.

He scanned the group of pilots gathered at the airstrip, some waiting until they knew for sure conditions would be optimum. They would leave later, after the sun had boosted rising thermals into first-rate elevators.

"Um, India, I have an idea that might work. Would you like to go along on one of the flights, if I can find you a seat?" Her face morphed into joy. She had become addicted to the overview, and would do about anything to get up there.

"Yes!" She exclaimed, practically spinning in place.

"Now don't please get your hopes up too much. It might not happen. Hang on while I ask around. All of these guys are very experienced. I would have no reservations about letting you go with any one of them. Most prefer to go it alone, but sometimes they like an extra pair of eyes to watch for traffic."

Since late the night before he had been in touch with Flight Service and watching weather reports on television and computer, monitoring weather systems crossing the US, fronts that might affect flying activities. There was a system threatening from the west, but it was still miles and hours away; they felt it wouldn't influence today's event. Even if it arrived earlier than expected, it probably wouldn't get there until late afternoon. If they were very lucky, it would arrive in the nighttime, give them a rousing dose of thunderstorms, and be gone by morning. He loved his lessons with India as much as she did and dreaded any cancellations or postponing.

"I'll be back in a minute," he said, striding off toward a small group by a parked glider.

THIRTY
SOARING WITH THE BEST

"*A*nyone here want a bit of ballast? Anybody like to have some good company along for the ride today? I have a student I'd like to introduce to soaring competitions, and it would be real helpful if she could hop in with someone. She's just ready for solo now . . . and awfully good at catching thermals. She's a natural. Do I have a taker?"

The men looked at each other, then over to where India stood, watching. Willowy and rosy, fetching with her ponytail spilling onto her shoulder, she shifted from foot to foot. They considered the possibility. More weight, eh? Nice poundage. Maybe yes.

"Do we need to draw straws or throw fingers?" they rumbled with friendly laughter.

"I got first dibs," exclaimed an older man. "I haven't been in the cockpit with any female under fifty in years!"

"Okay then," said Dave. "Come on over and meet India."

She watched them approach, assessing what she saw. Rangy Dave, broad-shouldered and handsome, walking beside a square-jawed shorter man, one with eyes that she knew would see as sharp as a hawk. She met his gaze, blue and clear, peering out of a nice rugged face under a cap. Ah—gray hair. Okay then.

"Hey, India. I'm Roscoe. I hear you'd like to see what the soaring competition is all about, and ride along with me today," he said, eyes twinkling under the brim of his baseball cap, thrusting out his hand to take hers. Tufts of gray sprouted out around his ears. No competition for me, thought Dave.

"Oh my gosh, I really would!" purred India, looking at the man, green eyes wide, keeping hold of his hand. "Could I go with you? Are you sure it's ok?"

"Of course. It would be my great pleasure. And I'm an instructor, so maybe I will let you have the controls from time to time. No promises, but it could happen," he said cheerily, watching her face break into a wide smile. She let his hand go, thinking how nice it felt. Like her Dad's.

He continued, "I don't know this territory around here all that well. I've come from farther east in Pennsylvania. You can help keep me oriented. And you will help watch for traffic, of course."

India's head circuits were overloading. Thoughts pummeled her brain, as she sorted out the new schedule for the day. Well. She'd better contact the pharmacy and tell them today wasn't going to be a workday for her. And call her parents, to tell of the new development. She had bid them good-bye in a rush; they would be expecting her home after work at the end of the day.

"When do you think we'll be back?" she asked Dave and Roscoe.

"Depends on when you take off," replied Dave. "What do you think, Roscoe . . . off in about an hour? The lift should have developed by then. I see a couple of telltale wisps forming over the ridges. Once you're off, it takes about two to three hours to fly the circuit, if all goes well. Could be longer, if you have to poke around a lot for thermals."

He looked at them. "Longer, if you land out."

Roscoe scoffed. "I haven't landed out since I was a kid. That's for rookies. Don't worry, India. We'll only have one landing, right back here. But if it happens, I'm a pro."

"Okay, then. But I'm just not used to being aloft for so long. Are you sure this is right for me, Dave?"

He frowned at her. "If you have to ask that, maybe it isn't. This is up to you and how you feel about it. It was just a last minute idea, after all."

"Yeah," said Roscoe, "We'll be up there a while. Be sure to make a pit stop before we leave. No ladies' room in my glider."

"I have the endurance of a camel. I can hold water for eight hours if I need to." India laughed. "No worries, Roscoe."

Turning to Dave, she said, "Well excuuuuse me . . . I will indeed go, and thank you for arranging it," she sniffed, tossing her ponytail and beamed at the pilot. Friendly vibes simmered between them, age notwithstanding.

Dave looked from one to the other. *Hey! They're flirting! Is he a horny old goat I've thrown her with? He doesn't look as harmless as I thought. Hell, she's my student, and maybe my girlfriend.*

"Okay man, take it easy with my girl, here. She's *my* student," Dave growled. India stiffened. *He had called her his girl. Well that's a step in the right direction,* she smiled to herself. *He made her knees go weak when he got close.*

India quickly called the Phelpses and let them know she would not be in this afternoon, apologizing for the last minute notification. They were fine with it. "We just appreciate all the extra time you're able to give us, India. Thanks for letting us know."

Her parents took the news with a certain fatalism; they weren't expecting her until late in the day anyway.

She felt giddy with elation over all this, and climbed quickly into Roscoe's sailplane before he could change his mind.

He and Dave both fussed over her, getting her arranged properly in her seat. This time, she sat in the back. The competitor would be the pilot in command; she would be the observer.

Dave bent to murmur his good-flight wishes softly into her ear, raising the hairs on her neck. He left his hand longer than necessary on her shoulder as he gave her a last look good-bye. Roscoe checked her belt too, before he hopped in front and strapped in.

The takeoff roll began, the towplane pulling at first slowly then faster . . . and then the exhilarating liftoff. Away they went, a farewell wing-waggle to Dave as they were hauled up and off the airstrip, on the way to release. Having waved them off, he watched until he saw the towplane dive off to the left, the glider climb to the right to start its slow circling. They seemed to have found the hoped-for lift. The tow pilot always looked for it, for the glider to release into.

Dave was looking again at the weather system on his iPad weather app; he hadn't checked it for an hour or so. What he saw ignited some apprehension. The front to the west had inched closer, with winds too high for comfort. It seemed to have met with some upper level steering winds.

He would radio Roscoe and let him know. Anyway, all pilots had radios and were aware of the weather. No one would leave unbriefed.

"India," said Roscoe, "You take the ship now and head toward that cloud over there and grab another thermal. See its concave bottom? We should pick up lift as we get to it. Note the bump on the wing, circle under it until we rise to cloud base, then head away from it to the next in the street. I have to call Flight Service for an update on the weather. You good with that?"

India gave her assent, and took the controls, smoothly transitioning one pilot to another. He was relieved to see her ability to do that. She had practiced with Dave.

"Glider Blanik 5-2-5-5, Valley base calling, Blanik 5-2-5-5 . . . Do you read me? Over." Dave was attempting to contact them before they got out of range.

"Roger Valley, Blanik 5-2-5-5 here—I read you."

"I'm looking at weather graphics, showing frontal progress eastward somewhat sooner than expected, with high winds along the line. We're sending out a general announcement on 122.8 and 121.5 to advise all gliders—Flight Service Station has it on Hazardous Inflight Weather Advisory Service. The last three entrants waiting in line have opted to cancel. Over."

Dave remembered Mark Twain: "If you don't like the weather, wait a minute." "Yeah," he muttered under his breath. "And if you do like it, wait a minute." Fickle, frustrating weather.

"Roger, Valley," Roscoe came back. "Just trying FSS to get the latest weather. Will continue to do so. Back to you when I've done that."

Roscoe turned to speak to India in the back seat. "Good

job keeping the course, but we may have to cancel the flight. Weather is starting to look iffy. I'll take it back," he said, taking the stick and planting his feet back on the rudder pedals. Their descent on route to the next thermal was minimal; when they got to it, they got another kick upward. He began circling and climbing at an invigorating rate. "Oh boy! I'd hate to have to quit on a day like today," he muttered.

India cried out and pointed down. "There's our first race checkpoint! Shall I take a picture of it?"

"Sure. Here's the digital camera. Just point and shoot!" He handed back his approved equipment, after first taking a shot of it himself, a line of tall windmills on a ridge. India was an attractive girl, but no sense putting critical stuff in the hands of this unknown rookie. The race clock was humming quietly away on the panel, he pushed the button on it to record the passage; they were making good time. With that photo snapped, he turned to a compass heading toward the next checkpoint.

"You know? We're doing well. I'll bet we can fly this whole thing. But take the controls again please—I still have to contact Flight Service."

With his attention directed to the radio, he failed to notice a kettle of hawks directly ahead. But India saw them, and ducked off to the right. The sudden movement of the glider startled Roscoe, and he yelped "What are you doing?"

India tapped his shoulder and pointed. They barely missed one of the hawks. The raptor took his piercing golden eyes off the land below and looked sideways at her. She would swear they had locked eyes.

"Holy crap! That could have been a mess for sure," said Roscoe, again taking the controls. "Good catch, India."

They avoided the birds, but lost altitude as they did so. "Now we have to get back some lift as soon as possible." He pointed the nose of their craft toward another promising cumulus on the route. No feathered Sputniks in that one. Soon a wing bumped up, he cranked her into the lift, and they were soaring upwards again.

Roscoe tuned his handheld to the proper weather frequency. "Altoona Radio, Altoona Radio, glider Blanik 5-2-5-5 listening on the Allegheny VOR."

Shortly a voice came up acknowledging the Blanik, and he got the data he needed about the front. It was two hundred miles west, moving briskly eastward at forty miles an hour. If he could make the second checkpoint soon, he could be heading back to base in plenty of time. Checking the distance to go on his portable GPS, it was a mere twenty miles ahead.

Race legs were fifty miles long. They had left at 9:30 a.m., it was now nearly eleven, having passed the first checkpoint. This could work out just fine. The prognostics were for a one o'clock frontal passage at the airport. They should be in no later than noon. He didn't yet sense any change in the winds; they would get active close to the front. It was a fairly short race, but it seemed long with the threat of bad weather. He looked at the chart to see where they could land out, if necessary. He had boasted that wouldn't happen, but one always needed a plan B.

THIRTY-ONE
STORMS AFOOT

"Valley, Blanik 5-2-5-5—you on, Dave?"

"Yes, Roscoe. Go ahead."

"The prog is for a one o'clock front arrival at Valley. We'll have finished the race by then. We're just ten miles now from checkpoint two, according to my GPS."

"Okay, sounds good. Dave out." And he turned to the pilots around him, the ones who had scrubbed.

"So, you heard. He's going to fly the course. The front will pass through early this afternoon. The current nice weather looks to last a bit; it will be okay for those who left early enough. We should be seeing some come back within the half hour. Are the assigned volunteers ready to wave them in? Better take your positions at the gate. Don't forget cameras and timers." The ones volunteering for that checked their pockets and neck lanyards for their equipment. Then they turned to walk to their posts, each set up with an umbrella table and chair.

Those were spaced at intervals along the side of the runway. The teams who would meet and help clear the runway were alerted as well; they held their hands as sunshades, scanning the sky for arrivals. The meet registration table was supplied with chairs, pens, and papers for the contestants to sign in on at landing, plus a collection box for their recorders for reviewing. The air was as yet fairly unmoving; they were sweating in strong sunlight. Umbrellas were all fully occupied. Nonflying observers were busy keeping iced tea pitchers full. Not much was moving in the quiet air. Occasionally a radio squawked with a transmission; they were all alert for returning competitors who would be announcing. Several were already back, about six more were due, including Roscoe. He would be last.

Dave looked at the umbrellas and scowled. They'd better be ready to take those down before the winds picked up.

The east-west Valley glider strip was aligned to take advantage of prevailing winds. But the slight headwind from earlier had dropped off. It was the calm before the storm.

"So, India . . . I make us about to cross the second checkpoint. You see it yet? It's a farm on top of a hill. We need to spot it. I have the coordinates in my Garmin, but I have to take a clear photograph of it." He looked down, all around, trying to spot it. No joy.

"Ah! I have it just at my four o'clock, Roscoe. We went past it."

Roscoe began a 360 degree turn to the right, to bring himself around to the place she had seen. "Ok babe, good job. That's gotta be it—nothin' else around," he commented, banking to snap the photo and click the timer. "Now let's boogie on home!"

They looked west, and saw to their consternation that the hazy line of the far distant horizon had moved significantly nearer. Now the western line was topped with a string of white buildups, a long silhouette of clouds horizon-wide, inching toward them. Burgeoning cumulus rose like far-off floating castles. Even these many miles away, a thick misty curtain or two of rainfall were faintly visible underneath, blotting out terrain below. The sun glinted off the front's dangerous beauty. Above one shadowy obscuration, a billowing pile of dazzling white clouds had risen high and flattened into the telltale anvil of a thunderstorm.

Above Roscoe and India, the sky was a still a benign, startling blue, but now noticeably dotted with more clouds.

"Whoops. We can't waste any time, can we? And he pointed the Blanik eastward toward a small cloud on the route home, hoping there'd be lift when he got to it.

There was. The midday sun was their friend, baking fields into nice thermal starters. They circled in that one to regain altitude lost transiting the landscape, then raced over fields below to the next one, repeating the process until Valley hove into sight.

"Blanik 5-2-5-5, Valley—how is your progress?" Dave nervously called Roscoe.

"I show us fifteen miles out, thermaling for altitude, expecting Valley in twenty minutes or less. Good lift, good forward speed, averaging fifty knots. Be there soon, bouncing in lift, gotta handle controls, Blanik out."

India turned around and looked back. "Wow," she called out to Roscoe. "Look at those sunbeams!"

Behind them, the sun's rays were de facto spotlights shining through occasional breaks in the approaching high dark overcast, sweeping down across the countryside like slow-moving klieg lights. India grinned. It was as if they were picking out this farmhouse, or aiming at that pond, to spotlight. She was transfixed and fascinated.

"Yep," said Roscoe. "You enjoy that. I have to mind the store up front here. I've seen those before. Good stuff."

By now, the wind had started to pick up, as it could be counted on to do well ahead of a cold front. At the airstrip, papers and pens were skittering before the wind. Four of the last gliders had made it back, landing quickly. Now all hands were rushing to stash umbrellas. But the welcome team was ready for Roscoe and India. They waved them in, taking the required photo of the finish line crossing.

As they had homed in on the airport, bumping about in intensifying turbulence, Roscoe mildly suggested she could do the landing.

"Really?" Eagerly, she took the stick, sitting high and peering around his shoulders to sight the runway. He slumped down to help her see better—and kept his hands hovering over his control stick (tandem seating, dual controls), waiting to catch an error if she needed correction. And down they slipped, into the crosswind, gently touching down smooth as grease, elegantly executed. But she was used to landing, and considered it the most fun of all. For a long time, Dave had not had to help her.

"Well done, India. We made it back by the skin of our teeth, I think. Nothing like a close call for a great adrenaline rush!"

A couple of pilots left the umbrella duty; they'd already collapsed and removed them so they wouldn't roll and bounce comically downwind, and ran out to hold the Blanik's wingtips, pushing them clear of the runway to tie down. The team clambered out in sunshine, but shortly a great shadow raced over the airstrip. The sun was quickly blotted out. Dave waved a happy thumbs up at them, and turned to fight gusts starting to pummel anything not well secured.

"The tables!" yelled Dave, as one flipped over, legs whimsically pointing skyward. "Get the tables!" All hands raced to comply. "Anyone else left to come in? I think we have one still out."

"I just got a call from my husband," said one of the women. "He got too low in some strong downdrafts and had to land out, but luckily at an airport. Guess I'll have to hook up the trailer and go find him. Anyone want to go along?"

Landing out. This often ended up being a rolling party. She had lots of offers. His landing field was not far from home base. They would meet back at Checkpoints later.

THIRTY-TWO
LOW-END RIDE, LOW-END GIRLS

To Vern, Mark was becoming worrisome. Between his hits, he showed odd little mannerisms. His fingers might twitch, and he sometimes laughed for no reason. Vern felt maybe he should extract himself from their lucrative partnership, but couldn't think of an easy way to do it. Mark no longer frequented Sam's bar where he could get the more benign cocaine—he felt uneasy going there. Not that he regretted his reprehensible deed, he just didn't want Sam connecting any dots.

"So, Vern—want to try another town for a while? I'm running out of easy pieces over here," said Mark.

Vern allowed as how that might be a good idea. On his part, he fretted that the Network might get wind of his little business and put an arm on him. It could happen, even though he kept his transactions low-key and out of sight.

"The big city?" he asked. "Want to peruse Pittsburgh? We should find something there."

"I'll have to get some permanent wheels, if we do that. I

could try to locate a high-time, low-price vehicle at a used car lot. One we could just dump when it breaks down. Keep trading along, as we go along. That could work. Especially if we keep making enough on the pills. Those have sure turned into gold for us."

Mark wondered about something. "Sure you don't mind that I'm basically just your getaway car? I know my job keeps me in cash and I don't need a cut from you, but I'm grateful for the odd pill you give me and feel I need to pay something. Fair is fair."

"Just round up some girlie action when I need it, and we're even," smiled Vern. "You have no idea how much I appreciate that." Mark reflected a second, and nodded understandingly.

"Well I'm in the same boat. I gotta get me some, too. Easy bar babes—party girls. Please Vern, no working girls. They don't usually come in pairs. Loose and easy party girls is what we want. I hear there are plenty looking for fun in the city, so yeah, let's go. As soon as I can get me a car."

They took a bus over to the Auto Mile, checked out the shined-up discards, and bought a monotone beige unit. It only coughed a little when it started up, then settled to a purr.

"No worries . . . the motor's just cold," swore the salesman. "She's a good deal—just ten years old, put in her time of good service. Her owner wanted something new. She's ok, this one. And cheap. You're lucky—no one really wants this kinda old lady car. When you're tired of it, come on back and I'll put you into something jazzier."

Mark pulled out some bills, collected the title and pending insurance papers. The salesman attached the plates, and off they went. The salesman would register it properly—a service of the agencies on Auto Mile. The price had included the minimum amount of insurance, to be quickly arranged with the company the car lot always used. They would take care of that, too. These pre-owned auto places had everything put together to make it easier to unload vehicles on their lots. And they made more money on the package, of course.

Mark, although jumpy about a paper trail, decided not to worry. Too bad about the insurance and registration. But he doubted he'd get pulled over in this little dobbin. Anyway, he had given them the address on his license—his parents' home. His parents were good with that, understanding his need for a permanent address in his shifting lifestyle. Later he would put it in his mother's name. But the license plates? He would at some point alter the license plates. And he would repaint the car.

One idle day a week or two later, he pulled into Buddy's paint shop.

"You want it gray? Gray, huh. How about a snappy black?" the paint shop guy had asked.

"Nope, just make it light gray. Doesn't show the dust so much," replied Mark.

"Well," said the painter. "This beige is as good as it gets for that sort of thing. Not that I don't want the money. Hey, I'll give you what you want."

Mark had not expected an argument. He nodded affably and hoped this wasn't making him memory worthy. He sure didn't want to be remembered.

"Yeah, you're probably right. But my girlfriend doesn't

like beige. She thinks gray is more, um, fashionable?" They had laughed at that.

In this idea of a smokescreen, of hiding himself, Mark changed apartments regularly. It was his nature. Made it easier to avoid unpleasantness. To a petulant face in front of him: "You were trying to reach me, babe? Oh hell, I moved out of that dump months ago. Had to—cockroaches. Yeah, we should get together one of these days . . ." and he would drift off, leaving the woman puzzled and ticked off.

Now, steering their newly purchased ride onto the highway to leave Auto Mile behind, he geared up to find new opportunities.

Mark said, "So, Vern, now we have decent wheels. She's a practical unit. Yeah, she's a low-end model of a certain age but she even has automatic transmission and AC. Here we go—but where? Got any suggestions?"

"Yep," replied Vern with assurance. "I figure we head for the big city, find a motel, and camp there while we case the hospitals and do a couple." He scratched his cheek and thought some more. "Maybe one with a couple of bars in the neighborhood?"

They located the cheap motels. The men were not into being roommates; they checked into separate but side-by-side inns. Easier to keep their activities private. The motels were close enough to each other that they could stroll back and forth. Not a block away began the line-up of bars and diners—neon festooned and lively on the outside, dark and covert on the inside, beer pulls and whiskey bottles handy to barkeeps. Peering into the bar's dark and smoky environment, they sauntered in with hopes of finding partners for the night.

Interested eyes pinned themselves on Mark right away, and of course she had a friend with her. Party girls rarely traveled alone.

"Hey, girl—whatcher name?" He came on to her, innocently.

"Patty. What's yours? This is my friend Greta."

Vern took Greta's hand, embellished it with a light kiss (tonight he was dressed like a banker). She simpered coyly.

Mark took the stool beside Patty. He wooed her with his eyes, letting his shoulder touch hers, and after a couple of warm-up drinks, he dared to caress her thigh. She let him, touching his hand with her fingers. She sighed happily, letting her mouth open slightly, and ran the tip of her tongue over her lips, lowering her eyes to his roaming hand. She wanted it. Her knees opened up as he stroked her thigh, and his hand moved to slide fingers inside her panties. She gasped at his brash move, then groaned and shifted her body toward him, looking at him questioningly. He smiled, kissed her lightly on the lips, put his arm around her shoulders, and whispered in her ear, "Yes. Of course."

Vern was making good time with the sidekick, a plain but nicely made-up honey who eagerly snuggled up to him on her barstool. Vern was amazed at how easy girls were these days. He hoped he wouldn't get a disease.

Mark was dreaming of the pill he had, and looked at Patty. Was she disposable? Could he get away with it, with Vern in tow? He thought not. Anyway, she wasn't slutty enough, not worn out enough. He had his standards.

But at least he could pick at the itch. He would guard carefully the high-powered pill for another time. It puzzled him how much he had enjoyed his killing.

Maybe that's what trophy animal hunters felt. Now there's an idea, he thought to himself. From pulling wings off flies, to burning baby chicks alive, a big step up from setting fuzzy tennis balls aflame (the parents of one of his childhood gang owned a hatchery business)—to bagging a gazelle for its trophy horns? Or whores? Jack the Ripper was famous for his serial killings of prostitutes. Justifiable in the Ripper's mind. And in Mark's. Besides, what a powerful ecstasy. And the Ripper didn't even have a special drug.

Trophies. Killers too, sometimes kept mementos, Mark knew. Not what he wanted. That would be evidence.

They left with their quarry in tow. The women were young, full-bodied, merry, and lusty. How could it be so good, the men asked themselves. And so they romped unrestrained, playfully, through the night, each in his own room, snacking greedily with 24-hour room service.

The girls sneaked out in the morning, leaving the studs sated and snoring. They met in the driveway, giggling, just a half-block from where they left their car. They hurried off to collect their wheels and go to breakfast, where they would discuss their evening's success. Would they see the men again? Doubtful, although they sure had been good lovers. It was not smart to get too close to pick-ups, however. Not smart.

And as handsome and arousing as Mark was, he made Patty nervous. She liked her action a bit rough, but once when his arm was across her neck, pinning her down, she saw something move through his eyes that made her buck him off. She was a strong woman. He retreated.

THIRTY-THREE
CHEERS AND BEERS

*A*ll gliders accounted for, the pilots made to set out for Checkpoints. Roscoe plainly was hoping for more company from India, but she only had eyes for Dave.

Well, he advised himself, she was a little young for him. He preferred to think of it that way, rather than his being too old for her. He was macho and vain.

"Roscoe, you are an absolute doll!" said India. "Thank you for the great experience." Murmuring her thanks for his compliments on her flying, she put her hand in Dave's and said how glad she was that he had made it happen for her.

They took their time around the airstrip and clubhouse, making sure all aircraft were either carefully tied down, hangered, or stashed in their trailers, and all loose items stored away. The disassembling of the gliders took time. But the wind was already brisk; they probably would be getting a bigger blow, and they wanted no damage.

With a crack of thunder and a burst of wind, it suddenly began pouring rain—and it was only just past noon. The front itself had not arrived yet, but as so often happened, a storm or two could precede it by up to a hundred miles.

CHEERS AND BEERS

It was maybe too early for beer, but they were all hyped up by the storm and narrow escapes. Bad weather was coming in way faster than predicted; the air mass had picked up enough speed to ruin any thoughts of more flying. What better way to celebrate a safe day than with a little cheerful elbow bending. And anyway, the burgers were tops at Checkpoints, and they hadn't had lunch. Hunger was the driving force as they loaded up cars and splashed down the road, now muddy and puddled.

India called home; the answering machine picked up. "Hi, Mom—just calling to let you know we're back and tied down, heading out now to get some late lunch. I should be in early."

The machine sounded with beeps like it was on battery power. Where were they? All of them out? Where was Eli? Oh, that's right, he's at JV lacrosse practice. Hm. She pocketed her cell phone in her shirt where she could feel it vibrate if they called. But practice would have been called off, she was sure.

"Everything okay?" asked Dave, still flustered from her putting her hand in his.

"I guess so," she replied. She pulled out the phone to see if she had missed any calls. Nope. "Nobody's home. Eli had lacrosse practice, but surely that was cancelled. Maybe they went to the movies or something. Usually we tell each other what we're doing, but I didn't miss any calls. Oh well."

They walked together to his car, wind and rain whipping them, where he flipped on the heater once they got going. It was only August, but the storm had blown in on a cold wind. Once at Checkpoints, the room burst into lively chatter about how close a call they had all had, everyone telling a tale, and how *It's better to be on the ground wishing you were in the air, than in the air wishing you were on the ground!* A saying on the walls of almost every flight school in the world.

India was on a high from her flight and the help she had given Roscoe. He was telling everyone how she had spotted the landmarks. "Hey—I flew right by the second one, and she caught it! Already behind us. I might never have seen it," he said, looking proudly at her. She was happier than she'd ever imagined, being accepted by these accomplished pilots.

But when would she solo? That was in limbo.

"Well, you've had quite the experiences today, India, and received approval from one of the best," Dave said, nodding at Roscoe. "If the weather's good tomorrow, I guess it will be your time to solo."

Her mouth dropped open, her eyes popped, and she whipped around to stare at him. Wha-a-t?

He took in her stunned expression.

"Well, why not? You've demonstrated an excellent understanding of this beautiful sport; you passed all written tests with high grades. You surely know how to land skillfully, and you can sniff out a thermal and hook into it as well as anybody. You seem to have learned well and easily. And you have logged the required hours. Yep—you're going to be on your own tomorrow, barring inclement winds. We don't fly when it's too rough."

Especially not the first solo, he thought to himself. It would be hard to let her go, even in the best of conditions. He wondered if maybe he was feeling too protective. But he had to let her go when she was ready, and undoubtedly she was ready. Nonetheless, uneasiness clouded his face.

Roscoe came over, leaned down, and whispered, "You

don't need to worry about that one," he grinned, gesturing toward India with his head. "I have to confess something. Today, India was the one who landed my plane. And she handled the winds like a champ. Don't look so shocked. Remember, I'm a high-time instructor."

Dave was dumbfounded. She was that good? Talk about affirmation.

He beamed at India. She looked back, questioningly. "Roscoe told me you landed his Blanik today. I'm impressed!"

"Hey, easy peasy, Dave. You taught me well. It was a thrill, bringing her in. The Blanik is a nice craft. I enjoyed it whenever he let me have the controls. I even saved us from a crowd of hawks! Did he tell you that?" She looked up at Roscoe, who raised his eyebrows. She coughed. "Of course he'd have spotted them if he'd been watching; he was on the radio checking weather. I guess I shouldn't get credit for normal see-and-avoid." Then she thanked Roscoe again for the pleasure of flying with him. It had been a sweet learning experience.

"Dave, I need to get home. My parents weren't expecting me to be this late. Not that I have to report in at a certain hour, but we keep track of each other. It's a family thing." He put his hand on her shoulder and nodded. "And they didn't answer the phone when I rang from the airport. Eli's practice had to have been called. I'm a little worried. I haven't been so trusting of the world since that assault."

"Okay," said Dave, "I'm ready to go. It's been a long day. It's only 4:30 p.m., but it feels like nine, after getting up so early." The crowd left its conviviality behind along with drained beer glasses and hamburger scraps, dashing out into the rain. Most were locals, but a couple of pilots needed to find a motel. They didn't want to drive their trailered sailplanes home in the full-blown storm. Dave made a couple of calls, set them up, and told them to follow him.

"I hope you don't mind a little detour on the way home, India. These folks need to get rooms and settle in for the night. I'm going to guide them to their motel."

On the way out, almost out of sight, a car sat idling, a man watching. They didn't seem to notice him in the driving rain. But he noticed them.

"What's the girl up to now?"

He had been going to go in and get a beer to scope the place out for him and Vern; they hadn't been to this watering hole before. But when he saw India emerge with the guy who had decked him, he stayed hidden. They pulled out. He put his car in gear and followed them.

He was surprised to see them head to the nearest motel, a higher-end chain hotel, just down the road. Was she going to go to bed with that guy? Then he noticed three other cars following them and turning into the drive, leaving India and the fellow to go on their way.

Never mind. He would see about her another time. But now he knew where she liked to hang out. Not that he could get to her there, but all the details could add up to something.

India tapped nervously on Dave's arm. "Dave, I saw something back at Checkpoints. The man who attacked me was outside in a car, and he followed us. I'm sure of it. I think he's gone now, but I'm scared." She peered through her fogged window, wiping clear a place to see out better.

"What? Let's call the police!" Dave jumped, and hauled out his cell.

"Wait, Dave. I can't prove I saw him. Maybe I'm wrong, maybe I'm just scared of my own shadow." She lowered her head, and looked at her clenched hands. "You remember him, don't you?" She looked at him; he frowned and nodded.

"I've often wondered if it was that guy from the accounting offices. I never had the chance to check him out," he replied.

Soon they were home, and the family's mysterious silence was explained. A lightning strike had knocked out the power while her parents were retrieving Eli from his practice, so they never got her message. Even the battery backup had failed. They were glad to see her, but they hadn't really been worried. They knew Dave would be in charge, and she had advised them early in the day about the meet and the later than usual homecoming.

They had ignited the cozy gas hearth fire and were cooking burgers on the gas stove, never mind the power outage.

The fire chief had sternly advised her when she wanted a gas stove: "Well you know what they say, Dr. Hammond. Go gas, go boom!"

She had snorted in good-humored derision. Never one to believe doomsayers, she had insisted on gas for cooking.

She remembered that, and felt smug.

"Too bad I didn't try your cell, Daddy, you could have joined us at Checkpoints! Aside from yours, Mom, Checkpoints has the best burgers in town. We're all fed," India said, patting her tummy.

They settled in front of the living room fireplace, which was dancing with flames from fake logs. They looked real enough, thought Dave, but he would never have those in his house, once he got one. They didn't throw much heat.

"Dave, why don't you have one of my burgers; a big guy like you must have some room left." If her mother was inviting, he wasn't refusing.

When they sat down together at that big table, cold fat raindrops pelting the window panes, he began telling the story of their day.

"You know, Sarge, it bothers me that we got nothin' on that wasted broad we found lying by the street, a coupla months ago. No info at all."

Sergeant Moore looked up from his desk. The officer's brow was scrunched up in concentration. They had just come back from lunch, and he was continuing a conversation.

"We never really probed the neighborhood for information on her. It was such a vicious beating she got, and now we got another like that over in Pittsburgh. The prostitute thing, some worn-out throwaway. Sad and sickening."

"Maybe the Pittsburgh police will come up with something on that one, then we can revisit our murder here. Maybe we should get at that now. Sooner rather than later."

THIRTY-FOUR
MARKIE'S NEXT KILL

When morning came around after his and Vern's conquests, he had been strangely unsatisfied. Yes, he'd gotten a good romping, but the bliss he'd hoped for was missing. He almost finished her, Patty. But she was young and strong and had escaped in time. He didn't think she knew how close her end was; he hadn't the chance to slam her around, and anyway she was too strong. He was getting soft, all right, for a babe to be able to throw him off. He'd pretended it was nothing, and proceeded to give her a good servicing, one that had her moaning pretty good.

When Vern and he met up again for a late breakfast, Mark announced he was going to drive him over and leave him off in the hospital district for a couple of hours, and go prowling.

"Vern, I don't like to admit this, but last night was not so great. Patty was into domination—of *me*. Not my thing. I gave *her* a good time, but I don't like to be controlled. Anyway, I'll have a bunch of time on my hands while you're doing your filching, and rather than sit on them, I'm going to poke around some. I might get luckier today."

Vern noticed his agitation. Mark was restless and had

pinpoint pupils. Geez, what was happening to the old Markie, the one he knew. He looked away, and sighed. Maybe the high-potency hospital supplies were too much, but he didn't dare say anything. Mark liked them. He got up for a pit stop before they left on their sortie. Mark sat and waited.

If Mark was concerned about himself, he didn't show it. He was pretty contained, giving off no hints. Why? Because what he was focusing on was finding a self-glorifying moment of supreme, extreme control. The ego shattering he got from the tootsie throwing him off had to be fixed. He craved, needed, this brutality to confirm his manhood.

His fingers drummed with impatience on the table as he waited for Vern. The dirty breakfast dishes were getting on his nerves. The place was short-handed, and the one slack-jawed waitress was not going to clear them soon. He passed a hand over the stubble on his face. He hadn't shaved. So what. No need to impress anyone.

By the time they got going, it was past noon. They found a convenient rendezvous corner, and Vern hopped out. They coordinated their watches. Vern, looking at the massive hospital complex, requested three hours. General Hospital here covered several blocks.

Funny, ruminated Mark, how hospitals were so often found in cities' sleazy, run-down neighborhoods. Neighborhood was not a good word. He felt 'neighborhood' implied nice neighbors, people who were friends, families, and old folks sitting on porches. Not here, he sniffed. His mouth contorted, looking at trash drifting in the streets, old brick office buildings, boarded up broken windows. ROOMS TO LET signs here and there. And the occasional inebriate tucked in by a dumpster. On the corners, neon lights outlined LIQUORS; in the middle of the blocks, scuzzy bars were open for business. Since nine in the morning.

Mark knew hookers would already be on barstools, looking to make money. Business could be good around hospitals. Unhappy souls seeking comfort would find them, and the hooker would have a hidey-hole to take customers to. He knew what he needed, what he'd do. He'd find a run-down whore, have that Scotch with her at the bar, and he would pop his drug. He would feel that telltale meanness begin to creep through his body, up his arms. It would start that wildfire in his brain. He perked up, thinking of it.

He drew on thin surgical gloves, getting ready.

He saw his prey, flashed her some bills. She nodded and motioned him to the stool beside her. She was allowed to fish from the barstool as long as she sold some drinks. He ordered and paid for his Scotch.

What's with the rubber gloves? thought the working girl. *Maybe the creep has scars or a rash or something.* She didn't care. If her inner voice was speaking, she wasn't listening. That cash was all that mattered. The bartender hadn't looked at him at all, placing the drink in front of him and collecting the money, all the while avoiding eye contact, looking off into the distance. He didn't like to involve himself in sleaze. He didn't want to see anybody. The less he saw, the better.

Mark stirred the drink, slurped a big gulp for the kick, and offered some to the woman after draining more than half. He wiped off his lip marks before he gave her the glass. No traces, please. Ah . . . such a feeling. The pill had gone down with his first swallow.

Mark hadn't counted on the pimp. He had just done her,

reveling in her agony, slamming her again and again on the floor after erupting into her scrawny body, shutting off her creepy mewing sounds. His violence had exploded with a harsh roar. His loud, satisfied guttural noises alerted and brought on her pimp.

Knife drawn, he burst in to see about his moneymaker. Appalled by the gore, the pimp hesitated. To his end. Mark, in his fury, did him, too. Fueled by chemicals, Mark grabbed the knife, drove it into his skinny chest with a twist, and watched as he grew limp and flaccid, as life ebbed from those chocolate eyes. "A twofer," he smiled to himself.

He cleaned up, washing his rubber-gloved hands, keeping them on for exiting the building. He had prepared for this—he would leave no fingerprints. Whatever blood had gotten on his clothes he rinsed out and blotted dry with a dirty towel, using the broad's hair dryer to finish up. Couldn't flash anything bloody at Vern. The prostitute hadn't commented on the gloves. He would throw them into a Dumpster somewhere.

Then he washed the knife, a long switchblade, and pocketed it. He would trash that too, but not in the same Dumpster. It was impressive, but he would not keep it. Maybe drop it into a river? He had three choices: the Monongahela, the Allegheny, or the Ohio. Pittsburgh was a huge urban pile at their confluence, the three rivers forming a de facto city dump.

He stepped over the bodies and let himself out. What a dung hole, he thought. He opened the door to the unlit corridor. Unseen by Mark, a shadowy figure vanished around a corner.

Mark slunk softly down the stairs. He met no one.

The activity had taken its toll on his muscles, and he

found himself shaking. "But oh, it was good, it was so damned good," he said trembling, pleasure sizzling in his brain.

It was hard to come down. He would have to snag some calming cocaine off the street before he picked up Vern. He hoped it would be calming. Lately it seemed to hype him up. Never mind. There would be some; you just had to know how to attract it. Where to look, and how to look like a ready score. In no time he was snorting up his fix. It was that kind of run-down city block. He slipped off the gloves and laid them on the seat beside him, examining his knuckles. Good. Not wrecked this time. He smiled at his cunning. And the hit had helped.

Driving back to pick up Vern, he swung behind a Walgreens, where he spotted a trash barrel. He saw he was alone; in went the gloves. Then he cruised along the Ohio and flipped the knife into its dirty waters. A driver or two saw that, but thought nothing of it. People were always throwing trash into that cesspool of a river. It was said of that stretch of the Ohio: "If it can fit in the water and sink, it's probably under there." Out of sight, out of mind, down among old cars and refrigerators, in low-visibility polluted water. That knife would never be found.

"You get some stuff, Vern?" asked Mark, calm and interested after his medicinal snort. Vern had quickly doffed the scrubs and the crammed waist pack, patting it happily.

"You betcha! I probably got two month's worth of high-livin' expenses right here." He looked at Mark for signs of . . . anything. "Uh . . . you find some action?" he smiled quizzically.

"Well, it turns out this isn't the area for easy pieces." The lie fell easily from his tongue. "But I figure we can find bones to hop when we look around for dinner tonight. Whaddaya think?"

The skies had been darkening, building in solid with gray clouds; it had started spitting rain here and there. Already it was midafternoon, sunset wouldn't come for another few hours. They talked it over and decided to head back to Valley. They had checked out already, thinking to try another motel elsewhere. No sense in leaving tracks.

They would return to their own apartments, and meet later.

And so he had found India exiting from Checkpoints, the bar and burger place, and had followed her for a while. But tonight wasn't the time for her.

The call came in later in the day; some pimp's whore had earlier discovered the bodies of her boss and a friend, slain in her friend's room. She had nothing else to tell them. No point in mentioning the guy she'd seen leaving. She couldn't describe him, anyway. "Just stay out of it, Effie," she told herself. Nobody else had noticed anything at the time. These were not people who had a neighborhood watch, or nosy busybodies snooping on each other's comings and goings, or even watching out for each other. This was the bottom rung of society. They had seen plenty of death, plenty of destroyed lives, including their own.

And they hated the pimp. He had been bullying, mean, and nasty, withholding what the girls felt were rightful earnings just because he could. He had a switchblade he had carved more than one gut with.

No, they were glad. Any one of them could have finished him off, but of course they wouldn't say that to the police.

"He was stabbed in the heart, right smack through the ribs. But where's the knife?" The police had scoured the room, the trash, and cursorily screened a two-block area. No knife. Didn't really matter. These dregs were no loss.

But it was curious. It brought to mind a killing over in Valley a couple of months before. Another whore. Did they have a Ripper on patrol?

THIRTY-FIVE
CHILDREN'S AID SOCIETY

*W*ith her inspired success the day of the meet (all had seen and admired her skilled landing) the club members had become even more interested in India and began to talk with her about her life. She told them about her involvement with Children's Aid and her wish to conduct outings to the airport from time to time. She needed chaperone-type volunteers. There were a couple of women who thought the idea was terrific and offered to help.

And so the first excursion was hatched. Permission slips went out and came back signed, relieving the glider club and associates of liability. A leap in trust, thought Paul Hammond, but what the heck. He wasn't going to argue it. The van was scheduled for a Wednesday. The motherly Audrey and Monica from the glider group had already signed up to help. Their schedules decreed what day it would be, and India was moving toward her first project, all obstacles dealt with.

Dave would be there. He said he couldn't round up the tow pilot, but he himself could allow the kids to take turns sitting in the towplane. A couple of pilots had been intrigued with the plan, and offered up their gliders. They would help the kids in and out of the cockpits, and demonstrate the controls before letting them handle them.

"India, there will be some strict rules about no touching, keeping their little paws off of things unless we say they can," Dave announced.

"Of course," nodded India. All in all, it seemed it would work.

She had long since prepared her first lesson for the children, nothing outside their range of comprehension. She would explain how the plane turned by moving the rudder and ailerons, and let them take turns moving them from inside the plane with the control stick (little legs wouldn't reach down to the rudders). Carefully, of course, no yanking. And she would show them how the air brakes, the spoilers, slow the plane, pushing up into and against the wind. She doubted they would understand the concept of lift, caused by a low pressure area formed by air flowing over the wing. But she would give it a try. There were only ten coming, so it would be manageable. They would spend no more than a half hour or so touring the field and gliders. It was a good introduction.

Her sister was on tap to stay with the littlest ones back at the Children's Aid building. She had proved herself to be an excellent replacement for India. India felt a small twinge of jealousy, but did not let it show. She was proud of Claudia.

"Hey India—look here!" exclaimed Dave. "See what I found in the storage room." He showed her a box full of little metal clip-on pilots' wings, bought for some occasion long ago and long forgotten. "How would it be to give out these wings as a reward for good behavior?" He turned that idea over in his head. "Or maybe even just as a memento." He reached for her collar, grinning, and put one on her, his fingers gently brushing her cheek in passing. "There you go, pilot lady."

"Ooh, that's brilliant," India blushed at his touch and sighed with delight. "What a perfect find. Things are certainly falling into place."

The charity was pleased to have their charges exposed to something in the world beyond the televised football games their parents watched on weekends, never mind the weekend kiddy cartoons.

Mr. Thomas Sanders, head of the organization, husband of director Janet Ollifant, offered to drive the children himself and "take a gander at the facility." He had always thought highly of India, and had observed how well she did with the children. Especially the tiresome of job of toilet training. She got a big secret atta-girl from him for that. And what a blessing that her younger sister Claudia turned out to be as wholesome and helpful, as smart and pretty as India? He felt grateful to the Hammond family for producing such winners. And the boy, Eli? He looked to be coming along well too, in sports.

"You know," he said to India, "I've always kind of admired those gliders, even thought about trying it myself. It just never was something I could arrange. Hope you don't mind my barging in?" He searched her face hopefully. He was looking forward to this field trip.

"Are you kidding me, Mr. Sanders? We'd be thrilled to have you along. What a treat for everyone. I know the kiddies like you. They'll be happy to see you. So you're on for next Wednesday afternoon at three o'clock, right?"

And the Phelpses? Not as upbeat as Mr. Sanders. To say the Phelpses had been less than enthusiastic about India taking off time for this pursuit with the kids was understating it. They didn't have a love of flight, couldn't understand it, and felt nervous about their highly valued helper getting caught up in it, and about her dragging in impressionable youngsters who might one day as adults get killed doing it. It was just plain unnatural to fly through the air. But India had the okay from Children's Aid, so how could they be footdraggers on this? At least India was no longer in the bull's-eye of that vile attacker.

Or so they believed.

THIRTY-SIX
MARK VERSUS INDIA

*B*reezes flowed pleasantly around her as she pedaled to the airport to meet her field trippers. She was wound up. And in a rush.

Usually, these late summer days, she would slow down to peek at August wildflowers, the golden tansies, wild asters, purple loosestrife, and sweeps of early fireweed coming out along the roadsides and coloring up edges of untended gardens. Soon milkweed would be bursting its pods, sending seed-fluff adrift to sow the countryside. She loved seeing milkweed's drifting seeds backlit by sunshine. The plant was a favorite monarch butterfly breeding host.

Once she followed the whole monarch growth cycle, from the leaf-chomping black and yellow caterpillar all the way through to the butterfly, from first leaf munch to the spinning and sealing of its glistening cocoon, to the fascinating chrysalis breakout, then the air-drying and unfolding of the dramatic wings. Her mother had almost ripped the interloping plant out of her garden, the one by the front steps. Granted, it was a rough-looking coarse cousin of the dainty flowers she had cultivated, but India had spied the caterpillar days before, and then the splendid sea-mist green chrysalis hanging under a leaf. She pleaded with her mother to leave it be. Once mother saw nature's elegant handiwork, she agreed to allow it life.

Claudia was little in those days, but observant and curious. "Lookee, India. That green is the color of your eyes." Wonderful, wryly thought India. Chrysalis eyes. "Well yours, too, Claudie . . ." she responded. "Your eyes, too."

Metamorphosis, she knew it was called. That caterpillar had been quite large and scary, but it morphed into such a splendid flying creature.

But today, speeding down her route, she was focused on the children, on arriving early to greet them, and in knowing just what she was going to say. She ran over it again and again in her mind. Dave had promised to be there, to conduct towplane tours. Two other pilots would be there too, to hand the little guys into their sailplanes. She would welcome them all, and introduce the volunteers. They would each, one by one, shake the hands of the adults and look them in the eyes. It was part of their training. She had seen to that. This was a very special grown-up thing they were doing this afternoon and she wanted to emphasize it.

Mark had a moment of time open to him between appointments and was idly puttering around the periphery of the town, thinking about not much, when a bicyclist appeared in front him in the road. He pulled out away from the cycler to pass—when suddenly he noticed who it was.

"Damn!" he exclaimed. He went rigid with shock,

but managed to continue driving, keeping the car under control. Even with her helmet on, he recognized her. India was keeping to the side of her lane as she was supposed to, but she hugged the shoulder even more when she sensed the passing car. She pedaled along, and continued with her thoughts. Her right turn came up shortly, and she wheeled down the dirt road to the airport.

Once he had gotten his nerves in order, Mark's head bobbed back and forth, checking the rearview mirror to scan behind him. Where was she? The roadway was clear. Where could she be? Oh, maybe she had seen him and scrammed home, the kind of thing a frightened female would do, after what he had done to her. He thought about that. What exactly had he done to her? He hadn't done so much. Not what he'd wanted to do, before he got rabbit-punched and had been driven off. Remembering her face and feeling the memory of her body in his arms, his loins started to itch, his member began to swell, and he grew hungry for a taste of her. He again felt her hair in his hand, and blood trickling over his fingers.

He was on fire. He wanted to find her, whip off that helmet, grab her gorgeous red hair and force her down into submission. She could beg, but mercy was not in him. He would have to plan this. Carefully. She probably would die after all, but not until he had pleased himself well with a satisfying rape and thorough beating. He panted as he drove, his face taking on a look of madness, his lips swelling with desire. Oh, yes, yes—he would kill her. Beauty be damned.

Mark had gone over the edge.

He was completely mad. Dark evil oozed cheerfully into

his mind, flames flickering on the edges, a hissing whisper urging him on. He suddenly longed to punch that angel face, rip it, make it gush with blood . . . until the bleeding forever stopped. He would watch the tear-filled green eyes plead until the light went out. He almost had an orgasm, thinking about it. His lips pulled back in a hideous grimace. He reached down grunting, and with his eyes fixed on a spot beyond the windshield, made that happen.

Someday soon, he would do it. He would do it.

Mark was, of course, a psychopath. He had begun his twisted life trajectory when he was young, long before his discovery of the delights of drugs. He had always liked to kill. When he was boy, it was frogs. He and other brutish little friends enjoyed making frogs' long tongues flop out and their froggy eyes bulge, all before their guts came out and they were dead. They would stomp on them, snorting and laughing. Messy, but fun. As he grew older, the stray dog would become a victim of lasso practice. He would pull the rope tight to strangle it, watch fascinated as it fought frantically for release, until finally it jerked quiet, dead. He had no idea then that he would find bliss from killing humans.

"Harmless," murmured his concerned parents. "Boys will be boys." They were aware only of his frog kills, at a loss to do anything. The dogs would have horrified them. They liked dogs.

A psychopath. Some could argue sociopath, terms often used interchangeably. Both lie easily, feel no guilt; can, with no drama, kill as well as contrive a theft. Nothing is ever their fault. One can occasionally find them in a lineup of politicians. They get there because they are highly intelligent, manipulative, charming, and good at getting others to do their work for them; and because they lie about anything and everything. A particular quirk? They enjoy the thrill of dodging discovery. A definitive characteristic is that they are delightfully persuasive. They often hide their psychopathy so well that families and fellow workers do not notice it. They can be fun to be around. But you'll be used. And of course not all are killers.

And there you have Mark, now planning his domination and the demise of India.

Mark felt his behavior was not particularly unusual, if he even thought about it. Television had shown him the bloody carnage of murder and mayhem all his life, and so he was inured to it. Monkey see, monkey do.

India braked quickly, skidding in front of the Valley Glider clubhouse. She was early, but Dave was already there. He smiled his hello at her as she came to a stop. "Whoa—you're going to take off right here, going that fast!" he twitted her.

She laughed and retorted, "If only!"

He was thinking about giving her a hug, but he was cautious about that. They were friends, companions, surely nothing more. And yet, there was a closeness and comfort in being together. Even exhilaration and happiness. They had taken in a movie or two together. Her companionship was so enjoyable. He found their age difference wasn't so much after all. First, they enjoyed many of the same cultural things. Also, happily, they had the same likes and dislikes. Getting along with her was easy. But he knew she had an education to complete before she caught up to him. Would she wait? Would he? He would indeed.

He had fallen irrevocably in love with her.

She was his first true love, despite girls he had dated in college. He hadn't felt like this about any woman before. Yes, India was a woman. Young, but a woman. One with a decency about her that made him hold off on coming on to her physically. Inviolate? She was sexy, no doubt about it. He couldn't put his finger on it. It was as if there was a protective aura around her. Sometimes he felt lightheaded from wanting her.

Her parents liked him a lot. They could see the affection he thought he was hiding. And hers. He had become a regular at the Sunday table.

Her goodness went with her wherever she went, an armor from the other side of this world's reality. Her guardian angel, perhaps. Does everyone have one? Something to help us fight off evil, or even do battle for us.

We speak of guardian angels, of instinct, of the inner voice or the nudging of conscience, a system guiding us through life. Believers call it God's communication channel, others His lifeline. Something we are called to listen to, hold onto. A gift, they say, from Him to us. Or from the cosmos? Take your choice. (Of course, it's usually not in our plans to listen or pay attention—way too inconvenient.)

India had felt this. She had sensed faint wordless guidance taking her into lit rooms instead of dark ones, nudgings to go into the right-hand elevator instead of the left, or even not to use the school's first-floor girls' room. Like that. She was tuned in.

She had listened with interest to the letter of Paul to the apostles, about when he was on the road to Damascus, the epiphany when he was blinded by the light. She was sure she had seen that light herself as a child, a cloud of light glowing at the end of her bed with the beaming face and figure of her Nana, when her beloved Nana died.

To India, it was as though there was somehow a world more real than this material one, more real than the table in front of her, a mystical reality beyond. She had heard of the Celts and their belief in the thin places between the two worlds, their explanation of apparitions. It was in among teenagers to talk of mystical things, of Ouija boards, of séances. Of ghosts. She loved all that. She believed. She paid attention. She stayed tuned in. Their pastor had preached vehemently against it all. "Dangerous business, Ouija boards," he intoned ominously.

And so the field-trip hour of the afternoon went by. The children happily hopped in and out of the sailplanes and waggled wings with the control stick, watching the wings as they did that. They listened to simple explanations of how things fly. They were well behaved and some even got questions right about lift and drag.

Best yet, they earned their clip-on wings. It was a huge success. Mr. Sanders was beaming, Ms Ollifant too. The volunteers lined up for the children's earnest handshakes, including a fellow from Dave's office. He thought maybe he might take up soaring himself.

"When can we come back?" was the eager chorus.

"Oh, pretty soon," was the cagey answer. India wasn't sure when she could corral the volunteers again, but her hope was for another sortie the following week.

The kids scrambled into the van and waved their farewells. India hopped onto her bicycle, after first thanking her volunteers for their super help. Well, they had had fun, too.

It was short and sweet and did a service for the children. They were well pleased with themselves. "We could get into this," they murmured agreeably.

And so goodness spreads itself out. It can be contagious. So can evil.

As India was pedaling home, Mark was watching. He knew this was not the time, but he was watching. He didn't see her come from the airport; he had picked up her trail closer to home.

Nearing the turn to her neighborhood, as she rolled past a group of parked cars, her skin suddenly crawled with alarm. The hair rose on her neck. What? She swiveled her head to look around, but she saw nothing, nothing threatening. A car was disappearing down the road behind her, having pulled out from its parking place across the street. A light-colored sedan. One she thought she'd seen before, but it was like so many. The strange chill faded as she moved along and continued on home. Dave was coming to dinner.

THIRTY-SEVEN
OBSCENE VILLAINY

Mark had found the guys he had known back in his childhood; the Terrible Six they had proudly dubbed themselves. The bullies, the sadistic frog-flattening playmates. They gathered over drinks regularly now, to brag and snicker over their perverted memories. Lots of "Remember hows?"

Mark enjoyed their company more and more.

Vern was not a part of this. Mark was getting tired of Vern.

Ever since his sortie to Pittsburgh, he had a yearning to talk to somebody about it, to brag. Coincidentally, he ran across his old friends from childhood. Dark forces at work? They understood; they were energized by the pleasures of ruthless brutality; they had learned it together. Some were recently out of prison, sent there for beating up girlfriends, or inhumanly, appallingly, setting fire to winos in gutters (while young Mark was garroting dogs, they were lighting baby chicks to watch them run and sizzle), or they were in jail for using broken bottles in bloody bar fights. There was a litany of cruel offenses. It seemed all his old buddies had served time.

Mark felt smarter than ever that of all his pals he alone

had not been caught at any of his crimes. Not even the shoplifting of his teens, snitching high-priced Nikes and Reboks. "Hey," he had told himself. "I'm entitled to good stuff."

Not that car thing either, when he'd been baited by a bunch of drunks. They wanted him to prove he knew how to hot-wire, a talent he enjoyed demonstrating. So, he had done it on a whim and a dare, hot-wiring and driving off with them in a slick Camry. That one he had crashed into a ravine. The carload of revelers were supposed to all jump out before it sailed through the guardrail. But one of the guys hadn't leapt out; too blotto, too slow, and had died in the crash's fire. Markie didn't care then, and he didn't care now. Not his fault.

He was a fun guy, outstanding company, but never close to anyone. He used people. Girls were eager to give it up to him. If they got pregnant, he punched them in the gut so they would miscarry. None ever charged him on it.

So now Mark was wound up, eager and tense. He wanted to tell them what he had done, but he wasn't sure . . . Someone would have to confess something appealingly dreadful first, before he would.

Finally, in a liquored up moment, one of the ex-cons said, "The dumb-asses never got me for the one I did in; they just pulled me in for punching one up. Not for the one I gloriously wasted," he said looking around, laughing to himself.

Mark locked eyes with him. Something dark flickered a message, one to the other. "Ah yes," it hissed. Mark thought he sensed something in his brain, and jiggled his head as if to shake something loose.

"It was really good, wasn't it?" he asked, nodding a knowing smile.

"Oh yeah, it was. But how do *you* know?"

"Because I've done it too. Slam-bam bitch-kill, twice." Mark's eyes glazed over, smiling slyly. "It was so good," he sighed.

Then they all, these criminals, started talking about their kills. It was the kids' club reborn. Mark savored the the horrors. One had cut his victim into pieces to dump into different parts of the river, a time-consuming job. Mark was in fine company.

A blackness surrounded them he hadn't noticed before. And a sense of gleeful evil. It seeped into his bones like invisible smoke and went into his chest. He felt for a moment that he couldn't breathe, and he panicked. But it slipped away, out from his lungs, leaving him puzzled and on edge.

"So. How'd you do yours, Markie?" demanded the chopper, a threat in his voice.

"Nothing like your hack job, buddy." Mark grinned. "But it was amazing."

They leaned forward, listening hungrily as he regaled them with explicit details. He spared nothing. Only Petey the child molester was disappointed. Interesting that even the hardest of them found him repugnant. But they put up with him. He knew too much.

The blackness gathered and entered his body through the top of his head, and his head lolled over. They laughed at his drunkenness. They all were aroused. Violence would be the only catharsis.

Markie came to, chilled by fragments of a vision, one of whirling about with demons. He shook his head to get rid of it, and frowned at his passing out. Gotta watch out for those ugly dreams, he thought. Then he fingered the pill in his pocket. Ah! He was surprised and happy to find two. How could that be? Never mind. He ordered a Scotch and suggested they go hunting. In the corners of his mind, he sensed a hovering elation, a bliss, waiting to happen.

This time it would be with the excitement of sharing, the thrill of a group kill. They would find a whore and slowly strip her. They would have her one at a time, each one taking his time banging and cutting her, delivering pain almost to the point of death. They threw fingers for who got to deliver the coup de grace. Markie won, but they would all intently watch her eyes roll back and go dark. He popped one pill, and saved the other. Where had the second pill come from, anyway? Vern must have accidentally given him an extra.

And so it happened as they planned.

The alleyway was unlit, full of shadows, empty, perfect for their terrible purpose. One of them had lured a streetwalker in by waving a tempting handful of bills, pointing at his crotch. She had nodded happily, and followed him into the alley. But she gasped and jerked back when two others grasped her waist, grabbing her by the hair. She fully panicked when two more gripped her arms. She struggled fiercely, writhing, resisting, and trying to scream. A hand clamped her mouth shut, and then her breath was shut off at the neck, just for a moment. They were pleased with this struggle, taking turns wantonly peeling off her clothing. Their fervor built, her resistance inciting them to crueler knife pricks. She bled, twisting in pain. She tried to arch away from each vigorous penetration, the men grinding her into the filthy paving stones with each thrust.

Oh, but the alleyway was not quite empty. Quietly hidden, there was an interested pair of eyes, seeing it all.

In the pitch-dark behind a dumpster, a dozing wino came to and blurrily watched the mayhem, listening to the grunts, thuds, and tiny muffled cries from the naked sprawled victim. Occasionally he caught glimpses of white skin, her knees bobbing up and down, flashing between the shadowy moving images of ravaging men.

It lasted longer than he would have believed. They taunted their victim with life, when obviously she wanted to die.

When they had satisfied themselves, after they watched her life go, they heaved her into the Dumpster. He heard a dull thud as she plopped down on garbage bags. Staying still as a corpse himself, he clung to the building's wall in the inky dark. Terrified, he wet himself as he watched and waited. He wiped his mouth, feeling vomit in his throat.

He waited a long time after they sneaked away before he dared to crawl out. Staggering, reeling up to the street, he called out to pedestrians, and shaking with fear and dread he pointed back to the alley, pop-eyed and hoarsely demanding someone call 911. It took a bit of convincing, because he was so haggard and smelly.

"Men, we have another one," announced the sergeant, shaking his head as he hung up the phone. A dirty slum alleyway death. "An ugly one. Another pro beaten to a sponge, bloody as hell. What's going on in this town?"

This time the police got lucky. They canvassed area bars. Sure enough, a bouncer had noticed a tough group murmuring and chuckling in a dim smoky corner, lingering and drinking a long time, and how finally they threw fingers and left together. He wondered what they were up to. It seemed sinister. He was glad to see them leave.

THIRTY-EIGHT
SUNDAY SOARING

The morning dawned clear and bright, drying up dew-strewn sweeps of lawn and delicate flower petals. It had rained a few days before; moisture still lingered in the soil. The sun would bake it out, taking it up to condense at good soaring cloud levels. India stretched and yawned, rubbing the sleep out of her eyes, then threw off her bed covers to rise and peer out her window at the misty loveliness.

She was thinking of what might happen that morning. She bet she would fly alone, go solo! She knew it. She absolutely knew it. Well, she hoped.

Church first. She shivered with happiness and eagerness.

It was an interesting morning at church. It was children's Sunday, and she was tickled to see a bunch of her Children's Aid kids in the congregation, those who had been on the field trip. She looked around, caught their eyes, and winked companionably at them. They were happy, sweet, and innocent. And wiggly. She was overjoyed to see them, and wanted to go hug each one of them. She would, later. Their parents were there too, having brought them, and caught her eye, smiling.

The children's exit hymn was played, "Onward Christian So-ol-diers," and out they marched, singing, to Sunday school, lessons in the back-of-church classrooms. As they left, she felt a lovely rush of rising goose flesh on her arms. There was a faintly visible glow of goodness around them. And encompassing her with a warmth. She was mystified. Could anyone else see it? As they disappeared through the door it faded; it had been faint. She blinked and looked again. She still felt that loving warmth.

"So you're Jamie's Mom, and Tommy is your boy, sir?"

So it went, after church. It was enlightening to meet the parents. They were good people, interested in their kids, and grateful for Children's Aid's help. They obviously loved their offspring, a revelation that cleared out India's foolish preconception of their being unloved. They were delighted to meet India, curious about her, and kind of wistful they hadn't been able to go on the field trip themselves.

"Well," India thought aloud, "Why can't we arrange a trip for you parents? I'll see what I can put together."

They gazed disbelieving at her, not thinking it could happen. Theirs were lives of hard work, supporting their families. They couldn't dream of a sport like soaring. But India looked like the kind of angel who should be airborne. They murmured encouraging remarks and said their good-byes, corralling their youngsters.

One mother leaned over to her and said softly in her ear, "Thank you India, for helping to potty-train my littlest one! Ms. Ollifant told me."

India gave her a squeeze and said, "Amy? She was easy. I just showed her how to hop on with the step stool and straddle the seat backwards, dangling little panties from one foot. She thought that was fun. Made going less scary, placing her hands on the tank. Sitting normally, facing out, she just *knew* she would fall in. I figured that out when I was a toddler, and then later passed it on to my little sister." They laughed together, saying final good-byes.

She turned back into the empty church, looking to find that glow she had seen. Of course it wasn't there. But it made her remember with a shiver the vision she had seen at the end of her bed, the one enclosed by the golden light, her Nana smiling at her.

Her grandmother had once admonished her to lock the car door as they were driving along. "You see, India, we must never be afraid of people—most people are good. But you have to know that although most people in the world are good people, there is a small percentage who are not. We lock our car doors not because we are afraid, but because we don't want to offer them opportunities."

India listened carefully and always locked car doors as she grew into adulthood.

She was due to report by eleven at the airport. She knew Dave would have gotten there early, setting up and already flying, probably with a student. He usually was off the ground by ten. Her parents were giving her a ride this morning; Dave would bring her home and they would all have Sunday dinner together. Unless he had more students. She hoped he didn't.

"Good morning, Hammonds," greeted a surprised Dave, as they came into the clubhouse.

Eli and Claudia had come too, wanting to finally see with their own eyes what was going on with their sister. This was their first time to the airport, a lifting of the veil of mystery for them about their sister's beguiling other life.

Well, he thought, if he was going to solo her, it would be fun for the whole family to watch. But were they staying? Maybe it would be too stressful, knowing how they truly felt about this activity. He wondered if he should offer to take them up sometime, one at a time. Maybe today? No. This was India's moment. He would go with the flow and not alter his plan.

He grinned and said to the family, "One of these days, if you like, I could take you up for a scenic ride—one at a time, of course."

Eli and Claudia practically orbited with excitement. "Wow!" they yelped in unison. Elizabeth and Paul, with their lifetime of cautious living, were much more restrained.

"Oh . . . well . . . that might be nice," her mother replied, halfheartedly. Her father looked more pleased.

Her family settled themselves on a bench outside the building. Soon India and Dave were being towed aloft, where almost instantly Dave made what would be his last surprise "rope break" and watched as she successfully brought the Schweizer 2-33 trainer down to a quick, smooth landing. They rolled to a stop. She looked proudly around at him. He nodded.

"Ok, kid, you're on your own. Set it up with the towplane. I'm outta here. Now you do a circuit on your own."

He jumped out and offhandedly waved good-bye. India was left staring at his disappearing back. She rallied herself, got out, and walked over to the towplane. Pilot Jerry grinned at her, giving her a thumbs up.

"So . . . shall we go now? I'll radio for the car to haul you back into takeoff position."

She gulped and nodded her okay.

Dave came back. He gave her a bear hug, laughing and pulling her off the ground and into his chest. "You're going to do a great job."

Like most glider clubs, this one had a clunker car for pulling gliders around, a rattling airport unit that was good only for that job, unregistered, not roadworthy. The team hauled her glider back into position for takeoff. They scooped up the dropped tow rope, hitched the two planes together, and got her set up for her flight. Audrey and Monica were her wing-runners. Pilots themselves, they were pleased to see one of their kind joining up. They had watched her progress, and watched the warmth grow in their eyes when she and Dave looked at each other.

Arms circling, the gesture was made to go, and rudders waggled in readiness. Off she rolled. Dave watched as they climbed, observed the release, held his breath as they separated properly, breathed again as he saw India obediently duck into the pattern to come back and land smoothly and easily. He met her on rollout.

"Bravo! You have done your first solo! I will sign you off now to fly at will."

India wallowed in her accomplishment, and wished she hadn't had to come down so fast. "Can I go up again right now?" she asked, still belted in her seat, looking up hopefully.

He scanned the sky, sensed the slight breeze, and agreed she could go. "But don't go too far, and don't stay up too long. Remember, your folks are here. Remember Sunday dinner! And it may be that another club member has scheduled this craft for use later. Do not take too long."

Glowing with happiness, India beamed up at him and promised she'd be back soon.

And so they hooked her up again, and watched her roll swiftly away to a gentle liftoff, climb to altitude, then veer away after release to catch a thermal. And around she went, slowly circling and climbing to her chosen cloud.

He strolled over to the bench where her family sat, waiting.

"There she goes," he said.

Their faces froze.

"What? Where is India?'

"Oh, she's up there." He pointed at a small object rising to cloud base, sun glinting off wings as she turned. "She's having her first solo flight today. I'm glad you could be here for it. The first solo is a huge landmark event in pilots' lives. You can congratulate her when she lands."

They went pale with fright. But then they were excited and pleased for her. They prayed together for a safe return. They couldn't help worrying.

THIRTY-NINE
LANDING OUT

*A*loft, circling wide with hawks as she had always dreamed, India was fairly exploding with excitement and confidence, exercising all alone the skills she had learned. By now it all seemed almost innate. She swooped and soared, streaming high over the land to find the wing-bump, sign of the next ride up. She watched her airspeed carefully, knowing overenthusiasm could make her exceed the structural allowance, that critical "never-exceed" velocity. Riding in a glider wasn't silent, despite the lack of an engine and propeller. The passing air brushed over the cowling and empennage, transmitting rushing sounds to the cockpit. As she sped up, the sound grew almost imperceptibly louder; she paid attention to it as a speed indicator, an early warning. Air had weight, mass, and pushed against the glider as it made its way through it, using it for wing lift. She looked down at storybook patchwork fields, roads winding like thin gray ribbons, neat tiny houses with trees and gardens, and chortled with pleasure at her freedom. It was almost like having real wings.

She rose higher and higher, rising above a low scattered cloud layer, seeing them as so many grazing sheep against the verdant background of the world beneath. Then, transfixed, she observed the altimeter pass eight thousand feet, nine thousand. Now she burst onto twelve thousand feet . . . higher than she had ever gone before. What? How was that?

Oh my. Maybe she was in a blue thermal, one without a cloud on top? They happened. Or could she be in a wave? It was a sought out prize that, if harnessed rightly, could be used to set altitude and distance records.

The horizon spread out far away, and she imagined she could actually see the wide curve of the earth. Was it visible? She felt that rush of joy that comes with the union of Me, Plane, and Sky, experienced by all who fancy the freedom of flight. Most likely kin to what deep-sea divers feel.

But also, she could have been feeling a heady touch of anoxia, oxygen deprivation. The atmosphere thins out of that life-giving element as the altitude goes up. Andean Indians in South America have large lungs from living at high altitudes. Regulations state that over 12,500 feet, a pilot must use supplemental oxygen after being up there for half an hour. She hadn't reached that half hour yet, but she still could have been getting a little head-funny and slow-witted.

Here is where her hovering guardian angel says, "Lord, hear me—I have my work cut out for me with this one. And, oh yes, I have that demon to wrestle. That one prowling the edges."

Blithely she flew along with the raptors, doing Dutch rolls and swooping turns, keeping track of where she was over the earth below. "What a wonderful world!" she sang out loud. Then caught herself and remonstrated: "I'd better not get lost and totally embarrass myself."

And so there she was, running high, way above the ridge, seeing views of the lands on the other side. She'd never been over there. Momentarily distracted by the sight of new geography, she finally veered back toward familiar territory. She glanced at the instrument panel.

She stiffened. She could not believe what her eyes were seeing. What's this? The altimeter was unwinding, not so slowly marking off her descent foot by foot. That could not be! The needle was passing by the altitude numbers inexorably, around the dial, down and down . . . Holy cow, it must be broken! She herself was not executing the descent. She checked the spoilers to be sure. Could the altimeter be broken? Nervously, she gently tapped it.

She had been a little concerned about being up so high, but now she was going down like an elevator. The land was rising toward her, slowly but surely getting closer, closer. She, India, was not mandating this descent. She was certainly in a wave. She was going down. She began to tremble, and gripped the yoke to control her shaking.

Dave had told her about mountain waves, the flow of an air mass going over a mountain range, rising and descending just like a brook over a boulder, up one side and down the other. That would explain her unexpected altitude gain.

He told her stories about powerful Rocky Mountain frontal waves surging aloft like an ocean tide, carrying even airliners up, up, up, then back down; and how air traffic control, instead of assigning one flight level, one altitude to stay at, an aircraft would be given a whole vertical block of air of maybe four thousand feet deep to travel in, to accommodate the strong lift and sink of the wave. An aircraft simply could not maintain one altitude. She had studied about them. Now she was in one. Had to be. But this time, the downward side.

Oh no, oh no, no! Dear God, she was going to crash!

Wait a minute here. Oh no, she wouldn't—pah! No dramas—she would simply land. She would find a field and land. Big deal. She would. Some place. Then a deeper fear settled on her. It was not so simple.

The inevitability overwhelmed her. She had never before experienced this kind of downward force. It was an important topic in the flight manual, and Dave had recounted tales of mountain waves, but all that didn't quite cover it. Executing a quick ninety-degree left turn, she tried to fly out of the wave and find lift again. Aha! There was a bump. But would it be enough? Nope. Gone. She gripped the stick harder, her knuckles turning white.

How could this have happened? She picked up the handheld radio and called, voice quavering: "Valley, Dave, this is India. Where's my nearest landing field? I can't get back to base—I'm in a wave, sinking, and have to land."

Holy crap, thought Dave. *How could she do this?* "Where are you?" he radioed back. "You disappeared."

"I think I'm near one of the glider meet checkpoints. I see windmills. I guess I'll have to land in a field. I don't see an airport." She surveyed her options. "There's a pretty straight paved road beneath me with big fields on either side. But the fields look plowed, maybe hard to land on. And trees line the roadsides. I don't think I should use the road. The wings wouldn't clear. Oh, man, I'm really getting low and I can't find any lift. I'm going to have to land."

Dave told her not to worry, just do what she knew was best; then she signed off. After he signed off from India,

INDIA, DAVID, AND THE DEVIL

Dave went into a high-speed wobble, his mind racing. He dug out his road map, shouted to others standing by, and radioed a general call to any gliders up who might sight her.

Now she had arrived at the critical moment; she chose the biggest field, and headed toward it. Fortunately, gliders didn't need much runway length.

Like an ocean wave headed for the beach, air currents continued to sweep her downward. She panicked, fingers rigidly gripping the stick. She desperately prayed, "Please God, don't let me crash."

As in foxholes, in cockpits there were no atheists.

Anyway, India wasn't one of those. A warmth, a light, came over her. Her skin tingled, and her mind cleared of all panic.

She sensed a thought, more than heard, "Be ye not afraid, I go before you always . . ."

Awed, she knew she would be all right. Those Bible lessons sure popped up at the right time, she laughed. The laughter calmed her too.

Still descending, she came upon and circled her chosen field. Watching the landscape coming up to meet her, she arranged the final approach to clear power lines she hadn't noticed until nearly the last minute. Skillfully she trained her flight path to align with rows of dried corn stubble, fortunately heading into the wind. Best yet, the wind was dropping off close to the ground.

On short final (just before landing) she eased the plane down with cautious use of the spoilers, touched the ground, and rolled out shaking with relief. It wasn't too much bumpier than the grass strip at Valley. She felt dry corn stalks rattle and bang the fuselage as she whizzed along, then the glider eased to a stop. Its wings tilted, one up and one down to rest on the ground.

"Whoof. That was not my plan for the day," she muttered to herself, her insides fluttering. The critical moment was over, leaving her completely unnerved. "Dave will never want me to fly alone again," she groaned. "He'll be furious with me, and mad at himself for signing me off to solo."

And her parents? She would just have to make light of it. Laugh merrily, and say she had just joined the special "Land-Out" club. "It can happen to anyone," she would toss off confidently. She took off her sun visor and shook out her hair—it gleamed like polished copper in the sunlight—then unbuckled her belt and swung her long legs up to climb over the side to check for damage. She did a walk-around and didn't see any. A sassy crow landed on the tail, teetered, and cocked his yellow eye at her.

"Okay then," she muttered to herself. "I'd better call Dave," and she reached for her cell. What was this? Her phone was dead flat of charge!

A man in cap and overhauls was walking toward her across the furrows. A dog was bounding zigzags at his side, tongue and ears flapping.

He hailed her with a call and a wave. "Hey there, missy, you okay?"

Apparently this was his spread.

"You ain't the first one to land here." He smiled widely as he drew close. The dog, tail stiffened, gave her a good sniff-over. Then licked her hand. She patted his back and scratched his ears.

"That downdraft off the ridge gets 'em again and again, even this far from it. Good thing you didn't whack any crops. That makes me mad and costs the pilot plenty. You need to make a phone call? Come on up to the house. My wife is waiting with a soda for you."

India reached out and shook his hand, finding her voice to return the greeting, smiling back her thanks.

"Thank you—but first I'll secure the plane. Won't take a minute." As she reached in to shut off the radio, she heard a transmission. Club member Ernie was apparently talking with Dave.

"Ernie here, Dave. I'm up at 12,000 feet, great ride! I can just make out the glider on the ground. She's down in the Brown's farm on that county road . . . Route 73, I think. I'm scanning with my binoculars. Yep. She looks to be out of the plane, with somebody. Better hook up the trailer and head over there. About fifteen miles from Valley."

India heard the transmission. After congratulating herself for not wrecking either herself or the glider, India got on the radio and called up, "Hey, I'm safe and fine, but my cell phone is dead! Can't call on it. Tell Dave" to Ernie, who relayed her transmission to Dave. She gave herself a silent "atta girl," turned off the radio, and closed up the glider.

Then she turned to her welcoming committee. As she did, she started weaving her web of ego protection excuses. None would hold up, but she had to think of something. She wiped her eyes of the silly tears that were starting. She would *not* cry. Then she thanked God for saving her behind.

As they strolled the quarter mile up to the farmhouse, he looked sideways at her.

"They ain't all pretty like you." Then he announced, "I'm Walter Brown. Your name?"

"My name is India, India Hammond," she said.

He did a double take. "Your Daddy is Paul Hammond?"

She nodded.

"Huh. I know your Dad—he was my lawyer for a little suit I had against me. Won it for me. A greedy idiot, a developer, wanted my land and thought he could just take it legal-like with a lawsuit." He snorted. "Didn't work out for him."

FORTY
BACK AT THE AIRSTRIP

They walked along through the corn stubble. Good thing it was Sunday. No need to cancel with the Phelpses. But, oh no! The roast in the oven. What would they do? And the neighbors coming for dinner? Well—her mother would attend to all that. She did not know that besides Dave, Mama and the rest were all coming to hunt for her.

Her family was scrambling into their car, unfolding their own road map. No *way* they weren't going along on the search and rescue. Dave hitched up the trailer, and off they went, all following him. The line of cars grew as others joined the queue. This was too good to miss. They'd heard she was probably ok, but they wanted to see for themselves. An off-airport adventure.

Dr. Hammond, seeing the way things were going, got on her cell phone.

"Edie? This is Elizabeth . . . we're at the airport and won't get back for a while. Can you go into my kitchen and check on the roast? I'd hate for it to burn."

Nobody much locked doors in their residential cul-de-sac, because everyone knew everyone who came and went. Thank goodness for that, thought Elizabeth as she rang Edie. They didn't worry about burglars. Their part of Valley was, so far, crime-free. Anyway, someone was usually at a kitchen window, looking out at the front drive, scanning the street, on the *qui vive* to spot something irregular. India thought they were foolish not to lock up. She believed her Nana. But Nana had been talking about car doors, anyway, and the dangers of carjacking.

So, back at the house, Edie, alerted by Elizabeth, opened the oven door, checked the roast, and closed it up again. What a heady aroma, that prime rib of beef! Had Elizabeth doused it with red wine? Surely extra butter with the caramelized onions. It needed another half hour, she figured. She turned off the heat but left the roast to continue cooking. She would come back in a bit to remove it.

Down the street a car was partially hidden by a hedge, a pair of eyes inside watching from under a baseball cap. The car had once been beige . . . now it was a nondescript gray. Edie caught sight of it out of the corner of her eye. Odd. Who would park there? Best she report it.

It had been time to change his look to one even less remarkable. He had worn old rumpled clothes and his fake horn-rims, a baggy tee and a worker's vest disguising his athletic build. He looked the hand-to-mouth construction worker part he was playing.

On any other day, he might have been a landscaper. Not

today. Not many in the residential area were home—they were mostly all at church. Nobody would notice him. He saw the woman walk over from another house, enter and leave the Hammonds' without a key. He thought it was not one of the Hammond family. He filed that away.

Mark's obsession was growing, and his fantasies were as well.

FORTY-ONE
THE HIGH-END HOUSE

Vern calculated it was time for another sortie with Mark. Vern's pill supply was growing thin. His clients were popping them indiscriminately, wasting money. And themselves. He was going to have to find some more users, maybe more professional people and fewer college students. Interesting how those youth seemed to have plenty of money. It was merely a community college, not a rich-kid magnet institution.

They met at a kitschy, pine-paneled local trough, one they'd been to before, passing through unremarked. Not where he met with the others. Looking like a couple of guys traveling through town, they ordered something to eat and drink, settling in to go over plans. A low-hanging Tiffany type lamp threw a circle of light over them, shadows hollowing their eyes. This time Vern pushed for a home burglary.

"Mark—I really want to exercise my little New York device," he said, referring to the remote control his son had given him. "It's quite the unit."

"Well, that sounds fine—but do you have an area in mind? I'm not sure Valley has the kind of homes you're looking for," said Mark. "You're looking for large mansions, estates, aren't you?"

"Not necessarily. Just affluence. The properties of those who were successful, those who made it big early on and blew their earnings on showcase houses. You know. They're into meth and cocaine snorts, the start of the slippery slope. I can clean up in those houses. They think they're safe behind their alarmed walls, but they usually forget about the garage sneak, trusting the remote control as if it were a crossbar to their castle." He snickered.

The excursion was planned for the Pittsburgh suburbs during the coming week. Mark would hover in dark streets a block or so away; Vern would phone when he needed a pickup. This sort of enterprise made Markie nervous. He was no cat burglar himself, and he was worried about Vern's abilities.

He shouldn't have been. Vern was as furtive as a packrat, as clever as a snake. There was no hole he couldn't filter through, leaving no traces. He thought of himself as the Houdini of his vocation, a Penn and Teller of his trade.

"I'm a magician," he said smugly, more to himself than to Mark, looking around and taking in what he thought of as self-absorbed clods populating the busy bar. "Those there are even possibilities," he said, making a small hand gesture at the room, discreetly just above the tabletop.

"They wouldn't bring in much, though," and chewed his burger. Vern liked the melted cheddar cheese, the way it ran into the juiciness of the rare meat.

"The best neighborhoods are on the north side. We'll have to give ourselves plenty of drive time to get there. And find a place to spend the night, like before."

Mark considered this. "I have a job to go to, you know.

THE HIGH-END HOUSE

I can't do anything during the week unless we wrap it up early and head back home here. Isn't it at least a two-hour commute to your target area? I can't see how this could work, except on weekends. Maybe you'd better find classy houses closer to us. We ought scope things out over the weekend, and decide what to do."

So they stored their ideas in the backs of their minds to develop, and made a date to meet Saturday morning. Meantime, Vern would review real estate records and see where the goodies might lie closer by. Mark would gather maps and plan routes to and from various areas. He enjoyed this stage of their capers, the initial planning. His kind of thinking. It was getting interesting.

They had duly scoped out the possibility of nearby hits, and found nothing appealing. Really rich people didn't live in their area. Never mind. They'd go for the long drives, the overnights in the no-tells. It would be worth it.

Vern found the internet to have rewarding links to his goals.

FORTY-TWO

RETRIEVAL, CELEBRATION

*A*s the afternoon plodded along, India exhausted the repertoire of subjects she could talk over with Mrs. Brown. She had run through her activities, and Mrs. Brown had informed her about the developer's lawsuit. They talked recipes and how to raise children.

They got restive, waiting for the posse to arrive and rescue her. It was already midafternoon. Whatever could be keeping them? As the shadows lengthened, along came Dave's car with the trailer, more cars following.

"Well at last," muttered India.

"Oh, my word!" exclaimed Mrs. Brown, looking from the porch at the bunch of cars. "So many people. What on earth?"

Dave ran up the steps and homed in on India, grabbing her up in his arms. "Thank God you're safe." She nestled her head on his chest thinking, *It was all worth it, for this.*

Her family joined Dave, hugging and wiping their eyes.

Mr. Brown finally had a chance to speak. He saluted Paul Hammond, offering his hand, smiling and saying, "Good to see you. Glad it was my field she chose. Nice daughter you have. And by the way, thanks again for your help with the lawsuit."

The rest stood by, wanting to hear all about it. But that would come later.

She pulled away from Dave, and turned beaming to her family. "Hey, it's great you're here too! Mom, that roast must be a sad shriveled lump by now, and am I hungry! Burnt offering or not, let's go get some."

"No worries, sweetie." Her mother touched India's cheek, explaining how Edie had saved the roast, and that all the regulars were awaiting their return.

"You know, there's enough to feed a combat troop. Why don't all of you come for some prime rib?" she said to the gang who had come on the rescue mission. Well they believed they'd like that—and off they all went. First to trailer the glider.

India said her good-byes and thanks to the Browns, then led the group across lots to the sailplane, now a roost for curious crows. She looked at the bird plips with horror.

"Never mind," said Dave. We'll clean it. Now help us get it ready for the trailer." They efficiently disassembled it and loaded it up. India hopped into the car with him.

"Boy, India, were we glad to get your message from Ernie, and to find you in one piece. We'd have been here lots sooner, but there was an accident not five miles from here. A bad one, and we couldn't get through for almost an hour. Emergency vehicles all over the place. I tried to call, but no cell coverage out there."

India nodded. "No worries. Mrs. Brown and I had a nice visit. And you trained me well. Once I got a grip on myself to tackle the approach and landing, it was easy. Normal, almost."

An hour later, they all were either at the table or balancing plates on their laps around the living room. It was a celebration of India's first solo and her skillful escape from disaster. Wine glasses were filled, and a toast raised to the girl of the hour.

"Hip, hip, hooray, In-dee-*yah*!" they shouted.

Dave looked at her affectionately, and silently thanked God for answered prayers.

She looked around at them fondly, catching Eli and Claudia's eyes. "So, what's your take on soaring, Eli? Too exciting?" She popped a small, baked rosemary-herbed russet potato into her mouth, and waited for his answer.

"Maybe, Sis." He snorted, raising his eyebrows at her. "And I don't see the joy of flight in landing with crows. That's for the birds. But I sure do see the thrill." Young Eli's voice was changing; it cracked as he cackled at his own humor. India rolled her eyes, groaning but giggling good-naturedly.

When she arrived at work the next morning, the Phelpses were waiting for her. Rollie had made up a certificate of accomplishment, complete with an eagle in flight at the top of the page.

"The Eaglet has Landed" it said underneath, with a cartoon of a sputtering, laughing crow. She couldn't wait to show it to Dave and the glider club.

"Are you sure you're back to earth, India? Wings folded, ready to roll up your sleeves and work? Not so exciting here." They looked at her concernedly, hoping to see a return of their affection.

In response she hugged them warmly. "Oh, I'm not looking for any more action like that," replied India. Holding the certificate out in front of her, she admired their clever creativity.

"Hey—wait just a minute! However did you know about my adventure?"

"Oh, India, you'd be surprised at how we're all connected. Mrs. Leticia Brown is a dear old friend," she informed India. "She was impressed with you."

The story of her landing out had raced through the circle of people they knew; the Phelpses were among the first to hear. Why? They had heard it right from the Browns, even before the Hammonds had started up their car for home.

By coincidence, Letty Brown was a friend of Maudie's since childhood. Naturally she couldn't wait to call and tell her about it. While they were waiting for the rescue crew to arrive, India and she had traded information. India told her about the Phelps Pharmacy job, but Letty had not divulged that Maudie was her friend. Oh no. This was too juicy. Letty could not wait to get to the phone. No sooner was the group out of the farmhouse door than she was ringing Maudie to tell her about it.

Maudie was appalled at what she felt was a frighteningly narrow escape, and someday would have something to say to India. But not yet. She wouldn't pop the bubble of success the girl must be floating on. Instead, they made up the fun certificate. They had become hugely fond of her.

By this time, India had long since told Dave about Mark Brissante the computer tech and his connection to the pharmacy through the pharmacy's accounting company, Ginsberg and Taylor. Mark was smart, but was Dave smarter?

After all, he was the elite Carnegie Mellon educated. And a systems analyst, as well as a programmer. She said Mark had been cleared of suspicion, but he wondered. Both he and India, in that dark alley, had not seen the perpetrator's face all that clearly. So even if Dave ambled into the accounting company's office and saw him, he wouldn't be able to swear to a positive identification of Mark. With no in-hand evidence of internet theft, he couldn't confront him anyway.

On his own time, he began his picking away at the seams of the web, poking along threads of bits and bytes of communications, promising leads into the far-flung fabric of circuitous connections. He had a hunch he would find a link to the accounting firm. It was interesting, challenging—and finally fruitful.

He took his information to the police.

FORTY-THREE
HOUSE HEIST

Meanwhile, Vern and Mark had planned to harvest a high-end home over the weekend. Weekdays just didn't make it. People were too often at home. Better on the weekends, when they were more likely to be off to a vacation home, or going to the theater or concerts in the city, or attending fund-raisers. Things that called them out of the house. Those activities the rich liked—women in designer outfits, subtle jewelry glinting at their necks and wrists, showing off to one another. Their children, if there were still any at home, often spent the night in friends' homes, clearing the way for Vern's treasure hunts.

By zip code, Vern had chosen the house to attend to first. They had perused the area earlier on, sighting the one they liked, then picked through publicly available data to find out about it. Information about residents was all open for viewing through public records, if you knew how and where to look. That Saturday they drove past their target again, then retired to a hotel cocktail lounge for the rest of the day. At eight o'clock they finished their dinner, called for the check, eventually paid their slow, awkward waitress—and left. They snorted. That waitress was as dumb as dirt and almost as blind.

Actually, that waitress had noted their demeanor, attire, and comportment. They had been in that booth way longer than most. Why was that, on a Saturday? she wondered, but never would ask. She was addicted to her mystery novels; those fired her imagination. Hm, she deliberated. The men weren't the businessman types this hotel usually had as clientele, even if one of them was dressed up like it. He was too plain and dull. The other, swathed in a hoodie, had drama all over him. There was a tickle in her brain that told her not to stare. She was a fanatic about her inner voice. She knew she was not smart, so she rallied all the help she could get. She always said her rosaries, and now she crossed herself when they left. They looked back at her, but she was already shuffling slump-shouldered toward the kitchen with their dirty plates. Her feet hurt. It had been a long day.

"A dumb bunny," muttered Vern. "Maybe I coulda had her . . . but ugh. No time, anyway."

Actually Vern would not have had a whiff of a chance with the waitress. Maybe she wasn't smart, but she was a decent girl, kind and dutiful. Instinctively she knew they were not.

The days were getting shorter; already at six thirty the nighttime had started seeping into the suburbs, creeping up house walls, sun's last rays flashing momentarily off windows. Now it was full dark. The selected target should be unoccupied; they knew this from their research.

All they'd had to do was find a name. Society pages had good names. Once a prospect's name was selected, it was easy to find an address; then it was easy to find his interests. Or hers, more likely. With a name, Mark could go to websites of charities and cultural organizations for their activities, and go to box office lobbies of the palatial concert halls and pick up programs. On these programs were donor categories, with lists of the best of the best. This was to encourage others to also give like the best of the best. Then you could easily see what those folks were up to on Saturday nights. Was there a special event for subscribers at the philharmonic? The opening night of the ballet? A famous soprano performing at the concert hall? The Heinz Auditorium was a fine and fancy restoration from a few decades before, a grand venue for pops and the classics. Their programs with donor categories were laughably accessible.

After all that clever legwork, they were chagrinned to find it wasn't yet the season for such events. But wait—it wasn't even Labor Day. These people were vacationing with their kids, or the kids were at summer camp and the parents were off on a tour. The children were all private school brats, not due back home until later in September. That's it! They just had to check all that out and come up with a winner.

And so they did. The backwards phonebook listed the owner of their choice as an attorney. He had a prominent ad in the yellow pages.

Mark called on the lawyer's place of business.

He wore wire-rim glasses, and his hair, now dyed black and gray-streaked for the role, was combed straight back, no part. Effete, confident, high fashion. Another, different look, very avant garde. It sat well on him.

"I'm sorry sir, he's out of the office until next week. Could someone else help you?" Mark peered down at a faked business card in his hand, ostensibly one the lawyer had given him.

"No, I think not. I should have called first, but he indicated he would be in the office. We spoke already of my problem; he said he'd like to discuss it. I'll call next week when he's back." He pocketed the card, thanked the secretary, and left.

The house had a few newspapers on the front steps; the housekeeper had not collected them. Whether she was out sick or whatever, it didn't matter. It was a sure sign of absenteeism. They had noticed that when they were checking out the place earlier in the day.

When Vern arrived, he wasn't going to pick his way over any old newspapers. He was going in hidden, through the garage at the end of the circular drive's spur, around back, using his fancy remote garage-door opener from New York. It had been months since he'd done a house, and he was almost giddy with anticipation.

Mark decided not to park and wait. This was a privately patrolled, enclosed—but not gated—community, and he would look suspicious. What he would do was roam slowly about the whole hilly area, winding around the estates, giving Vern enough time to do his deed, but not ever be so far away he wouldn't be within a moment or two of a quick pickup.

For the first time in their heist history, he felt uneasy. The car. He should have gone for black, like that painter said. His car gleamed in the darkness like a blob of white bird turd.

Well, he had an emergency plan. If he was stopped, he would explain that he was a process server, looking for a particular residence.

"No, sorry officer, I really wouldn't be able to tell you who. That's privileged and private. The citizen wouldn't appreciate it, now would he?" The guard would huff a bit, and Mark would waggle the paper under his nose. It was a real form, with engraved swirls and curls in the right places.

"Well—don't get too lost in this maze." And the guard would slowly drive off.

That's how it would go, but Mark hoped he wouldn't have to fall back onto that.

But he did. And it went off well. The patroller didn't even blind him with his flashlight.

Vern activated his control unit, aiming it at a small box at the upper corner of the garage door. Quietly the door slid up, and a light went on inside. He muttered an oath. He didn't want any lights. But there it was, and now he would have to scurry. He darted in, found the switch, and lowered the door. He stood very still, listening for possible sounds of approaching police, or anyone. Nothing. He was safe. Now where was the kitchen door? Ah yes . . . over past the storage cabinets.

It was locked, of course, but he had acquired a master key for standard doorknob locks. He knew if worse came to worse, he could use the awl on his Swiss Army knife to jiggle the lock open. But click-clunk, and open it went. No mess, no fuss; the door obligingly opened into the pantry. Making sure his balaclava was covering his face, in he went. Good thing, because there was a security camera at work, one trained on the doorway from a large bag of dog food on an upper shelf. If he'd perused the pantry, he'd have noticed the bag and wondered why. These people didn't own a dog.

In a few weeks, Vern's dark figure would be viewed on tape by police, unidentifiable. In time, patrolling security would remember the car and that process server. But it had been dark, and he couldn't describe the man.

Vern made his way upstairs by flashlight; the house

layout was traditional, overblown, exaggerated Cape Cod. Very twee on the outside, a predictable floorplan inside. He rifled through the master bedroom, checking behind and under drawers to find its tidy trove of illegal powder packets. He pocketed them and scoured the master bath. Nothing there. He left things just as he found them.

But the safe behind a curtain in madam's dressing room held promises. Carefully his gloved fingers turned the dial, his stethoscope trained for the telling clicks of tumblers. It swung open. What a lovely mess of trinkets. Untidy. It would be difficult to note what was missing, and with luck it would take weeks for her to notice anything.

Vern picked over the lot, plucked a diamond pin and ruby ring out of the mess that he could fence, closed the safe, and made his way back downstairs. Creeping quietly through the pantry, he exited as he had entered, this time letting himself out a side door, even though that meant he couldn't slide the dead bolt over from the outside. But no sense raising the garage door again, putting on that risky light.

"Okay, I'm ready," he murmured into his cell phone.

"Be right there," responded Mark.

Shortly, Vern was climbing in and they were easing their way out of where the best of the best made their homes. They didn't see the patrol car again.

Later on, the lawyer and his Mrs. each blamed the other for not securing the garage side door. But it wasn't for a couple of months that she said some jewelry was missing, and they checked the tape. There was the shadowy masked figure coming and going.

So that's how my drug packets disappeared, murmured the lawyer to himself.

She couldn't be sure she hadn't lost her jewelry herself, but reported it stolen to her insurance company. It was they who investigated and reviewed the security tape. It was old history by then.

Mark and Vern wandered farther afield, successfully burgling affluent neighborhoods, always escaping cleanly. But Mark was getting antsy again, constantly scanning seamy bars for a possible score. Vern's pile of plunder was getting high, and he was thinking of that Caribbean vacation. He too was checking out the babe buffet, looking for a possibility. One night at a no-tell motel's next-door bar and grill, they flirted with a couple of Hispanic imports.

"No papers? No green cards?" queried Vern.

"*No, hombre, no papeles,*" they giggled.

Mark tucked that into his brain and thought that was very good. No tracing the body.

Vern, however, viewed that information with dismay. That was one señorita he couldn't take with him on his dream vacation, because she wouldn't have a passport. He wouldn't bother with her. He told the three good night and went off to bed, sullen and disgruntled.

Mark gathered his lusty find to his side and went off into the night, leaving the other bimbo to get herself home. He strolled aroused, leading the woman along, following dark demons to his room. The pretty *muchacha* was disturbingly willing to play. A total turn-on. There he wooed her with tequila and nips of booze from the room's little bar supply. He wooed her, warm-eyed and reassuring, till she was super compliant. Then he tied her up for agreed-to sado sex.

He exuberantly ravaged his prey, her dark Latina sex well worn out with his vigor—and then murdered her. But this time he didn't draw blood. He let her asphyxiate as she was climaxing. He was supposed to ungag her, but he didn't. Any screams were cut off by the gag. Her eyes bulged wild and pleading, her panicked body bucking and writhing against the toweling ties. He grinned as death happened, as her body went limp, as her eyes rolled back.

It was good. Not as good as the first time, but satisfying and fun. And it left no marks. He untied her, rubbed her wrists to make sure there were no marks, and went to sleep beside her still-warm body. In the morning he checked out, leaving the corpse apparently asleep. He'd shown a fake ID to register, not that the man at the desk had even looked at it—and he left.

The cleaning maid who came in around noon was rightly shocked when she found a woman in bed that she couldn't awaken. Her body was quite stiff.

Emergency responders said it was probably an accidental suffocation brought on by kinky sex—there were almost indiscernible marks on her wrists and ankles. The diagnosis was confirmed by an on-call doctor who made a cursory examination. No identification. Why explore it? They were tired of these. She stank of booze.

He and Vern had a nice breakfast at a café along the highway back to Valley. Mark said he'd had a fairly good romp, despite the fact that the girl had actually seemed sort of weak and ill. He hoped he hadn't caught anything contagious. He'd been unable to awaken her when he left—probably should have reported her to the manager, but that would have caused problems for them both. Vern agreed it was best he'd left her where she was. He looked at him thoughtfully.

Mark knew Vern had to be needy, wanting some time on the mattress too. So that night they patrolled downtown Valley saloons, dark and smoke-filled, searching for something willing. It didn't take long. At first, Mark got the pretty one, of course, and Vern settled for her overly made-up, pimply sidekick.

But when pretty-babe heard Vern say he was a stock trader, she dumped Mark and with warm eyes cooed sweet whispers into Vern's ear. They giggled and hip-bumped each other out into the night.

Mark and pimples stared at each other. Mark mumbled an offhanded "See you later, sweetie," and got out of there. Vern could by God find his own way home. He texted him to get a cab.

Vern cheered when he read the get-yourself-home text, crowing to himself, "I got the pretty one, I got the pretty one!"

Her name was Josie, a pretty girl's name.

The death made a small mention on a back page. The reporter who picked up the police radio call went by to investigate, to see if there was a story. He decided not. What to report? An anonymous illegal, a boozing, sadomasochistic death, in a sleazy motel? No.

But the police were turning it over in their minds. Another easy woman dead. Was it part of a string of serial murders? This one did not appear to be anything more than an accidental death.

Mark carefully checked the television news for the next few days. Nothing. He was also relieved to see only a small mention in the papers about the death. He'd gotten away with it. Again. Maybe. He was getting cocky.

FORTY-FOUR
THINGS TIGHTEN UP

The pharmacy's new back door had been installed. Siren howling, Chief Baxter had come around to see that it was done according to code. Good job. He signed the permit he'd brought and then left, calling attention to himself with the blaring siren.

Mr. Phelps shook his head. "Some firemen never outgrow their little-boy dreams."

But now the delivery man could not simply arrive and open the door. He used to just walk in with his boxes, call out, and plop them on any available surface. Someone would step up and sign for them. Deliveries were always an interruption anyway. Somebody would either have to abandon a customer, put a computer entry chore on hold—or scurry back from coffee. It was all so tiresome, an unwelcome distraction. This was undoubtedly safer, but more bothersome. Fortunately, most supplies came around the same times of day, mid-morning or late afternoon; they got used to planning around that. But they didn't like how they now had to be hauled in through the rest of the store from the front.

When India reported for work, the Phelpses were busy tidying up an early delivery. The FedEx man was waiting, needing a signature. He had to come in the front, through the store. They noticed he was wearing a gun. Was that new?

"Have you always packed a pistol?" asked Rollie. "I never saw that before."

"Actually, yes, I have. But I carried concealed. Only recently have we been carrying them showing. Even encouraged to." He cleared his throat. "Ever since that incident here, and a few other events at other places around town, I've been prompted to carry and show, to discourage robberies. FedEx distributes a lot of valuable drugs."

Maude sighed and nodded. Then shaking her head in disgust at the woeful condition of the world, she signed the delivery forms. Then they discussed the awkwardness of the front-door process, hauling stuff in through the main store, and what to do about it.

"Could you call us as you drive up, or give us a special coded ring on the back doorbell? That may sound silly, but it would be better for us both," said Rollie. The driver was quick to agree.

"Yeah—I would be the only one to use it—any substitute drivers would not have the privilege," he responded, hand resting reassuringly on his pistol.

The Phelpses and he agreed on a signal and bade him good-bye.

In the meantime, the police were checking on Mr. Brissante. Sergeant Moore stroked his chin and picked at a tooth, looking over Dave's printouts assembled on his desk. The data was pretty damning, but spread out like that it meant nothing to him. Dave had taken pains to explain, but it hadn't helped much; the Sergeant's pride didn't let him show how computer illiterate he was, but Dave knew. No matter.

There was the proof. But it had to be demonstrated that Brissante was the one actually making the computer entries. "That shouldn't be too hard," the chief figured. He thought some more. "Besides his being the prime suspect in the drug heists from the pharmacy, this guy might be the killer we're looking for. You never know." Then he shook his head and muttered, "Probably that's a stretch."

There had been the initial call from someone near Pittsburgh about the flophouse murder of the pimp and his jane.

Later, tipster Effie had gotten bored with her life. Without her pimp, she had gotten restless. It was hard to get clients on her own, and she missed him. He had been a good agent. She began to nurse an attitude toward the killer. Damn him, anyway. That pimp had been her livelihood, even if he was a mean-minded cheat.

She needed to stir a pot.

So, she decided to call in what she had seen, the man sneaking down the hall. She had already reported the two bodies—she had seen his gory messes, spread out on the floor. But there was more. She had also peered out the window and watched the man getting into his car. She hadn't seen his face, but she copied the numbers off the car's license plate.

That wouldn't help, because some time ago cagey Mark had altered the numbers, making an eight into a three, and a six into an eight.

It had not been hard. He had smiled to himself, humming a little hum, while he applied stencils lifted from a crafts store. He rubbed dirt onto his handiwork; no sense in making the plates be cleaner than the rest of the old car. One day, to while away the time, an idle hospital security cop had run the numbers on the slow-circling vehicle and had been puzzled by the result. Some yokel in the far eastern part of the state owned that number. And that car was newer than this one. He shrugged it off as an error on his part. Nothing he actually needed anyway.

Not only that, the Valley police noted that there were no particular drug thefts reported during that time, certainly none from the hospital near the murder scene. Vern was always careful to cover his tracks and not take too much. Substances were never missed until a few days later, when an inventory was done. The staff would always suspect one of their own. They would not report it. Those incidents went to in-house investigations.

Vernon did not know about the license plate legerdemain. The less Vern knew, the better. It still did not sit well with Mark that his devious burglar friend had tootled off with the cutie-pie, leaving him with Miss Pimples. Well, it was no use brooding about that. But he wasn't going to tell Vern about the made-over plates. He might have questioned him, asking him why he thought that was necessary, leading Mark to reveal the path to his sadistic activities. Vern had been a little too probing in his queries about the dead señorita.

In fact, Vern was pretty sure Mark had done her in, but felt it best to let that one lie. Especially when he sensed the wall that went up around the subject. *The criminal mind has many facets*, thought Vern. *Murder and mayhem, robbery and greed. You never know.*

Of course Vern never considered his own mind to be so criminal. Self-awareness was not one of his traits.

INDIA, DAVID, AND THE DEVIL

——◆——

It may not have been one of Vern's, but it was one of Dr. Hammond's. She was fully mindful of her motherly anxieties about her daughter and from where they sprang. She was anxious about the relationship between India and Dave. She feared for her daughter's passage into adulthood through her attraction to the young man. She had never told anyone, least of all her daughter, but when she herself was quite young she had had a boyfriend who had impregnated her, then, terrified, bolted away, leaving her to deal with it alone. It had been a nightmare, one that ended in a spontaneous abortion, a miscarriage. A lucky thing for her, such a young girl, but that was never a given. It was a personal tragedy she wept over quietly in the nighttime for years. Her parents never knew.

This, of all things, eventually pushed her onto her path to psychiatry. Why should she be so distraught over a miserable bit of protoplasm? She hated to admit it to herself, but probably Freud had been right about anatomy and destiny. At least as far as the psyche, the emotions, went. India, in her mother's observations, seemed to be of a cooler makeup, not hot-blooded and not likely to repeat her mother's errors.

She hoped.

FORTY-FIVE
RELATIONSHIPS

Summer was drawing to a slow close. A few maples were already flame-orange in low-lying swamps, and bright fields of waving goldenrod, laced with companion ragweed, were firing up outbreaks of hay fever. It was both a beautiful and a wretched season. India was shivering with anticipation; her flight test was coming up in a couple of days. She didn't want to think beyond it. Well, that was her characteristic flaw—putting off the inevitable.

Her wall of maturity had a chink in it. She had not applied to colleges; she had daydreamed herself into a year off from all such responsibilities. She and Dave had become a definite couple, spending many evenings with her family or out on movie dates, sometimes having a restaurant dinner together, talking over their views of the world, the supernatural, baseball, football, or the world of art. Sometimes, even the disciplines of technology. That one was a tentatively probed subject. India was not educated in the intricacies of computer programming or computer languages, but she appreciated that Dave was. In other words, they were dating. Courting. Her great-grandparents would have called it "keeping company."

INDIA, DAVID, AND THE DEVIL

She was foolish with love. And feverish, like a dog in heat. Dave made her almost topple over with desire, a blinding feeling she didn't even understand. But he did. And he ruminated about what he should do about it. Unaccustomedly flustered, he went to an off-the-main-drag drugstore and got himself some protection. For both of them. It amazed him how condoms were so lavishly displayed, and what a splendid selection there was. He was glad he didn't have to ask; his voice was raspy with emotion and embarrassment.

He was not a virgin. Like many handsome adolescent boys he had been roped in by a lusty teen queen, an experimental girl eager for action—the one who plucked his cherry. But he surely was not a player. His years in college had been mostly celibate, except for a brief liaison with a prowling husband hunter who dumped him when she discovered he was a boring scholar. She wanted to wear an athletic sweater and get "pinned." The fraternity pin he could provide, but he was no quarterback. They said their poignant farewells; she had already goo-goo eyed a muscular football player with hot looks for her. He had thighs like fire plugs with a neck to match. She could wear his letter sweater, she bet. Maybe even marry him.

One evening, Dave had brought India home tousled and red-cheeked from hot kisses. India said good night to Dave and her parents and went upstairs.

Paul, flushed and enabled by wine with dinner, abruptly grabbed his arm as Dave was about to leave. "You'd better not get my little girl pregnant!" Paul Hammond declared to Dave, confronting him.

Mrs. Hammond watched, aghast, and paced about,

wringing her hands. But she was glad the subject was being addressed, however ineptly.

"Good God, sir!" exclaimed Dave, straightening his shoulders. "I would never do that. I'm a responsible adult. Your daughter's virtue has not been nor will it be compromised by me!" He glared at Mr. Hammond.

Then he leveled his eyes at the older man and said, "At least not yet. Not yet. That's up to her. But I will tell you this—I love her dearly."

He added, "Nor, sir, is she a little girl anymore, in case you hadn't noticed." Then he softened. "Please. I mean no disrespect. I understand your concerns, truly I do. But I am absolutely not going to get India pregnant. Do not worry about that."

Paul studied Dave's face, and nodded. He was surprised at his own outburst, but reassured at the results. He smiled tentatively at Dave. "I really like you, Dave. You seem to be a good person, and I'm glad that if there's someone India has to fall for, it's someone like you. I accept your assurance that you will take care of her."

In the background, Elizabeth Hammond put her hand to her chest and swallowed nervously, then quietly spoke. "Dave, maybe you can understand our positions. India is a treasure, a magnificent human being. We trust you will be good to her."

Upstairs, India was unaware of the flap downstairs. She doffed her clothes and slipped into her pajamas, then burrowed into bed. Claudia knocked on her door.

"Come in," called India.

"Did you hear Mom and Dad and Dave just now?" she

asked. The younger sister had not outgrown lurking in the stairwell to spy on goings-on below.

"No. I came up to bed. Dave didn't leave? What's going on?"

"Oh, the parents were grilling your boyfriend. I think he came through with flying colors. But watch out, India. Things are heating up."

"Don't I know. I will be careful. Thanks for the heads up, little sister. Keep an eye out for me!"

Families are the initial practice arena for the world at large. They can be good for each other, or not so.

Elizabeth Hammond had practiced good psychology on her children and they truly loved and enjoyed each other. She had seen the opposite, when kids and parents were pitted against each other, making for miserably unhappy lives. All that foolish, annoying, whiney stuff. "He keeps touching me, stop him!"—"Daddy, he hit me!"—"Ow, Mama, he pinched me!"—"Hey, she tripped me, she did it on purpose!"

Mother Elizabeth paid attention. She had her ways of pleasantly distracting the altercations and giving them all positive reinforcements. She liked doing it. They adored her.

Dave could see that, and he wanted to be in on that world. It was not unlike the family he knew, his own parents and siblings. He was not church-raised, but his mother and father were otherwise conservative and old-fashioned, holding to their traditions as firmly as he could see the Hammonds gripping onto theirs. His parents had been hard-nosed with his sisters, but they were older. They had done their parenting practice on their first children and were fairly relaxed and lenient with him. Being a son helped. His sisters had pretty much spoiled him with their doting care and attention all through his childhood, but they were big sisters with all that entailed.

As youngest and male, he and Eli Hammond occupied the same family position; he could relate well to young Eli. He knew what the boy was thinking most of the time, even though Eli was the jock Dave had never been. Dave was strong and athletic, but no gridiron star. There was no data about women Dave did not know. No secrets. He liked women because he liked his sisters. With all their differences, he liked women. It's said that men who like their mothers and sisters make the best husbands. India couldn't do better. But she was still young, by the day's standards.

He would do nothing to subvert his chances with her. But oh, how he yearned to take her into his arms and show her in his male way how much he loved her.

Nature had its mandates. So did love. Hard combo to fight.

FORTY-SIX
PARENTS' FIELD TRIP

India had organized a Saturday afternoon tour for the mothers and fathers of her house apes, as Dave wryly called them—a step up from rug rats. House apes would at last graduate to human.

After seeing how nicely they comported themselves during their little tour, all whee'd up with excitement but their restlessness under control, he confessed to a better impression of that age group.

"But it was only for a short time, India," he pointed out. "I doubt they'd deliver good behavior for a longer period."

But he found them likeable, and got along well with them. *A good start*, thought India, smiling to herself.

The parents' visiting time would be after the day's soaring activity was wrapped up; it would never do to intrude on that. The club members had discussed the idea of offering rides, but they figured a ground tour was needed first, and then they could see if anyone would be up for a ride some other day. Those demo flights were merely a haul up to a release altitude, then a slow circling descent to land, a fifteen minute scenic overview. No catching any lift because thermals

PARENTS' FIELD TRIP

would be done for the day. The late afternoon was a perfect time for the scenic ride, shadows dramatically modeling the landscape.

Most of the pilots could afford to donate a ride, but it would have to be discussed further among themselves. Would it be a good thing? There had been sniffs and grumbles from the townies over the years about airplanes overhead. Maybe a whole day given over to free scenic rides would be a good idea. They would offer some positive exposure to the mental discipline and studies required to be licensed. Weather, for example, and aerodynamics. And they could experience the bird's-eye view of their homes, their town, and their valley. Nobody didn't like that.

There would have to be some publicity, and appointments scheduled. There would be limits to how many could be accommodated.

It was getting complicated. It could open the door to nut cases. They chewed it over, recalling an instructor friend from earlier days, a woman who had been killed by a depressed male student. He had grabbed the controls; she wrestled futilely against his crazed strength. They plunged to their death in the Virginia foothills. She had radioed a desperate Mayday, her last words.

That had been in a little Cessna trainer, an airplane with an engine. But a glider flight could also quickly become fatal by exceeding the allowable structure speed. It could break apart in flight, sending the pieces hurtling to the ground. That had happened to a high-profile retired head of the FAA, a war-hero retired Navy pilot, a man being given a ride in a friend's high-performance glider. It was on a splendid Colorado Rocky Mountain day, towering ranges silhouetted against the sky, peaks etched on brilliant blue, and tidal waves of clear air masses surging over their tops. Local lore had it that they had been doing loops and lost track of how many times the needle had gone around the airspeed indicator, finally reaching the structural disintegration velocity. Darker opinions were that the aircraft had been tampered with.

They decided on no open day for PR freebies. The inner voice was speaking; they were heeding. There was a rush of shared relief at the decision, all pleased to be released from public relations work and freed from the threat of danger. India in particular was glad. She was thinking of the one who had whacked her head.

The selected parents' afternoon had sported a shower or two that cleaned the air and moved on. It was otherwise a delightfully benign day. Claudia had offered to babysit the group's kids at one side of the airport, entertaining them with games of tag and hide and seek while the adults got their tour, a job aided by a couple of her friends.

It all went so well they decided they would have to do it again. Next time, with a cookout while the weather was still nice, before it got too autumn-nippy.

"Maybe we could have a cookout at the field after the next orientation, for the whole group, Dave!" suggested India. "What a fun end to the afternoon. At sunset we can gather around a campfire and roast hot dogs and have our sodas. The kids will already be here. It would be such fun!"

Dave thought for a moment then said, "We could even toast marshmallows." The innocent all-American summertime pastime.

How could it possibly be a setup for evil?

FORTY-SEVEN
VERN'S GIRLFRIEND

*V*ern was away on his dream vacation with his cutie-pie . . . the one he'd partnered up with a month ago. It was now September, a time of discounts for Caribbean beach hotels. He and Josie had flown off for their margarita-based luxury vacation. She was good company. He had been busy raising his ante with hospital and hotel sleights of hand, no thanks to Mark. He and Mark had drifted apart once Markie had found his old friends from childhood. Mark would occasionally procure drugs from him, but he paid.

No matter. Mark had become distracted. Off-put by his vagueness, Vernon quietly turned to public transportation, thereby fading from Mark's world. A bus, if used cautiously, was a fine way to and from his targets. He abandoned home burglaries. Bus service didn't seem to route itself to and from upscale neighborhoods. But that was all right. He liked working nice hotels better anyway, and hospitals were always reliable sources when he needed particular high-potency drugs. He preferred working alone. His ability to blend, to remain invisible, was his forte. He was a master of undetectable movements, a magician of camouflage. He blended quietly into backgrounds. And he didn't wish to own a car and leave possible trails. Moreover, he didn't need Mark as a pleasure facilitator anymore. Josie was his old lady now, and Vernon was happy.

Josie didn't ask many questions, and she had taken a liking to Vern's easy ways and bland demeanor. That fit in with her image of financiers. Although she suspected some of his activities were shady, she never sensed any danger. She didn't mind. Adjustments could be made. Mark had been too much the macho cowboy for her. She and Vern settled into a contented, satisfying relationship. Under that suit, she found he had nice shoulders, decent pecs, and lovely biceps. And he was generous. She cracked her gum and considered her good luck. Pretty Josie too, was happy.

She and Vern would have a nice life together, without Mark. He had gotten too creepy.

It was a good decision.

FORTY-EIGHT
MARK SCHEMES

During hours when he was not tied up with computer work at the office, Mark cruised the town in the company car on Ginsberg and Taylor business stops. He continued to be valued by his company; they still saw him as a fine fellow, if preoccupied. Ginsberg attributed the added tension in Mark's mien to his needing to ramp up his care of their clients' accounts. His job was important to him. That was reassuring to Mr. Ginsberg. Little did he know.

Often after work Mark hunkered down over drinks with his scurvy ex-con buddies. They held back on committing another murder. The news coverage over that back-alley episode had them on edge and careful. They no longer went to that bar. Although Valley was not a large city, there was a plethora of seedy joints with willing women. On a few occasions they engaged one who liked a group deal; she would have a room in an old slum hotel, one where she could make as much noise as she liked—and they liked. The guys liked lots of salacious sound effects.

Mark reflected on how nasty women could get to earn money. He took them as they did themselves—worthless, useful only for sensual, sexual satisfaction. Those working girls offered up an interesting, creative kaleidoscope of stimulation, even selling the perverted pleasure of excruciating pain. It pleased him to see how far they would take it and still hang on. It was a game. The bar scene kept him fairly sated.

But it wasn't enough.

"Mark, I know you dig hurting them girls," said pedophile Petey, listening to some of Mark's boasting. "But they only do it from hunger. Ain't you got no feelings?"

"This coming from a guy who sodomizes kids? Gimme a break," countered Mark with a sneer.

When not otherwise occupied, he explored the town in his unremarkable gray ride. He fantasized about India, and began making a plan to have her. He would need to be more than usually careful; she wasn't a convenient, accessible, worn-out prostitute. It would be tricky; it would be elaborate. The challenge inspired him.

Through surreptitiously following her, he had become aware of her airport activities. "Ha! The sweet little angel is flying," he cackled. "I'll pluck those first-class feathers," he snorted.

He drove into the airdrome late one weeknight when it was unattended. Lights extinguished, he slowly motored down the landing field.

With his remarkable night vision, he noticed rabbits hopping into the woods, drawing his attention to a couple of faint trails. Deer paths most likely, made by their wandering in from the far side's deep woodlands and crossing over to the street side of the airport. Deer were tough nighttime road hazards. Hitting one could cause significant damage, while the deer itself might leap away apparently unhurt. But not always. Often enough, their corpses were found lying on the roadway. Generations of deer hadn't evolved much since storybook Bambi and Faline. Deer fell victim to automobiles, items not in their genetic history. They seemed to wait for headlights to illuminate the road for an easier crossing; they underestimated the auto's arrival time.

The runway's open field approaches were noteworthy. Maybe he could get at her that way, and force her into the woods for his sadistic designs. He could hike in and conceal himself among the trees. When the opportunity came he would pull her deep into the shadows and do her.

He could wait, still and patient, for as long as it took.

Mark loved the night, especially night without moonlight. He felt akin to it, at one with the forms behind the gleaming eyes of predators.

Each time he dreamed of this scenario, he would become aroused, and double over holding onto himself, breathing heavily. He enjoyed his cruel dreams. In his mind's eye he had her naked, spread out like an X in a square, her feet and hands tied to corner trees, legs spread wide. Or maybe he would pull her legs up, bending her knees akimbo, exposing her with the most indignity. He imagined her whimpering through her gag, moaning as he stroked her. The delicious evil damage he planned for her was making him almost wet himself. He stepped out of the car to relieve himself, scaring off a grazing rabbit. He watched it bound away.

But India was not an evening airport user. No one was; there were no runway lights.

This would require a lot of thought. He planned on enhancing the experience with an extra pill. Yes, he would do that, it would raise his ecstasy to a whole new level. He, Mark

Brissante, clever self-made man, deserved the reward of such intense pleasure, the brain-fired bliss with that toothsome beauty. He deserved her, he needed to destroy her.

In the woodland darkness around him, a deeper blackness moved through the camouflage of night. It eased into his brain, guiding his thoughts to vivid, obscene visions. He lurched and sank to the ground.

Chemicals were drumming a tattoo on his synapses. He lay there a long time, unmoving and out cold, even until the owls stopped hooting and the sky was beginning to lighten. He awoke disoriented, scrambled into the car, and rolled out of the airdrome before anyone could see him. Well . . . not quite.

The night watchman, hired to keep an eye on the valuable assembly of gliders, spied the gray sedan drifting like a ghost, emerging from a faint mist of ground fog, then glide almost noiselessly down the airstrip, into the drive. Then it headed toward town. No lights until the car turned down the street.

What the . . . ? the watchman asked himself. *Guess I better go check the aircraft and clubhouse. What could a trespasser be up to at this time of day?* He fingered the pistol on his belt and passed his hand over his jaw, feeling the stubble. *Jeez—I never heard nobody drive in. Weird.* He checked around and found nothing amiss and shrugged it off. *Probably a couple making out.*

He didn't think he would report it. It would make him look bad, and he didn't want to risk losing the easy pay. Also, the job gave him the right to wear the gun. He liked that.

He should have reported it.

Mark figured he would survey the terrain before he formulated any plan. He would roam the hills around the airport to find the best way in, find the right spot to trap her, and finally, the right place to lay her out and have her. He had caught sight of an old foundation when he was prowling the deer path. He would have to check that out. People had lived and left several times over during the past couple of hundred years—there was history here. The remains of bygone habitats could be found in surprising places.

Getting her into the woods was another problem. How could he accomplish that?

Clearly he was not going to be able to drive in as he had the other night. He would need to go up into the wooded hills, trek down and across lots, and then make his way through the forest to finally arrive at the airstrip.

A single-minded hunt for a certain prey, he told himself. He would scope out the dense copses to locate some old rotting cellar hole, the perfect place to take her. He would have to track like an Indian over rough terrain and through brambles, leaving no traces. He reckoned to do this soon. His lips pursed in a malevolent smirk.

FORTY-NINE
INDIA AND DAVE

One afternoon after the crew had left the airfield, India lingered to help Dave close up. She hated to be away from him. Abruptly he turned to her and grabbed her into his arms. They had kissed before, something that India had found maddeningly wonderful. All she could think of any more were his kisses and how she ached for his touch. Now, alone in the shadow of the hangar, he glowered down at her and fiercely pulled her to him, thrusting his hands inside the back of her jeans, feeling her nakedness, pushing his hardness against her, kissing her roughly, sensuously. She buried her head into his chest, smelling his skin through his shirt.

He took her by the hand, and they left.

It was the start of a new level of communication. Time and love moved on. They had reached the need to be alone, away from the world.

India sighed and stretched in Dave's embrace, arms locked around his neck. She wanted, needed, to experience their love physically, and oh, how she loved him. They had gone to his apartment—but they were not on his bed. They weren't there yet, if ever they would be.

He had slipped off her shirt, her silky skin now pressed against his bare chest. He bent to move his lips over her, breathing her essence. A warmth of passion swept through her. Her mind was fuzzy with desire. Her body relaxed and opened to him, demanding his touch. He looked lovingly at her face, and reached to her opened jeans, pulling them down and off, stroking her stomach, tenderly caressing the mound that rose to meet his hand. Her hips moved instinctively, to help him get her where she needed to go. She tensed and arched her back, her legs falling apart, inviting him to probe the mysteries of her femaleness. Their desire for intimacy was overwhelming.

"Oh please," She whispered at each touch.

The flower of her virginity could be his; he knew it. His mouth on hers, he reached down and spread the tender folds, then began rubbing her gently, watching her eyes dilate, hearing whimpers of pleasure as she joined his effort. He moved away. She looked at him questioningly. He responded by bending down and placing his lips and tongue on those most intimate parts. She gasped in surprise and shock. Breathing in her muskiness, his hands reached behind her to draw her tightly to him. She arched her back, then relaxed and took his head into her hands, fingers grasping his thick sandy hair, hips pushing, moving, a reaction so automatic it took her over. A wave of passion washed through her, clouding her mind with joy and love. Soon she was pulsing with a bliss that rocked her body, leaving her crying and gasping. As she climaxed, he drew back and watched her, reaching to cup her breasts in both hands and squeezing them gently, escalating her bliss, low sounds coming from her throat.

INDIA, DAVID, AND THE DEVIL

She and Dave had clearly arrived at the intense fondling stage of their love, now sharing their bodies as they had their minds, their ideas. They had moved beyond the warm-fuzzy, fact-finding tête-à-têtes and were now well into the physical stage. But she was still unpenetrated, technically virginal. He was senseless with loving her, with wanting her.

She sucked on his lower lip, then her tongue licked his, reaching into his mouth, her hips still moving in a lingering aftermath. He was maddened by her uninhibited movements, her luxuriant hair cascading around her shoulders. She took his large, engorged member in both hands, holding and stroking him while looking into his eyes, until he too climaxed with loud gasps of pleasure. Petting at its ultimate.

Where were they ever going, in their love life. Love life? Oh yes, they were in love. They were, indeed, de facto honeymooning. Almost.

In a sane moment in her brain-fogged love delirium, India remembered what she had sworn to her mother. "I will not be victimized by love, by urges."

So much for that, thought India.

Foggy with love, India realized she had not had the faintest notion as to how powerful was the demand of the species, of life, to reproduce itself. Because, of course, that's exactly what it was all about. Love, commitment, desire, the wave of passion that weakens the knees so you'd topple over and have at it, ensuring the advent of the next generation. Generation? So you fall down, spread your legs, and generate a new generation. Now that was a revelation to deal with. She, India, was not going to go all the way until they were married. She didn't know what she was going to do about it.

Marriage certainly had not been in her plans.

Dave knew what to do. He felt around in his pocket and pulled out his nervously purchased protection. Horrified, she looked at it with something akin to revulsion.

"But Dave, I just can't." Her eyes welled up, and her lips quivered. How she adored him and wanted that union with him. "Sexual intercourse is for marriage—I just cannot use this desire, this love, as a device for mere pleasure. As much as I want to, it's against my upbringing. I don't know how I can reconcile it."

He smiled at her definition of sexual intercourse. As if what they were doing was not in the realm. She was hanging her argument on a technicality. He enfolded her in his arms and drew her close. "I love you with all my heart, you know," he said.

She shivered and sighed at his words. "I love you too, Dave. But there's so much more to it, isn't there?"

How did her high school girlfriends do it? She knew some were not virgins; she had heard giggling, bragging, about this boyfriend and that one. How fabulous it was. She had been taken aback at their cavalier attitude toward lovemaking, sex. She had been so out of that loop. Now she thought she understood, finally, their snickering references to Saint India.

Well, that's what I am, she announced to herself. *I will be true to myself.*

It was her mantra. She clung to Shakespeare's Polonius, who said in *Hamlet*, "This above all: to thine own self be true, and it must follow, as the night the day, thou canst not then be false to any man."

India valued that play, *Hamlet*, so full of every blindsiding passion man can suffer. She had played the role of Ophelia in their senior production, chosen, she felt, more for her looks than her acting ability. Never mind. She had thoroughly wrapped herself around all of the play's words and actions. How was it that Shakespeare was so knowing, so clever? When taken as a source for life's lessons, she found it to be about as good as the Bible. And the Bible was pretty thorough.

So, she decided. Dave must understand that to be true to him, she must be true to herself. But she wasn't going to quit the heavy petting.

He could absolutely live with that.

He would marry her.

Dave was not unfamiliar with the Bible. He particularly remembered St. Paul's advice: "It is better to marry than to burn." And Dave was burning.

He looked down at her in his arms; she was dewy with the heat of desire. "I don't know how we're going to work this out, India, but you're going to marry me."

She froze, her brain jammed.

"Sooner or later, we're going to be married," he announced. "What we feel for each other cannot be dismissed. We are meant to be husband and wife."

FIFTY

THE FLIGHT TEST, THE FUTURE

*F*inally the moment had come. She was going to fly under the critical eyes of the FAA flight examiner.

It was September. The sky should have been a brilliant blue, a day sparkling with autumn sunshine. But it was not. The day broke flat gray with a high overcast, but at least no rain was forecasted. India scanned the sky in vain. Not a single ray played out under the ceiling to sweep over the fields. And no lovely rising thermals, either. No sun, no up-elevators.

She was scheduled in the early afternoon for her flight test, and the weather was plenty good enough for the examiner's requirements. To accommodate test maneuvers, today they would be towed to a higher than usual altitude for release; she would demonstrate her ability to handle the plane with turns around a point, stalls and recovery, and more. She would do turns by compass, turns by selected points on the horizon, Dutch rolls, and maybe even lazy eights. She would execute the emergency landing with a simulated rope break. On the ground, even before they went for the flying part of the test, she would answer selected questions on weather, regulations, and aeronautics. She knew her stuff. Today she would have her license.

And so it came about.

The FAA examiner smiled his congratulations, and signed her paperwork. There was hilarity and there were cheers, there was back-thumping and an enthusiastic endorsement of India by the other glider pilots.

They went to Checkpoints, where she had to buy the first round of beer (good thing it was payday) and they sang "For She's a Jolly Good Dol-ly," their amusing tweak of the old hoorah. She clicked her glass of sparkling cider on all of their beer bottles, and took a bow.

And then it was over.

What a letdown. What now?

Most new pilots would have simply set their sights forward on the exhilarating work of earning medals of altitude and distance, because they were sportsmen. India would love to do that, but she had other concerns, priorities.

One evening soon afterward, in a fit of impatience with herself, India sat down and intently, determinedly, filled out five different college applications along with the required essay. The essay necessitated considerable thought, but she had been turning the subject over in the back of her mind for days. She predicated it on what she had learned about herself and life, about the responsibility of her generation to attend to the business of righting wrongs in the culture.

She had grimly told Dave she had to do it and waved him off. The next morning she sent the forms along with the fees, money she had set aside from her earnings. The recommendations from teachers? She had run those off in multiples at school. She had to dig through her jammed file cabinet to find them, stored on the bottom of a drawer to keep them flat and neat, hidden under a collection of aviation data, materials on the subject of her new pursuit.

She was shocked at herself. Passions had to be controlled. India the Responsible, India the Good, India the Grownup—Saint India—would not lose herself to anyone or anything that would keep her from her goals.

That made her sit up. Goals? What goals?

She suddenly realized she had no concrete goals, none whatsoever, beyond learning to fly. How dumb. Travel and discover the world? What was that? Hardly a goal, or an accomplishment, or a career, or a way to make a living. She would have to think about this, something she had procrastinated doing.

In the world nowadays a woman's prime goal was no longer to find a husband and housekeep with kids around her ankles. Her mother hadn't, and she wouldn't either. But what? It was all very well to make lofty statements on admissions forms—but she hadn't a clue where to start. Perhaps in college she would find the veil of mystery lifted and see a path into the future. To find her way, especially one where she would love the work. That would be primary.

She saw that she had already started on her path, with her work at Children's Aid. But childcare was not going to be her life's project. She was interested in chemistry, and in research. Medical research. That was it. She quickly turned on to this idea, one that would satisfy both her interest in children's welfare through working on cures for diseases, and her intellectual curiosity about the way the world is put together, on a microlevel. She nodded and smiled to herself with satisfaction. She finally had a goal, and college would help her see her way to it.

Premed was available at all of her college choices.

Dave was in a funk. College? Of course there would be college—that had been clear from the outset. But he had not wanted to think about all that. In their head-crazy lovesick state, their cloud-nine bubble, they ignored the elephant in the room. He had pushed that whole scenario out of his head. Stupid, stupid, stupid. He hadn't even asked her where she wanted to apply, he was in such denial. Maybe she would settle on one nearby. He had only known her a bit more than three months, and he already wanted to make his future with her. He could not imagine life without her.

The two of them put the subject out of their minds and applied their energies to the next parents' airport afternoon, this time with a cookout.

FIFTY-ONE
A HIDEY-HOLE

*P*uffing and wheezing in a way that annoyed him—he'd struggled much less than this when he'd idly hiked the hills a couple of years ago—Mark forged an inconspicuous trail across the hills to the airport, although more detectable than he'd have liked. He had lost muscle tone since he had given up the YMCA's running track. He would need strength to overcome Miss India. Well, he would be powered up from his pleasure pills. Yes, pills, plural. He was going to heighten the experience with two. He determined he would need that, to fulfill his obsession, his warped, brutal craving.

Warped? He didn't consider himself at all warped. There were too many examples throughout history of brutal behavior for him to believe he was unusual. He thought of the prime one, the Marquis de Sade. What joy that character had found. Mark wanted to savor all that too. His compulsions were strengthening.

She was just so perfect, so extraordinary—in fact intimidating. That infuriated as well as bemused him. He didn't want any subconscious golden overrides to his evil plan

INDIA, DAVID, AND THE DEVIL

("She's too pretty to kill," or "She's too good a person to 'off.'"). The chemical fire in his brain would deflect any of that. He wanted to watch life ebb from those beautiful green eyes.

Yes, those eyes were beautiful, and he would be the last person she would see with them. He became aroused, imagining it, and laughed at himself.

He had found a perfect hidey-hole in the thickets, a stone cellar ruin that he would use. No remnants of a house foundation anywhere—it must have been a cattle shelter. Traces of rotten wood didn't matter. It was a shallow place. He might need to make her climb down the few stone steps he'd cleared of overgrowth.

During his prowling and exploring, his thoughts went to his intrigue, his fascination with this woman. His interest had grown; his appetite for her overtook him. She was a fantasy now, a larger-than life creation of an imagination stirred by lust. His desire for domination was overwhelming; he needed to crush her. Demons had fed all that. Mark was sometimes faintly aware of them, waiting on the edges of his mind. When they sensed that, they stilled themselves. It was not fruitful to be known. Demons managed their evil best when they slipped into the subconscious, which here was aided by drugs. They needed to destroy India and her goodness.

Goodness could be their nemesis.

A while back, police dispatch had received a call about a strange car parked in the Hammonds' neighborhood, but when they'd gone to check it out the car had moved on. The neighbor had taken down the license plate number, but when they ran it through the registry, it made no sense. Dispatch mentioned it to Sergeant Moore in passing. A red flag popped up in Moore's head.

"What information came through when you ran the plate?" he asked. "Who owns it?"

"Oh, someone over in the eastern part of the state, a newer car. Not a fit."

The sergeant thought a moment and said, "How about the car model? What was reported?"

"It was turned in as a good-condition sedan, probably twelve years old. Gray, but it could have been painted," responded the officer. "Again, not a fit."

Moore agreed, but something occurred to him. "Old car, good condition? Go to Buddy's Paint Shop, and talk to him. I've got a hunch. I know there are lots of paint shops in the metro area, but you can start in Valley."

Moore paused, then said, "And see if those plate numbers are ones that could have been easily altered. You know, like closing the sides of a three to make an eight. And a six into an eight. Like that."

The chief was a born sleuth; he reveled in these things. A puzzle always intrigued him. Like a bloodhound, he loved to track, he enjoyed the pursuit. Drooping jowls and pouchy bags under piercing black eyes finished the picture, observed the young detective, returning to his desk.

The detective desultorily toyed with the plate numbers and looked them up, expecting nothing. But what a surprise—there was a name, there was an address. The name? Marilyn Brissante. The address was of a Marilyn Brissante. He told the chief.

Someone would go around to the house and have a conversation.

Moore put this information on hold for the day, and waited for his investigator to come back from Buddy's Paint Shop. When he did, there seemed to be no need to search further. He confirmed that Buddy had indeed turned a beige sedan to gray, but he didn't remember for whom or when.

Dave's computer data search had finally revealed a clear but extraordinarily convoluted trail to the accounting firm where Brissante was employed.

The net was tightening. Why would Brissante be lurking near the Hammonds' if not to look for India? The chief was alarmed. If this was indeed the car that had been sighted in Pittsburgh, the car at that grisly double-murder site, and it appeared that it was, there was a lot to be alarmed about.

The initial tipster, Effie the prostitute, had finally supplied that important piece of the puzzle. She at last came forth with how she had glimpsed a man soundlessly creeping down the dark hallway, shoulders hunched, then from her window she saw him getting into a car. As he drove away she got the plate number. Something about the guy made her do that. After that, she had gone to her friend's room and seen the bloody horror and called 911. At that time, she called in just the bodies, nothing more, keeping the plate numbers to herself. She hadn't wanted to get more involved. Possible witness stuff in court that she didn't need, and all that. But finally she gave it up.

Moore was cheering over that information, coming from a source he never expected. But he had noticed over the years that if he was patient, in most cases people let go of hidden things. For whatever reasons, it was too hard to keep silent.

A HIDEY-HOLE

Moore immediately put people on India for her protection. It could easily be that this was the guy who had once attacked her. And when Dave had come in with his incriminating research, he had told the sergeant about how when he had come upon India being attacked behind the pharmacy, the man was yanking down India's pants. Dave told about how he had pulled them back up after flinging the attacker away from her.

"Sergeant Moore, he had knocked India out, and she knew nothing of this, and I didn't tell her. It was horrendous enough to be whacked; there was no need to frighten her more. But I believe you police need to know. Maybe I should have told you sooner, but the moment passed."

FIFTY-TWO
THE COOKOUT

The afternoon had been a positive experience, even heartening, for the families of the Children's Aid Society. The youngsters had raced around the open airstrip, gasping and laughing, playing tag and kick-the-can. Claudia and her friends had given them a challenging romp, joining in the children's gurgling laughter.

Claudia had also given them a good talking-to before they got into the fun and games, explaining the dangers of the closeness of the woods, about the rattlesnakes and bears that were known to be in there. Texas had nothing on Pennsylvania for rattlers—they were the most dangerous denizen of the state. They needed to mind the rules and stay close to camp.

Some listened better than others.

The cookout campfire was blazing, and the grills were fired up to cook burgers and hot dogs which would soon be sizzling. The aroma of hickory smoke wafted over the airstrip, precursor to the cooked meats. The fold-up tables and chairs used at glider meets had been put into service, and the grownups were sitting and talking over their afternoon's

THE COOKOUT

orientation, some actually discussing the forces of flight and moving their arms and hands to demonstrate.

India was reflecting on the scene, thinking a contented prayer of gratitude, enjoying that interesting glow she often felt, an energy that invaded her heart. What was that all about, anyway? Sometimes she even sensed a benign presence hovering on the edge of her mind. It was nice.

The sun was slipping down behind the tall pines, throwing spiked shadows like armed specters as it went, flat black figures inching silently across the strip. India shivered at how inky those shadows were, like bottomless holes. Something didn't feel quite right. She tried to shrug it off, but the sensation persisted.

The moon was a bright crescent sliver, like a chair rocker. It wouldn't give much light, but the stars would shine brighter. Her scalp prickled as she peered into the darkness. She felt as if someone were watching her. Well, of course there were several someones. The kids were now playing hide and seek at the edge of the copse, dodging back and forth behind tree trunks. Claudia had been correct about the snakes. Maybe she'd better haul them in and get them to eat. The food was about ready.

"All-ee all-ee in free!" she hollered, "Hot dog time!" And they came running.

Except for one pair of eyes, deeper in the woods. He must wait.

His fingers touched the tablets in his pocket. What a fine setting for his plan. The way to the cellar hole lay just behind him. He had it well fixed in his mind, just how he would do it. They would be well-hidden in this hidey-hole, until possible searchers passed by, and he could haul her out and continue with his ugliness. He had a vile, repellant odorant in his pocket just in case. So offensive a rotting stink it would drive anything away.

The cookout was a feast of fun and song. The adults remembered camp songs from their childhood summers at the YMCA camp down the highway, and chorused their happy memories. Mark listened and watched as the light faded from the airstrip and the shadows became one with the nighttime.

FIFTY-THREE
CLOSING THE NET

Out of a deep concern for India, Sergeant Moore had put his best tail on Mark Brissante. It was now obvious to Moore that Brissante had to be the killer they were looking for. He went over the facts. There were the altered plates on a car registered to the mother, there was the sighting by Effie—and there was more.

They had rechecked the neighborhood of the first murder, talking with bartender Sam and learning about an apparent addict who had once made a liaison with the murdered prostitute. The bartender had been vague at first; Sam naturally did not want the cops to know he was dealing, so he didn't speak of that bit. When he at last figured he could escape detection, he came forth. The man who had been seen by Sam picking up the working girl answered Mark's description.

What about the gang rape and murder? That was a mystery. The frightened old wino hadn't seen enough of the men to identify anyone—just that he had seen their shadowy actions and heard her desperate weak cries and knew they had hurled her body into the dumpster. He had heard the thump.

It had been interesting. Detective Thomas reported

that in following Mark, he noted that he had begun hiking during off-work hours, curiously disappearing into the hilly woodlands. It had been quite impossible to follow him in there. The detective was not exactly the fabled silent Indian that Mark seemed to be, but with careful surveillance he deduced the man was going to end up at the airport. He had observed that Mark seemed to show up on the periphery of all of India's activities, whether it was near the pharmacy where he hung around the parking lot or at Checkpoints where he watched her come and go from around the side of the building. Sometimes Thomas came upon him sitting parked on the roadside to her home and near the airport where he lurked in a turnout. Clearly Mark was stalking.

Although no silent Indian, the detective himself was a skilled tracker and watched Mark unnoticed. Detective Thomas swapped around a few different dumpy little cars while following him, as a precaution. Besides that ruse, he had a novel ability, a gift of an almost shifting veil of opacity, one of a puzzling "now you see me; now you don't." When playing hide and seek as a kid, he flummoxed everyone.

India and her family were completely unaware of all of this. Sergeant Moore did not bring them in on it, feeling it best that they not be alerted or alarmed. They mustn't be looking over their shoulders. He didn't want their behavior to change; that might be a clue to Mark that the Hammonds knew of his actions, and that as he was watching, he himself was being watched.

FIFTY-FOUR

LOST CHILD

"*A*my! Amy!" they hollered, "Where are you?" But the little girl was nowhere. "All-ee all-ee in free!" they called, just in case.

She did not come running. She had come in with the rest when called to eat, but had slipped away when nobody was watching. Fearless Amy was curious about the things in the forest.

Frantic, they all gathered flashlights and set out to comb the forest as the night came on, calling loudly and urgently.

"There are old decaying cellar holes in these woods," declared one of the parents. "She could have fallen in. We'd better call the police and get a search squad going."

Claudia and her friends had been so attentive, so firm in their instructions to stay close, but as the day wound to an end and the shadows deepened, it was not easy to keep track of them all. One slipped loose.

India couldn't believe this; her excellent plans had gone so hideously, dreadfully awry. She clasped her hands to her forehead, looking into the woodlands. A terrible apprehension overtook her, and she began to tremble. What could she do, what could she *do*? Dear God, poor little Amy. Desperate, India grabbed a flashlight and headed into the woods.

How nice. Mark observed his prey delivering herself right into his trap. He had seen the little girl drifting away from her group, peering into the woods with inquisitive eyes. Initially he brushed off any idea of redirecting her, but he could see a problem arising. If he didn't somehow send her back to the cookout, searchers would present obstacles to his plan.

And that's what was happening. So he hissed like a snake and growled like a bear, and with such noises rounded her up and back like an errant sheep to her flock. She ran wide-eyed and terrified out into the runway, into the arms of her parents.

"Mommy, Mommy, there's bears in there!" They hugged and scolded her, giving a swat to her backside for being disobedient. They gathered her into their arms, and wiped their eyes in relief.

"Amy, why on earth did you go in there?" they asked, looking at her in amazement.

"I wanted to see a snake," she whimpered, sniveling into her father's neck.

But in the meantime, India, not knowing the child had reappeared, plunged deeper into the dark woods, calling and shining her light about in desperation.

The group looked among themselves for their leader, their India. She was not there.

Dave rallied them to follow him, to look for her. She was now as great a concern as Amy had been. He began to feel a deep fear come over him, and started to run.

Mark watched her coming toward him, stumbling and calling. He quivered with anticipation. He reached into his pocket and found his stash, at the same time noting the swelling of his arousal. He fingered it and the pill, smiled to himself, opened his mouth wide, stretching his lips back from his teeth, and with a flourish placed the chemical under his tongue. That way it would enter his bloodstream more quickly. His face was distorted; he looked like a living gargoyle. He undid his belt and drew it out; he would use it to snap around her torso and pin her arms to her body; his interfering clothing would then be ready to remove. He watched her face as she came closer. The flashlight played across her hair, giving it glints of gold.

In a quick movement he had her.

She kicked and thrashed and tried to cry out, but his hand clamped over her mouth and nose, cutting off her breath until she fainted. Like a satyr he threw her over his back and carried her toward the cellar hole. The only sounds he had made were soft rustlings of underbrush, nothing to attract attention.

Predatory animals became motionless, putting a hold on night prowling. The bear and the wolf raised their heads and pricked up their ears. They hearkened throughout the woods, listening, licking their chops. They would soon feast on the forbidden.

The wood frog, too, suspended its calling, sensing something . . . something.

Mark knew he would not have to get rid of a corpse. Having seen tracks of mountain lion and bear, he planned it that way. They would take care of that. He would take his time. Her body, a carcass, would be hauled off to a lair for a group feast.

He was well hidden, he thought, safe in the deep night,

deep woods. He would keep her alive until sunrise, tied up, caressing her nude body, making her moan in ecstasy despite herself. He would have her at leisure throughout the night, plunging into all her orifices. He became breathless, thinking of the thrill of such domination. Torturing her with knife pricks until finally, at daybreak, he would stab her deeply and watch her die.

Madness had affected his common sense.

First, he had underestimated the potency and harmful properties of the chemicals. He had outsmarted himself. And second, in his arrogance he had underestimated the police. When questioned by Sergeant Moore, he had sneered and snickered to himself over Moore's bloodhound face. Such a cliché detective face, those droopy jowls, a silly caricature.

He snorted, swiftly pushing away a disturbed rattler at his feet. He was in no way intimidated by the rattlesnake, especially not now. He kicked its head as it poised to strike, stomping on it with his boot, shifting India's limp body on his shoulders.

"The woods are full of dangerous things," he tittered softly. "You shoulda been more careful, Little Miss Redhead."

The hyper pharmaceuticals kicked into overdrive. Mark's muscles began to quiver uncontrollably as he held India. He trembled and shook violently. There was a glow around her that pushed back the hissing demons in his brain, the slithering darkness in the shadows, that powerful force battling against her. The aura expanded around her, and he dropped her as he began to thrash. His body contorted, and in a massive, grotesque orgasm he jerked in the throes of death.

India's erratic flashlight movements as it sailed from

her hand to the forest floor had led Dave and others to the frantic actions.

Even as Mark crumpled, Dave caught India as she rolled out of his grasp. Mark's eyes, drugged pinpoints now black holes, rolled upward into sockets over his evil grimace.

India was unharmed, uncompromised. Despite all Mark's efforts, her life force was unaltered, her mind untouched by his foulness. It was a complete blindside that had happened in a second. In the darkness she had not seen a flicker of him, neither before nor as he threw the belt around her and drew it tight, pinning her arms in helplessness. Dave quickly undid her and gathered her close.

She was coming to and looked puzzled, squinting at the moving lights. The others stood around them, shining their flashlights on the dead man at their feet. Face down on the dirt, his gaping mouth drooled foam into the leafy detritus.

"That is one ugly dude," said one of the men. "Let's get out of here and get the police."

Lights flared up around them.

"We're here," said a voice behind him. "Been right on you. Detective Thomas called, advising us to come fast. That guy had only seconds left before we were on him. We were called as soon as the little girl didn't come back. Thomas has been tailing this man for some time. My men are also coming in from the other side."

They stopped and listened as the woods echoed with crashing branches, the sounds of backups coming through.

"He didn't have a chance," said the policeman.

INDIA, DAVID, AND THE DEVIL

"That's one for me," proclaimed the angel, wrapping her loving aura around India and Dave.

"Yeah? We got one too," gleefully retorted the demons, kicking Mark's terrified soul into the yawning mouth of Hell.

EPILOGUE

"Dave, I think we should ask the heads of Children's Aid, don't you? And possibly the parents and children we took on the field trip?"

India and Dave sat beside each other at the Hammonds' antique secretary, going over their wedding invitation list.

It was just after Thanksgiving, a feast they had celebrated with the Ridgeways at their home on the outskirts of Pittsburgh. It had been time for the two tribes to meet and size each other up.

It had not been easy for Elizabeth to hand over control of a cherished tradition to another women, but she did so graciously. She admitted it was a grand success, and one she enjoyed fully. She liked the Ridgeways. It was there that Dave and India announced their engagement. And they wanted to marry soon.

They planned a Christmas wedding, one with the church festooned with tiers of red poinsettias and white lilies. India's pastor had counseled them carefully and was reassured that his favorite angel of the congregation was ready to assume the duties and challenges of married life.

Mother Hammond had tried futilely to ward off or at least postpone these nuptials. She thought it was way too precipitous. She believed that if it was true love, they could wait at least ten months to test it. The cloud of sweet new passion would pale a bit by then, and perfections would show cracks. Would they be reasonable? Nope. They were having none of it. The couple was so adamant, so perfectly suited to each other, so in love—reason capitulated.

College? India was also ready to start premed at a Penn State campus. October had been a busy month. She had taken the initiative to investigate and interview at Penn State, declaring that her first choice. Her scholastic records were top-notch, and they admired the glider rating. *I was right about that*, she thought. She was accepted and enrolled for the following fall term.

The months ahead before she started classes would give her and Dave time to set up housekeeping. Life as a couple was beginning to set its course. How well would they steer it? They were so besotted with each other, they could see no impediments.

———◆———

India had bounced back quickly and easily from her near disaster with the psychopath Mark. She had learned when she was a toddler about overcoming the shock of the blindside. She well remembered her grandfather. It was his gift to her.

Grandpa had taught her this first lesson, initiated her first epiphany.

It had come early. She had stumbled, cute toddler sandals catching on the garden hose. Down she went for a chubby-cheeked face plant. At two, she didn't have far to fall. But to her it seemed a big deal.

Howling in surprise and outrage, she wailed into the

grass tickling her nose while at the same time peering with interest at the ants marching past her eyes. Her mother rushed toward her, holding out her arms to gather her up, to console and wipe away tears.

Grandpa stood in Mama's way.

"Aw, stop squealing like a pig stuck under a gate, India. You're not hurt," pronounced her scowling grandfather, standing over her.

India had been brought to the old farm to be shown off, one of her monthly visits, to be dandled on Grandpa's knee and coddled by her Nana. Turning off her yowling, she considered her two-year-old self, realizing that, surprise of surprises, she was not hurt.

Grandpa's lesson would rest in her heart always, to be remembered whenever something blindsided her. Was she hurt? Not usually.

And not this time.

*A*ward-winning author Cabot has used her wide-ranging literary talents to spin an intense tale of love and the chillingly macabre. In weaving this tale of a young woman's frightening transition into adulthood, she draws from a variety of experiences: hours working at a psychiatric institution, time as a Court-Appointed Special Advocate investigator on behalf of abused and neglected children, and meditation and guidance at a Cistercian abbey.

Cabot's writing credentials range from publisher of an aviation magazine to years of published restaurant reviews for a New England newspaper. In 2016, she won a coveted IPPY award for nonfiction. She is a member of the Writers' Group of Alamos, Sonora, Mexico.

Cabot holds a commercial pilot's license, single-engine airplane land and glider, with tow pilot endorsement. She has logged more than five thousand hours of flight, adventuring with her husband throughout the northern hemisphere, including parts of Alaska, Mexico, the Bahamas, and Central America.

Cabot was born a Texan, and spent much of her youth living around the world in foreign posts with her US Air Force command pilot father and southern mother. About her flying she says, "It's genetic. Like my father, I was born to be airborne."

CPSIA information can be obtained
at www.ICGtesting.com
Printed in the USA
BVHW07s1053260618
520037BV00001B/3/P